Lion Girl

Gina Augustini Best

For those living in the shadow of circumstances beyond their control.
Wishing you light, love, and *Lion Girl* energy.

Chapter I

I willed my mind silent, but it ignored me, like everyone else in this house. Dialogues squawked inside my head, words I needed to say on an endless loop, rattling my brain.

I took a deep breath and folded into a crunch, a fire screaming deep in my belly. Held it for twenty, then let go with a grunt.

Pushing hair out of my eyes, I strained to see the digital clock, a hand-me-down from Grams, half-buried under a clutter of fantasy fiction paperbacks on the bedside table. In nine minutes, like always, Dad would put on coffee, drop Pop Tarts in the toaster and start breakfast before calling me. I made a move to get up, groaned, and flopped back on the carpet. I was fifteen going on forty-five.

I'd been up pacing for hours, still in my night shirt, dropping to my bedroom floor for impromptu planks and crunches. I'd contemplated spots on the walls—but saw nothing, really. Always working the puzzle, searching for a way out of this mess. Fumbling with various combinations of what I needed to change or make happen to sort it out. Make pieces fit together into one cohesive form—like the colored squares of a Rubik's Cube. But my life wasn't like that puzzle. I couldn't retrace my steps, make different moves, change what I'd done. Or what I *hadn't* done.

It always came back to that.

It was like that unlucky mosquito we learned about in science class. It landed on tree resin a million years ago—and *boom*—it was trapped there forever in a chunk of amber. One horrible mistake perfectly locked in place. Poor bug. I could relate.

I forced myself to my feet. God, I needed sleep. I nibbled at the ragged cuticle of my thumb, tugged at the sliver of skin, a stab shooting up my hand, as a glob of red formed and edged its way down the side. A copper taste coated my tongue as a calmness settled over me, a warmth draping across my shoulders.

I reached for a tissue and wrapped it around my bleeding thumb. The clatter of dishes and utensils grew louder from the kitchen. Dad ate breakfast before our morning runs, but not me. I preferred running on an empty stomach that time of day, knowing I'd eat right after we finished.

I knuckled the spot between my eyes. I needed to talk to him, but he made it so difficult. One glance at his sad, watered-down blue eyes, and I'd swallow my words, each one like jagged bits of glass. It sucked.

"Em—better get a move on if you're going with me," Dad called through the door. "OJ's on the counter."

"Coming!" I hollered back.

I pulled crumpled running clothes off the chair, carefully balancing the bloodied tissue on my thumb, then slunk into my bathroom. Rummaging through a drawer, I found the last Band-Aid and slapped it on before turning on the faucet and splashing cold water on my face. I quickly tamed my hair with a brush and yanked it into a tight ponytail.

In the hallway, I slipped on worn-thin running shoes and headed for the kitchen. I gulped down juice and grabbed a handful of almonds from a bag on the counter. A rumble of snoring caught my attention, then a tumble of dark hair on the arm of the family room couch. I walked over, nibbling almonds, and stared down at my puffy-faced, rumpled mother still in yesterday's sweats. My shoe hit the tip of a blue bottle peeking from under the couch and a medicinal stench rose to greet me. I held my breath, tugged the bottle free and marched it to the kitchen sink.

I had just poured the vodka down the drain when Dad walked in. He stood silent, focused on the floor. With the empty bottle in hand, I waved toward my mom.

"She's at it again," I snapped and hurled the bottle. It crashed inside the bin, but the lump on the couch didn't stir.

Dad raised his brows and blinked. He glanced over his shoulder, shrugged with a deep sigh, then looked back at me, his mouth easing into a straight line, as flat as the half-eaten Pop Tart he'd left on the counter.

I could have predicted it, but still, his response gnawed at me. He hated conflict as much as he hated reality TV shows. My dad was brilliant in so many ways. An astrophysics professor at a university in Dallas with students who worshipped him. But from my point of view, he lived in a bubble—one filled with beloved theories about wormholes, black holes, and countless faraway galaxies that collided with and consumed one another. But the collisions and implosions that occurred within our own family seemed to bounce off some protective force field of his, zapped into nothingness.

I couldn't help myself. "Really?" My voice was a thin squeak. He rubbed the stubble on his chin with the back of his fingers.

All these years I'd tried to be like him, tried to appear unaffected by my mom's moods, which cycled weekly between mania and depression, hot and cold, round and round. But my insides were a different story—a pressure always pushing from the inside out, knotting my chest and stomach, acid inching up the back of my throat. Always a fluttering heartbeat, wispy and nimble, like hummingbirds' wings revving for flight. I struggled to keep from ripping off the Band-Aid and gnawing at my cuticle. The urge to feel something other than *this*—this helplessness, this disappointment, this *rage*—was powerful.

"You ready?" His voice was brisk as he moved toward the back door. "I have an early meeting."

That's right. No talking. Not about anything that mattered, anyway. Not about how far he had drifted away. Not about Mom and her episodes. Not about what I'd done this summer. And certainly not about what had happened six years ago—that moment our family shattered into tiny pieces, into particles smaller than atoms.

My dad disappeared through the back door, and I followed, rounding the corner of the house, past the thorny rose bushes that bloomed despite neglect and through the side gate that led to the front yard. He took off at a light jog. I trailed close behind, long-legged and slender like him.

We'd started running together a while back, after our family had been blown to bits and the panic attacks began. I'd have them at school or at my best friend Sophie's house. Wherever. Whenever. They'd start with a tingling in my limbs, then morph into a feeling of overwhelming terror. I'd try to run from it, I would, but sometimes I'd freeze in place, unable to move or even speak. Trapped like that mosquito. All the while my heart would race as if it were on a countdown to explode.

Back then there was this droopy-eyed school counselor named Mrs. Davies who'd called countless meetings with my parents, even though they repeatedly blew her off. Once, she came to our house unannounced. My dad invited her in, offered her a cup of coffee. The counselor's voice quivered when she spoke.

"Your family has experienced a tragedy beyond *traumatic*," she'd told my parents, "and in my professional opinion, you would all benefit from counseling." Before she could get out another word, my dad had laughed so harshly the woman and I flinched in unison.

"Psychology isn't too far removed from that self-help mumbo-jumbo they peddle on afternoon talk shows," Dad had said, fingers drumming against the side of his NASA mug. "It's pseudoscience—there's no scientific data—did you know that? They've yet to discover universal human psychological processes. It's all too subjective to be considered science."

I kept my head low but the counselor had turned to my mother, who looked as if she were made of marble—pale, unyielding. Half-moon shadows under glazed eyes, Mom stared hard at the fidgeting woman, then shook her head no. Just no.

Dad had risen from the table. The meeting was over.

"Emma will be okay," he'd told Mrs. Davies as he guided her toward the door. "We'll get through this." I'd felt sorry for the woman as she tottered toward her car, shoulders sagging.

Grams, my mother's mom, had even tried her southern *Steel Magnolia* edge to convince my dad.

"For God's sake, she needs help, Richard." I'd overheard them arguing one night when they thought I was asleep in my room. "You think you can handle it, but hon, *that dog don't hunt*! Your way isn't working!"

"She'll be fine," he'd snapped. "We all just need time, Dorothy." End of discussion. He'd deflected and obliterated Grams' plea like any other incoming emotion threatening his bubble.

A couple of weeks later, though, he'd asked me to run with him. Neuroscientific research showed the benefits of running so that was his solution. Of course, at the time, no one had asked what I needed, if I wanted to talk to someone about what had happened, how I'd let everyone down. Even if they had, I wasn't sure I could have known what to say. So, I'd held it inside as best I could, and I ran.

This morning, it wasn't enough. After my fumbled attempt to stop the pain last month, as in trying to end my life, I'd been sent to Austin for three weeks, where the counselors at Serenity Oaks Hospital encouraged me to talk to my parents. Even if it terrified me.

And God, it paralyzed me! I couldn't explain why. But today, I forced myself to at least try to express myself. I pushed to keep up with my dad.

"Uh—like I said, Mom's not doing so great," I tried. A flash of irritation crossed his face. I pushed on, my voice smaller. "This is, like, the third morning in a row." No response. "She's in another funk, Dad."

He tossed a flinty glance my way. "It's difficult, Emma." He massaged his temples as he jogged. "Just—don't. I can't explain." His pace quickened. Mine did, too. "Just—please—leave it for now, okay?"

"The counselors told me to start, you know, talking about stuff instead—"

"You don't know what she used to be like," he said, his voice louder and sharper than usual. "You don't remember her before—before—"

"Yes, I do," I interrupted, breathless. "I remember lots of things." Icy fingers snaked around my throat and chest, slow and deliberate, increasing in pressure, even as I ran. I forced air through tightened vocal cords.

"Sometimes, I just need to talk—about things." I brushed away the sting in my eyes.

"I'm sorry. I just—" Dad cast his eyes downward. "Listen, Em. I can't do this right now." And that was that. He took off.

"But I—" I mumbled at his advancing back, "Please. Don't leave." I had about as much a chance of reaching him as I did the moon.

As if on cue, a cottontail lit out of a clump of shrubs, a streak of taupe and white zipped across the street where he had just passed. Then it was gone. On our morning runs, I often spotted the rabbits, which constantly dove down holes and ducked into nearby bushes for cover. They never seemed to find peace either.

I slowed to a stop and slipped on earbuds. I needed to reset. To work loose of the tightness that gripped me. I put on my favorite playlist and started jogging again.

Rubber soles hit the pavement, a spongy rhythm massaging the bottoms of my feet. *Inhale—One...Two...Three. Exhale—One...Two...Three.* I picked up speed and lost myself in the strum of guitar, the cadence of breathing, the blur of houses that slipped past.

I found my pace, and then I didn't dwell on the heaviness. Life was as simple as the blood humming through me, the to-and-fro swing of my ponytail, and the burn of leg muscles taking me forward. I crossed a small playground and dashed down a wooded footpath that descended onto the tree-lined jogging trail. Endorphins kicked in and I sailed on, one long stride after another.

For a second, I caught a glimpse of Casey. An apparition full of joy, bounding alongside me, a bouncing blur of dark, curly hair. Then, like most mornings, my little sister vanished. The sudden appearances never frightened me. Instead, I longed for them. The piece of the puzzle I'd lost long ago. But I never told anyone about seeing her, not even Grams. I knew what they'd all think—that I was even more whacked than they already thought.

Chapter 2

I slowed to a walk, stopping at the edge of our front yard. My dad, hands on hips, stilled as I approached.

"Good run?"

"Yep." I dropped to the grass, under the shade of the broad red oak in our yard. I stretched my legs and fiddled with the neon yellow tips of my shoes. I loved the feeling just after a run; my muscles loose, the tension melted away. We didn't talk about what I'd brought up earlier—*surprise, surprise*—both of us silent, pretending to focus on our cool-downs. I hated the pretending.

A jab of anger punched within me. I tried to stifle it with a few deep breaths, tried to hold onto the feeling of lightness. I looked up as my dad studied his watch.

"I'm headed in." He chewed the corner of his bottom lip, a habit when he wasn't sure how to say something. "I just wanted.... It's just, I'm—" He chewed some more, glanced at the watch again, then went silent.

"What is it?" I asked. *Why couldn't he talk to me? Was it that difficult to look at me?*

"Nothing." He pivoted and stomped up the porch steps. "Can't be late today. Gotta jump in the shower."

The storm door shut behind him. I straightened my shoulders and leaned into another stretch, aware of suburbia awakening. Sprinklers sputtered to life, misting yards in synchronized twists, tiny rainbows sprouting in soft morning light. Garage doors rumbled open and closed. A few cars hummed past. A middle-aged Asian man, a neighbor from a few houses down, left his house, dragged along by a tiny white-and-brown Shih Tzu that lifted its leg every few steps. I didn't know him but gave a small wave. He returned the gesture before being yanked in the opposite direction by the puff of fur on the leash. I smiled as they zigzagged away.

We should have gotten a dog. Maybe that would have made a difference.

I finished stretching, then like always, I avoided the driveway, taking the long way around to the back door, where I slipped into the kitchen. I was famished and quickly scarfed down four slices of bacon my dad had left in the frying pan Then I fixed oatmeal, making sure to slam the microwave door and scrape the kitchen chair across the tile floor. I stared hard at the top of my mom's head. The mass of curls lay still on the couch. I popped up from the table and grabbed the frying pan from the stove, slamming it hard against the countertop—not once, but twice. Nothing. I glared at her. A thunderous bass line of snores was the only thing convincing me she wasn't dead.

I bobbed my spoon in oatmeal, my appetite lost. Dad soon appeared in a dress shirt and pants, an unknotted tie slung over his shoulder. I watched him pour a cup of coffee. He cut his eyes away, set the travel mug on the counter and squinted at it as if it were the most fascinating object he'd ever seen. He cleared his throat, then moved away.

"Guess I'll see you at dinner tonight?" He studied the leather wallet cradled in his palm, then slipped it into his back pocket. He reached for the coffee and keys. I nodded and gritted my teeth. I couldn't make myself look at him even if I'd wanted to.

"Okay. See you then," he said, then left the house with a jingle of his keys and a hushed click of the door.

My family hadn't always been so over-the-top Crazyville. I studied the wooden tabletop in front of me, its surface smudged by scissor scratches and permanent-marker scribbles left from simpler days when I'd sit for hours painting flowers or coloring Dora the Explorer's happy round face.

A thick, red mark marred a spot on the table, and I ran a delicate finger over it. A memory of when I was five settled over me. I recalled my mom's face from that time—smooth olive skin, an easy smile, her clear eyes joyful, not guarded. Back then, I'd felt so lucky. Like I'd found the winning golden ticket secreted inside a wrapped chocolate bar. That's how magical she'd been to me.

"Whatcha doing?" my mom had asked. She'd moved closer, allowing me to inhale the scent of flowers and cinnamon tea mixed with the faint tang of Kodak fixer she used to process photos in the darkroom, the way it was done before digital cameras came along. At the time, she worked from home as a freelance photographer. She wore her favorite jeans, ripped at the knees and stained with chemical splotches, and a white t-shirt under a flannel with missing buttons. She'd reached for the drawing and studied it, her lips curving upward.

"Who's this?" she'd asked, pointing at the stick-figure girl with a rec-tangular camera that covered an eye. Behind the girl stood a larger stick figure with a giant head and crazy curls piled high on top, the shape of a beehive, with a camera dangling from her neck. Butterflies flew nearby and violet flowers bloomed at their feet.

"That's me, Mama," I'd told her, "And that's you. See? We're on an adventure!"

Mom had chuckled and kissed the top of my head. "I like the way you think, girlie." I had warmed under her eyes, my body had curved toward her, like a flower drawn toward sunshine.

That Emma would have never fathomed, not in a million years, how her adoration would transform into contempt for the shell of a woman now on the couch. The light she'd once shared with me had long since flickered out.

Was it possible I'd imagined that moment with my mom? Even though I didn't want it to be true, I considered the possibility I might be just like her—dreaming up conversations and situations that never existed. Like the vision I'd seen on my run this morning. Was that Casey real? Or a glitch of neurons misfiring in my head? I couldn't be sure either way.

I shook my head, determined to get free of those tangled thoughts. When I left the room, I refused to glance back at the snoring figure on the couch. Instead, I pushed myself toward brighter thoughts. Grams and I were going shopping today. She was supposed to be here in forty-five minutes, but since she was always early, it would probably be more like twenty. My mom could continue thundering like a train, for all I cared. I had better things to do than worry about that stranger on the couch.

I turned on the shower in my bathroom and grabbed a ragged-edged towel from the jumbled linen closet, placing it by the sink. I checked my shampoo. The bottle was all but empty. I'd be washing my hair with shower gel again. Like the rest of my life, something was always in short supply. Mentally, I started another grocery list for me and Dad since my mom couldn't be counted on for anything.

No. I didn't imagine that day. I used to have a mother—I'm certain of it.

When the water was hot enough, I stepped inside, positioning my face in front of the jets, eager to wash away the griminess on my skin, along with the sticky thoughts that clung to my brain.

***

As soon as I shut off the water, I heard muffled voices coming from the kitchen. It sounded like an argument—Grams' forceful tone against Mom's raspy voice. I couldn't make out what they were saying, so I wrapped the towel around myself, and with water still dripping off me, I tiptoed to the bedroom door and tried to open it quietly. The hinge creaked.

Crap. Dad never fixes anything around here!

I froze, hoping no one had heard. A minute passed with no reaction. I leaned in closer to the crack of the door. I wanted to hear what my grandmother was saying.

"...get a grip, Rosemary," Grams' voice cut through, "you're drunk as Cooter Brown most days. But you're not the only one who's suffering 'round here." A kitchen chair groaned against tile. "Emma's hurting, and you're part of the problem."

I couldn't make out Mom's response.

Then Grams raised her voice, close to yelling. "For Christ's sake! It's like hugging a rose bush with you! Your daughter needs you, clear as day, and if you can't be there for her, maybe she should come live with me."

"Like hell," my mom said, loud enough for me to hear the bitter bite in her words. "You know *nothing* about what I've gone through. You've never had to...." There was silence, then muted sobs.

"Please, Hon. For the love, *please* let me help you." Grams' voice softened. "You have an illness. Nothing shameful about it. Yeah, it gets ugly, like diabetes or anything else. But self-medicating like this? It doesn't fix a thing, Rosemary. It just makes it that much uglier." Silence. "Let's find a doctor like we did after you had Emma. Remember? You liked her." Grams pushed on. "Maybe you get back on those meds so you feel better. You won't need to—"

"Shut up!" my mother yelled. Her intensity frightened me. "I don't need you—or your damned psychiatrists. What I want...what I need is *never* coming back!"

As I jerked back from the door, the hinge screeched louder this time. I froze again, my heartbeat clanging so loud in my head, I was sure they could hear it, too. It was quiet in the kitchen except for my mother's sobs.

"Emma, hon, is that you?"

Grams.

But I didn't answer. My heart continued drumming in my ears.

"Take your time," Grams said in a singsong voice. "Me and your mom—we're fixin' to have coffee. Just making small talk!"

"Yeah. Okay, Grams!" A fake brightness lit my voice. What else could I do?

I closed the bedroom door and returned to the bathroom. I could still hear muffled shouting but didn't try to listen anymore. Instead, I started another playlist and blared the volume on my portable speaker. The sound of "Survivor"—one of my favorite girl-power anthems performed by Destiny's Child—pulsed so loudly in the bathroom, it vibrated my back molars.

I glared into the cloudy mirror, my image distorted by condensation on the glass. *Do not cry. She's so not worth it.* I grabbed the hairdryer and attacked my wet hair, painfully scraping my scalp with each stroke of the brush.

Grams was *way wrong*. I might need a mother, but I sure as hell didn't need *that* woman. My mom—the one I remembered from that day long ago, the days when I'd felt loved—had disappeared six years ago, the exact same moment my little sister's heart had stopped beating. And ever since then, I'd been left floundering on my own.

Chapter 3

Grams clutched the steering wheel of her big Buick. She slowed to a crawl when the light changed yellow, but long before it blinked red, the car shuddered to a halt.

"Enjoy your jog this morning?" Grams stared straight ahead, preoccupied, oblivious to the cars passing through the intersection.

"Sure." I glanced away. "It was great." I didn't want to upset Grams more by mentioning my dad's weirdness. Or the argument I'd overheard between her and my mom afterward.

Michael Bublé's "Fire" played on the car radio, and Grams drummed her fingers to the beat on the steering wheel. She loved Michael Bublé, whose last name she mispronounced as "Bubble," even after years of me correcting her. I focused on her elegant fingers, topped with bright, sculpted nails.

"Nice color." I nodded toward her hands.

"Cherry Bomb." Grams wiggled her fingers and her brows simultaneously.

I folded one hand over the other to cover my mangled cuticles. Bitten down to nubs, the jagged tips accented the inflamed skin around the nails. Kind of my own version of "Cherry Bomb." I pursed my lips and watched the cars behind us in the side mirror.

I plucked at the fresh bandage on my thumb and tried to twist it. My compulsive chewing drove Grams crazy, so I did my best to hide it. I couldn't remember exactly when I started, but for whatever reason, found it soothing. Somehow, when I tore the skin off in slivers, and the nerve endings stung all the way up my arm, the world mellowed. But it was a nasty habit. Two years ago, I'd gotten a staph infection in my left hand and had to take antibiotics for a couple of weeks. I'd heard my parents' angry whispers about a possible blood infection, each blaming the other for not noticing sooner. Like either would notice a damn thing with me. But unlike them, Grams paid attention. I crossed my arms and buried my fists deep into my armpits. For the fifteenth-gazillion time, I made a mental note to figure out a way to stop.

"Excited about your first year of high school? Just think, in three short years, you'll be a graduate of the Class of 2019!" Grams tried again. The light turned green. She inched the car forward. The traffic was stop-and-go-congested near the mall.

"Yeah. I guess." I shrugged. "I don't know. Maybe I'm excited. But I'm, like, kind of nervous, too. I hope Fi and I have classes together."

Grams scrunched her brow, then shot me a quizzical look. "Where is Sophie? Wasn't she coming with us?"

I gazed out the passenger window and shrugged again, faking an interest in the black sports car in the lane next to us. "I never got around to texting her. We haven't talked since this summer."

My tongue stuck to the roof of my suddenly dry mouth. I didn't want to admit I hadn't had the courage to call my best friend when I'd gotten home from the treatment center. Sophie had been at camp when it happened, and I knew she'd detonate the minute we were alone. She had sent a "Get Well" balloon to the hospital with the words "Love You" scribbled on a small card, which came the day before I left for

Austin. That was it. A balloon! The same thing you'd send a snot-nosed ten-year-old who just had ear tubes put in. Her silence spoke so much more. I couldn't blame her for being angry. It wasn't like she had any idea I would gulp down a bottle of Tylenol while cradling Bear, my little sister's favorite stuff animal. *Tylenol? Really, Em?* I could hear Fi groan in disgust.

A rush of heat flushed my face and burned the tips of my ears. I pushed my chin into my chest and pressed my eyelids shut. I tried to block out the searing pain of that day but couldn't. The humiliation and agony of the plastic tube forced down my throat as the ER staff administered activated charcoal directly into my stomach. It was supposed to absorb the excess Tylenol, but in my case, it also forced up a black porridge of vomit that covered the yellow hospital gown, along with most of my hair and face. Endless streams of sticky black everywhere, until I had nothing left inside, my entire body curled into itself, wracked by dry heaves. Casey had been sitting next to me. Her dimpled chin rested on intertwined fingers, her presence more in focus than ever. I'd tried to speak to her, reach for her, but a dark heaviness dragged me under. When I woke hours later in a hospital room, she was gone.

I wished I could find the words to explain just how empty and lost I'd been that day. The intense pain piercing my chest. How my heart physically ached for Casey. It had been six years to the day of her death. Had I been a better sister, she would have celebrated her ninth birthday. How could I explain the rawness I'd felt? Torn and exposed. Like these bloody cuticles. I stole another glimpse at them before folding my hands again on my lap.

"Oh, darlin'." Grams' husky voice interrupted my thoughts. "Take my advice. Don't dig up more snakes than you can kill. Please. We all make mistakes—sometimes they're biggies." Her voice was as warm as the hand she planted on top of my cold ones. "But you know what I've found out? The people who truly love us, well, they forgive." She leaned into my shoulder. "They might be hurt and all. But they *always* forgive."

I couldn't meet her eyes. Instead, I concentrated on her beautiful hand covering my ugly one. The way the cubic zirconia on her ring sparkled with the slightest shift. She finally spoke into the silence.

"Em, you have to explain things to Sophie." She squeezed my hands again. "You owe it to her—and to yourself—don't ya think?"

I teared up, a welling in my eyes that spilled onto my cheeks. Grams was right and I knew it. I'd text Fi later today. Maybe we could hang out. We'd been through so much together—Casey's death, and everything that followed, including Sophie's parents' bitter divorce, which left her camped out with her mom and little brother at a Holiday Inn off the interstate for more than a month. So much history. I had to make it right.

My grandmother reached for a tissue in her console and gently held my chin. She dabbed at the dampness, and I let her dry under my eyes, pat along the sides of my face, let myself sink into the comfort of her touch. After one last dab, she kissed the tip of my nose.

"So, now that that's settled, let's shake off these blahs." She cocked a brow at me. I couldn't help but grin in response. "We deserve a little retail therapy, don't ya think?"

I nodded. Grams had a way of making it all seem better. At least for a little while.

Ignoring honks behind her, Grams crawled into the parking lot. Everything about her was youngish, except her driving. Most girls I knew wouldn't be caught dead shopping with their grandmothers. They'd choose gum-chewing, phone-carrying, boy-ogling packs instead. But me? I'd take Grams. She wasn't like most grandmas. She had young tastes in clothes and a wicked sense of humor, which belied her seventy-one years.

The honks from behind continued as Grams set her sights on the first row in front of Macy's. She braked abruptly for a woman meandering to her parked car, accompanied by a small boy who skipped around her. Grams clicked on the turn signal, put the car in park and hummed along to Bublé while she waited. The lot was packed. A few angry drivers pulled around and gave Grams the stink-eye.

"Oh, for Christ's sake, people," she muttered, "Relax!" One driver in an orange, midlife-crisis convertible pulled alongside her and shot the finger as he passed. She returned the gesture, a flash of Cherry Bomb, but just as quick, placed her hand back on the wheel.

"Grams?" I giggled. "Oh. My. God." I burst into full belly laughter, which immediately made me feel lighter, happier.

"What?" Grams' finely arched eyebrows disappeared under silver bangs. She shrugged with a smile. "Honestly—some folks make hornets look cuddly."

She pulled into the parking space and gathered her purse as if nothing had happened. Still chuckling, I climbed out. I linked arms with her as we strolled toward the entrance. Yeah, life sucked most days. But every now and then, during moments like these, life was a lot less sucky.

Chapter 4

I checked my phone again, even though I'd looked at it two minutes earlier. *Nada.* After Grams dropped me off last night, I'd texted Fi to find out if we could hang today. I sent another this morning after my run. No response. True, it was only eleven-thirty. But still. Fi always carried her phone with her.

Ignoring the urge to nibble a fingernail, I got up from my desk and paced. I reached for the bottle of bitter clear nail polish I bought yesterday and rolled it between my palms. It was designed to help toddlers stop sucking their thumbs, the cashier at the drugstore had told me, and added in a stage whisper, "I hear it tastes like earwax." I wrinkled my nose and placed it back on the dresser. I wasn't ready for that just yet. I moved away from the dresser mirror—and the reflection I still didn't recognize. Grams had surprised me with an appointment at the hair salon in the mall. My natural reddish-blonde hair was cut to my shoulder blades and tipped at the bottom in about four-inches of rose-gold. It was still long enough to put in a ponytail but angled around my face.

Despite my grumblings, Grams also had strong-armed me into a cosmetic store for a makeover. Usually, I didn't wear much unless Fi pushed me into it for a special occasion. Most days, I opted for sheer foundation and lip gloss.

"C'mon! Let's try something new for high school," Grams had said. Her eyes had widened as she clapped her hands together like a little kid. "It'll be so much fun!"

In the end, I was happy I'd given in. The new look—light blush-colored lids, and contours and highlights—made me feel less "Walking Dead," and more like I had a pulse. I'd even tried to put on eyeliner and mascara this morning, but it wasn't as good as yesterday. I'd have to practice at it.

"Your eyes are, like—wow," the twenty-something cosmetics technician had told me. She'd brushed foundation on my face in layers until my skin appeared to glow. Then she'd chosen a palette of warm neutrals and pulled another makeup brush from a hip holster, twirling it like a gunslinger. "A little color will definitely make them pop." At first, I shrank back into the seat, but after a few minutes of pampering, I let myself relax. When she had finished, my turquoise-colored eyes—probably my best feature—definitely popped.

I raked a hand through my hair, peeked at my phone screen again, then flung myself back on the bed. I started another text to Fi. I knew she was pissed at me, but I wasn't giving up—I needed to explain everything. Like Grams had said, I owed our friendship that much.

Me: *Hey again. Where you are? Wanna chat? Miss you.*

It took a good ten minutes to compose the simple message, and another five minutes of debating whether to hit 'send' before I finally did. During the past few weeks, it had hit me how much I missed having a best friend around. Grams was right. Facing Fi might be scary, but it was worth it.

I flipped onto my stomach, kicking my legs behind me as I scrolled through old photos on my phone. I found the ones I was searching for, a couple of selfies Fi and I had snapped the first day of ninth grade. In our school district, which was one of the largest in the state, ninth graders went to a freshmen center for a year before entering high school. This year we'd be mixed with the upper classmen. It would be like *real* high school. Fi and I looked so young in the pictures, and I snorted at the duck faces we'd made for the camera, somehow thinking at the time we looked cool.

My phone pinged.

Fi: *FaceTime for a sec? Can't hang today. Have other plans.*

I chewed on my bottom lip, then sat up and reached for the laptop. On the third ring, she answered.

"Hey." My voice sounded overly bright, even to my ears. Fi's face filled the laptop screen; her dark-brown hair longer since I'd last seen her. She'd also had her eyebrows done. The sleek black arches further emphasized her striking face.

"Hey," she said. "Wow. Awesome hair!" She squinted and leaned closer to the camera, her face looming large on the screen. "Did you put on mascara? Amazing."

"Thanks." I patted at my head, self-conscious under her gaze. "You know—Grams insisted."

"Love it." She pulled back from the camera. "I'm not sure I would have recognized you." Ouch. The subtle dig was her specialty. Awkward pause. A tight, fake smile curved on her lips. "So, what's up? How are things?"

"You know. Same stuff." I adjusted and readjusted the laptop screen. "Just waiting for school to start. What about you?"

Another awkward pause. Her lips tightened, and her serious eyes bore through the screen straight into mine. "Em, I can't do this pretend crap. Not with you." I braced for a punch in the gut. She sat silent, her face closed, before she finally spoke.

"Okay. So, what's up with me?" She rolled her eyes. "Huh…I don't know, my best friend tried to off herself about a month and a half ago. Did you hear about that? Yeah. Crazy, right? I haven't heard from her since it happened, though. Not. One. Fucking. Word." Her eyes were moist. "I'm furious—you know, like *beyond* pissed. But only because I love you, and I'm selfish, and, you know, I just don't get it. I mean *why*? Why would you do that? What would I have done if your dad hadn't found you, and you had actually—you know—left like that?"

I bowed my head, unable to speak or even swallow. Hearing the pain in her voice, knowing I had caused it, shook me. A tear splattered on the keyboard's space bar. I wiped it off with the hem of my shirt.

"I want to fucking scream at you, you know, like throw something at you—but I'm afraid if I do, you might try that shit again." Fi cleared her throat. "So." A cough, more sniffling. Another pause. "So. That's how I'm doing."

She dabbed at her face with a tissue while I wiped away tears with the heels of my hands, black streaks down the sides of my face. *Damn mascara.* I tried to calm myself. My throat squeezed tight as I swallowed back sobs. Sophie watched from her end, hurt radiating from large, watery eyes.

"Fi, I'm so…sorry. I…wasn't really thinking about anyone…except Case. She would have been nine if I—" I stammered, my voice coming out raw. "You were gone, and Grams was gone, and…I was so alone." I pulled my hands away from my face. "God…I can't even." I pressed a fist against my runny nose and bit my knuckle. "Please…forgive me. I never meant to hurt you. Ever. You never have to worry that I'll do that again. I swear."

Fi wiped her nose with the corner of her bedspread. She worked her jaw, her lips stretching into a tight, straight line. The silence lingered on. Her eyes were cast down, so I couldn't tell what she was thinking.

Then she looked up with a guarded face. "So. You promise?" Her expression was solemn as she blew her nose again. "Pinky swear?"

"Yes. Pinky swear, Fi." The pledge meant I still had a chance. I rubbed my drippy nose with a sleeve and stared hard at the screen. "I pinky swear."

"But, Em, if you ever scare me like that again—" she said, interrupted by someone entering her bedroom. She beamed at whoever it was. I knew it wasn't Fi's little brother, Jacob, because if it were, she'd be cursing, not staring away with gooey eyes. Then I heard an unfamiliar, deep voice.

"Hey!" I heard a voice that wasn't her mom's. Fi glanced back at me. "Um, Em, I have to go. We'll—" She slapped a reaching hand away. A masculine hand.

"Hey, stop it—" she giggled. Half of a boy's face appeared on screen.

"Hey, yourself," the dark-haired boy said, a playful smirk on his lips. Then he squinted at me. "Who might you be?"

I had to have resembled a fish, eyes bugging out, mouth opening and closing. Or maybe more like a raccoon ensnared by a beam of light, a mascara-smeared bandit caught in the act. Frantic, I grabbed tissue off the nightstand and wiped around my eyes.

"Emma, this is Tyler, my new… friend." Fi grinned. She rested her head on his shoulder. "Tyler, this is Emma. I wanted you two to meet, not necessarily like this, but—"

"Hey," I managed softly.

"Oh, yeah, you're Sophie's best friend, right? You do exist!" He had white teeth, made brighter by dark, wavy hair that touched his collar. His mossy-green eyes, framed by dark lashes, seemed to "pop" without the need for eyeshadow. I continued to stare with my mouth open. I couldn't help it. I was in shock.

"Em?" Fi said. "Hello? Emmm-mmma?"

"Huh? Oh, right. Yeah," I said. My voice sounded raspy and far away. "Okay. I'll let you go. We can talk—you know, uh, we can talk more about that other stuff later."

"Yeah, sure." She tucked a strand of hair behind her ear. "Hey, Em?"

"Huh?"

"Glad you texted. Really. We've got lots to catch up on." Her voice wasn't as warm as usual, but it sounded like she was trying. "Maybe we can hang tomorrow?"

"Okay. Sure. Whatever. We'll figure it out." Then, for a reason I'll never understand, I gave them a double thumbs-up—*Oh, my God. A double thumbs-up? Why?*— then ended the session.

Mortified, I sat unmoving for a few minutes. Thoughts swirled inside my head. What *was* that? Apparently, I'd missed a lot this summer. A lot. This was what I knew. I might get my best friend back. I mean, she just might forgive me, so that was good. It also appeared Fi had a boyfriend. That was just plain weird. Neither of us had ever had serious boyfriends. Sure, we'd had crushes, some more intense than others, but not actual boyfriends. I had never shared Fi before, not with a boy.

It was *a lot* to process. I changed into running gear, pulled on shoes and laced them tight. Down the hall. Out the back door. The pavement under my rubber soles. Legs striding forward, measured at first, building in speed. I ran for close to an hour. But try as I might, I never caught up to the thoughts that raced ahead of me.

Chapter 5

On the first day of school, Sophie's mom drove us since neither one of us had gotten our driver's permits yet. The thought of getting behind the wheel to drive overwhelmed me. I discreetly yanked at strands of hair on the back of my head. Fi recounted something that had happened at her father's house over the weekend, and she and Ms. Zohar cackled together. They made it appear so easy, that mother-daughter thing. I watched, my eyes drawn to the ease with which they touched one another as they spoke, Fi's hand resting on the back of her mom's headrest. They weren't always this agreeable, but even after intense battles, they always circled back to each other, the bond unbroken.

It was nothing like the relationship I had with my mom. The Watters women kept our distance from one another, more like sparring partners who rarely engaged. Most days we avoided eye contact, much less clever exchanges. And when my mom did take a rare glance at me, the weight of unspoken accusations settled heavy on my shoulders. I tugged on another piece of hair, welcoming the brief pain.

"So, what do you think, Em?" Ms. Zohar watched me in the rearview mirror. She gave off a professorial air with her chunky-framed glasses and salt-and-pepper bob.

"Huh?" I lurched forward. "Sorry, I didn't hear what you—"

"God. What's your deal? You're so zoned out today." Fi shifted around to stare at me. Ms. Zohar, brow furrowed, shot her a look.

"What?" Fi widened her eyes and then grimaced.

"She wants to know what you think. High tops with this skirt or black combat boots?" Fi asked. Her words were robotic, her eyes rolled upward.

I slumped back into the seat. "High tops. They're the bomb."

"See," she said to her mom with a smirk. She lifted one of her white-and-black checkered sneakers and admired it. "I thought so, too, but Mom liked the boots."

Ms. Zohar flipped between local radio stations, one of the few people on the planet who refused to pay for streaming service. DJs bombarded the airwaves with moronic morning chatter and forced hoots. She settled on the guitar twangs from a country station despite a withering glare from Fi.

I bobbed my knee up and down and chewed the inside of my cheek. I wasn't sure what to expect at school. Would everyone know what had happened this summer? I offered up a silent prayer that no one had heard about it. It wasn't like we lived in a small town, and my family certainly wasn't close to other families. Unless the Zohars had talked. I eyed them as I brought a thumbnail to my mouth and bit down. Saliva puddled under my tongue as my taste buds puckered. I sputtered.

Dear God. It does taste like earwax. Maybe worse.

I scrambled for my purse, dug through a bunch of crap inside, thankful to find a beat-up peppermint at the bottom. I brushed away the lint and popped it in my mouth. It didn't cover the entire taste, but at least it kept me from throwing up.

Fi asked her mom to drop us off a couple of blocks away from the high school.

"But I wanted a first day picture of you two in front of the school. We've taken one every year since second grade." She jutted out her chin and pushed her glasses up higher on her nose. It was the closest I'd ever heard her come to whining. "Next year you'll be driving. This is probably the last one I'll get."

"Absolutely not. No way." Fi screwed up her face as if she'd just sucked an extra-sour lemon. She motioned to stop the car. "This is good. Seriously."

"But it's a tradition," Ms. Zohar said in a shrill voice.

Fi glared. "Mom, please. I do *not* want anyone seeing us posing in front of the high school like kindergarteners." She exhaled loudly. "God. We're sophomores now."

"But, Sophie, I wanted to—"

"No, Mom." Her voice rose to a shrill of its own. She then added a soft but firm, "Please."

"Fine, but I—"

"Right here is great." As soon as the minivan came to a stop, Sophie lurched out. "Thanks for driving us. Love you."

"You girls have a great day! I can't wait to hear all about it," Ms. Zohar called after us and I heard the hurt in her voice. "Good luck today!"

"Yeah, thanks." Sophie gave a careless wave and started speed walking. "See you later!"

I grabbed my backpack and quickly climbed out the back. "Thanks for the ride, Ms. Zo. Have a great day!" I flashed her my brightest smile.

Sometimes Fi embarrassed me when she acted like that. She had no clue how lucky she was to have a mom who actually gave a flip. But whatever. What could I say that didn't make me sound like a total zero? I caught up to Fi.

"Love those Vans. Whole outfit—goals." I was desperate to reconnect. I knew our recent video chat hadn't earned her forgiveness just yet.

In the past, we would have spent weeks before the first day of school planning outfits. Fi always pored through my back-to-school wardrobe and loved putting ensembles together for me. Another tradition to bite the dust this year. I'd put together my own outfit: rolled-up skinny jeans, gray suede Adidas sneakers, and a flowy poet blouse. I'd gotten up earlier than usual, gone for a run with my dad, and spent the extra time fixing my hair and make-up. I worked hard to make sure neither one looked overdone.

"You look great, too. That haircut is sick," Sophie said after an appraising glance.

"Thanks." But I knew her too well. I could tell by the way she held her chin up, by the arms-length distance she kept, that she was still ticked about this summer. It would take a little time before we could return to the comfortable friendship we'd shared in the past. I got that.

"I wanted to talk to you," Fi said. "So—about Tyler—that was totally weird the other day, right?"

"Uh, yeah. Kinda." I cleared my throat. As usual, she blurted out whatever was on her mind, and again I found myself taken off guard. I wasn't sure how to approach her about this boyfriend thing. "So, are you dating him or what?"

We walked side-by-side, in-sync. Fi grinned to herself but remained quiet for a couple more steps. I'd grown even taller over the summer, so I found myself towering over her. She had always been shorter than me.

"I don't know." She shrugged. "Maybe. I guess." She tucked a long strand of curly, dark brown hair behind her ear, her beaded earrings dancing with each step. "He's hot, though, isn't he? Like California dreamy, right? Or is it just me?" she asked. "I don't know. I think I'm still crushing on Ben, but you know, that's never going to happen. Not with Kiley always hanging on him." Her nose wrinkled in distaste. "Tyler moved here with his mom from San Diego, California over the summer. His parents got a divorce—or maybe they're separated? He lives in our neighborhood, you know, not too far from Grams. I met him at camp."

"Oh. That's great." I pretended to concentrate on avoiding cracks in the sidewalk. "So, you don't know him that well?"

"Well, I wouldn't say that." Sophie played coy. "We have been hanging out."

So that's what Sophie had been doing all these weeks while I was trying to pull my life together? That's why I hadn't heard anything, not even a text, after she'd sent a useless balloon. Wow. A spike of jealousy pierced me.

It's not like I can blame her. Enjoying summer, hanging out with a gorgeous guy. Who wouldn't pick that over a depressed, suicidal friend? I'm sure I'm a lot to take.

I longed for that kind of summer myself—the kind of existence with no cares in the world other than deciding whether to lie by the pool or go to a movie. But that wasn't my life. Far from it. An unusual bitterness flooded my mouth, and it wasn't from the nail polish.

I tuned back in when I heard Fi's voice rise in a question.

"Huh?" *Busted again.* "I'm sorry—"

"Seriously. What is it with you today? You're acting so strange." Her face had the same pinched appearance it had had earlier when her mom wanted to take the photo. "I asked if you're good with Tyler sitting with us at lunch."

"Sorry. Just fuzzy this morning," I said. "Couldn't sleep last night." I forced a fake yawn for effect. "Lunch? Sure, I'm good with that."

We were steps away from the front door of the high school. Sounds of excited yells, bus engines running, and the slamming of car doors enveloped us. We waved at familiar faces. A few girls bobbed up to hug us before bouncing away. I wasn't sure whether it was the leftover taste of nail polish or the bus exhaust fumes that made me queasy.

"Here we go," Fi said. Her hazel eyes lit with excitement, her anger temporarily forgotten as we were swept into a frenetic wave of students funneling into the building. She called out to me, "I'll see you at lunch...or in between classes."

"Sure. I'll find you in the cafeteria," I called back. My heartbeat zipped with anxiety as I lied to Fi a second time that morning. I had no intention of sitting with her at lunch. Not if Tyler sat with us. Not yet anyway.

The counselors had told me this summer to start speaking my mind—to be honest with others, as well as myself, about my feelings. I'd have to work on being more vocal with Fi, but I wasn't quite ready for that confrontation. If I were 100 percent honest with myself, I'd rather down a bottle of that crappy-tasting nail polish than sit next to the guy who might steal her away from me. I'd already lost one sister; I wasn't sure I could stomach losing another.

Chapter 6

Shutting the locker door for the third straight time, I retried the combination again to make sure I had it right. Satisfied, I entered the flow of bodies as students made their way to classes. A heady mingling of cleaning supplies, perspiration, and pungent colognes assaulted my senses, and I held my breath when I hit concentrated pockets of it. Chemistry was next, and I welcomed the extra blowing air from fans inside the lab.

"Damn, girl. Looking hot!" Lacy O'Neil called out when she spotted me. "It's like I didn't even recognize you. Like you're different, but the same, you know?"

"Thanks." I laughed, not sure what to make of that observation.

Lacy had a fine-boned face and unnaturally bright blue eyes, framed by beautiful spun-gold, loose-waved locks. She had been a *fashionista* since grade school.

I stepped back to create some distance. Lacy was one of those who invaded your personal space. She'd move in about three inches from your face, entangle her arms around one of yours, and cling like a baby koala. Except for that annoying tendency, I'd always liked her. But I had to admit, being under the Lacy microscope was unnerving.

We'd grown up in the same neighborhood and attended the same schools since kindergarten, but we were just casual friends. Lacy's mom, Mrs. O'Neil, hadn't liked my mom since the first grade when the two were room parents together. The final falling out had resulted from a winter party craft activity. Mrs. O'Neil had wanted the children to only use black felt for snowman hats. Period. My mom had a different vision. She'd instructed the children to use pink, blue, purple—whatever colors they wanted. Bickering in the back of the classroom had ensued, with my mom's final eruption.

"For Christ's sake, Kay! Really? Let the kids choose whatever damn colors they want!" she had barked. "God forbid they actually *use* their imaginations!"

Mrs. O'Neil, too refined to yell back, hadn't uttered a word. Instead, she stiffly gathered her purse and daughter, then left the classroom. All of us students had sat with mouths agape. Unfazed, my mom had cranked up the volume on the holiday tunes and picked up right where we'd left off. That year our class had the coolest snow people on the first-grade display wall, some of them psychedelic or fluorescent green with multicolored felt hats, gloves, and scarves. I'd never been so proud of my mom, even if it meant the end of future invitations to Lacy's epic birthday parties and sleepovers.

"So?" Lacy sat down and motioned for me to sit next to her. She leaned in close. I could smell spearmint gum on her breath. "What happened to you over the summer?"

I sucked in a quick breath as heat flooded my cheeks. I moved a fingernail to my mouth but stopped short when I remembered that wretched polish.

Oh, God. I'm going to vomit. Did Fi tell her? Does everyone know? Everyone knows.

Crap.

Since I couldn't chew my nails, I again pulled hard at individual strands of hair at the nape of my neck. What could I say? I struggled to compose a coherent sentence, but Lacy didn't seem to notice. She went on.

"Oh! So, I met Sophie's new guy." She placed her notebook and pen on the lab table in front of her, as she wiggled her perfectly waxed eyebrows up and down for effect. "Adorable. And so funny, right?"

I nodded and gritted my teeth. "Yep. Definitely." I hoped Lacy wouldn't notice the lie. It was too embarrassing to admit I was the last person on Sophie's list to meet California Dreamy.

Before Lacy could continue, Coach Cox, a brawny grim-faced man with a reputation for strictness, strode into the classroom. He scrawled chemistry lab rules on the dry eraser board. At that moment, I thanked a higher power for the first rule written in his big blocky handwriting: No talking in class when Coach Cox is at the board.

***

Someone tapped on the classroom door. A smallish girl with a blonde pixie-cut poked her head in, interrupting the coach in mid-sentence. He furrowed his brow and nodded her in. She carried herself with the superior indifference of a senior as she handed him a note. He read it quickly, then peered at us.

"I need Emma Watters to go to the front office," he said. He scanned our faces. "Emma Watters?"

Lacy lowered her chin and looked sideways at me with wide eyes. I shrugged and stood up, woodenly making my way to the front of the class.

"Take your stuff in case you don't make it back here. We only have fifteen minutes left," said Coach Cox.

I almost tripped on my way back to the desk where I hastily stuffed chemistry notes into my backpack. I could feel the hot vibrant pink of my face.

"Hope everything is okay," Lacy whispered. "See you later, right?"

"Yeah. For sure." Avoiding stares from the other students, I sensed them sizing me up until I shut the door behind me.

"Follow me," the sprite-like senior said. She walked on her toes a couple of steps ahead. My guess was she was on the dance team. Over her shoulder, the girl informed me that the high school counselor needed to meet with me. A woman named Ms. Poskey.

"She's cool," the girl said. "Everyone likes her."

I had an idea the counselor would want to see me, but I wasn't expecting to be summoned on the first day. The muscles along my jaw tightened, so much so that I wondered if I'd be able to open my mouth. Not that I planned to do much talking. Ahead, the senior snaked down unfamiliar hallways and past a maze of offices. She deposited me inside a larger office in front of the closed door to a smaller one.

"Just wait here. Poskey's with someone, but she'll probably be done in a sec." The girl hurried away. "Good luck."

I heard murmured voices inside and jumped when the door sprung opened. A tall boy blew past me. I peeked into the open doorway.

"Emma?" Ms. Poskey stood up from her desk and gestured for me to come in. She was tall, maybe six feet. The counselor's voice was warm, her brown eyes kind and genuine. "Come in. Please. Take a seat."

I sat down in one of the faux leather armchairs in front of Ms. Poskey's large oak desk and placed my backpack and purse in the chair next to me. The woman would know everything, I figured, which made me want to cry, but I worked to keep my face blank. I gnawed the inside of my cheek, careful not to bite down too hard.

Ms. Poskey sat in her chair and scooted closer to the desk. "So, Emma, how's your first day at Roosevelt High going?"

"Fine." It sounded flat, even to my ears. She'd probably make a note of that.

"Good. Good." Ms. Poskey nodded and cleared her throat. "I won't keep you in suspense. I was told about what happened in July. A case-worker notified us. Standard procedure."

Ms. Poskey tapped her pencil, eraser-side down, on the top of the desk. The *rap-rap-rap* of the bouncing pencil distracted me, but I shook it off and focused on her. She had blackish hair with silver streaks that framed a heart-shaped face. Deep laugh-lines extended like starbursts from the corners of her eyes and mouth. "So, do you want to tell me—in your words—what went on this summer?"

I shook my head no and looked down at my lap. Every sound was magnified. I could hear myself swallowing, sure that she could hear it, too. Ms. Poskey waited, the rhythm of her pencil slowing down, stopping.

"Emma, I read your file, so I have a decent idea of what happened. Not the why, but the what," Ms. Poskey said. "I want you to know you have someone here to talk to. If you're feeling overwhelmed or upset about anything, you come in and talk to me. Okay?"

I stole a peek at her from under the veil of my hair. Ms. Poskey slipped the pencil behind her ear and leaned forward in the chair. She cocked her head as she appeared to weigh her words.

"This time of your life—you know, the whole high school scene—can be a difficult transition for students, even under the best of circum-stances."

I spotted the colored forms scattered about Ms. Poskey's cluttered desk. She seemed real to me, messy desk and all, which I found comforting. I inhaled through my nose, closed my eyes, exhaled through my mouth. I recalled the sessions I'd had with counselors in Austin. How they'd encouraged me to be honest, to express myself. It hadn't worked with my dad when I'd tried talking to him a week ago, and this morning, I'd been afraid to say what I really felt to Sophie. So far, I hadn't had much success with the whole "express yourself" thing.

"I understand you don't know me well, and Emma, you don't have to confide in me," Ms. Poskey said. "Mainly, I just want to help you, make sure you're okay."

Behind me, the wall clock ticked off minutes, a loud reminder of how time plodded ahead, a steady *tick-tock* march, whether I joined in or not. More than six years had passed since Casey's death, and my family—Mom, Dad, me—remained tethered to that moment. I didn't want to be stuck there forever, couldn't bear it. My front teeth scraped against my bottom lip as I raised my face, eyed Ms. Poskey. Could this total stranger help? Or would it be another miserable fail? I mustered all the inner courage I could and took a chance.

"I wasn't trying to 'harm' myself this summer, ma'am." I kept my words precise. "I was trying to stop how much it hurts. It's been so long—" I stopped, working out in my mind how to continue. It was important I make her understand. "I just want to live without all this pain," I said as I motioned at the space in front of my chest. "But it's not that easy. It's way more complicated than that."

Ms. Poskey regarded me as she reached for the folder with my name typed name on the tab. She glanced at her watch a second before the bell rang.

"Miss Watters, do me a favor, please, and shut that door."

"Sure." I stood and closed it, then returned to my seat, leaning forward with my elbows on knees.

"Now, let's get acquainted. Maybe there's a way I can help make it all a little less complicated," she said. The lines around her mouth deepened as her lips curved upward toward her cheeks.

My eyes started watering, but I didn't care.

Maybe— just maybe—I could reclaim my life.

CHAPTER 7

Four days had passed since I'd confided in Ms. Poskey, and I still hadn't broached the subject with my parents. We'd met for an hour that first day, and afterward Ms. Poskey handed me the business card of a therapist. She said he specialized in families who'd experienced extreme tragedy and trauma, even helping family members who'd lost loved ones in 9/11. I told her it didn't matter how great he was, my parents would never, not in a million years, go for family therapy. But she wouldn't let me leave until I agreed to at least discuss the possibility with them.

"How else do you plan on changing the things you don't like about your life, Emma?" Ms. Poskey had drummed that damned pencil on her desk. "Do you have another idea?"

I hadn't answered. My hands were knotted so tightly together on my lap, my fingers were white from lack of circulation.

"You don't get it." Just thinking about it had drained me. "My dad, he thinks this kind of stuff—you know, talking about how you feel and all this psychological stuff—that it's a joke. No offense."

"None taken. Nothing I haven't heard before." She shrugged, then tossed the pencil on the desk. "Have you ever let him know what you need—what would help you work through this?" She cocked her head. "Have you even asked yourself what you need?"

I rested my head against the wall behind me and counted the speck-led-white ceiling tiles. Thirty-two in all. I squinted at a rust-colored water spot in the corner—the stain was shaped like an octopus, splattered tentacles reaching outward. Ms. Poskey moved from behind her desk.

"If it would help, I'll talk to your dad." She sat down next to me, reached for my right hand, which was balled into a fist. She unfolded my fingers and placed the therapist's card on my open palm, then planted her own hand on top. The woman's entire persona—her big eyes, the comforting clasp of her hand—oozed compassion. "I can't imagine how any of you have coped this long without professional guidance."

I gently tugged my hand away. The idea that any of us had "coped" was laughable. I stuffed the card in the front pocket of my jeans. It was a long shot, but maybe I could convince my dad to at least meet with this guy. I wasn't kidding myself. I knew I needed way more help than a school counselor could provide, even one as nice as Ms. Poskey.

I'd held back from getting into anything too deep with her, but I'd mentioned the panic attacks and how running each morning helped. Ms. Poskey had suggested I meet the school's new track coach, maybe join the team. I'd been skeptical but said I'd think about it.

"I think you and Coach Rodriguez would click." Her voice had been animated. "She's a veteran of the Iraq War. Spent two tours over there. She doesn't broadcast it, but some of the things she experienced...well, I think you'd be surprised."

I planned on finally tackling the therapist topic tonight with my parents, primarily with my dad. And I had fortifications coming. Grams was bringing homemade lasagna for dinner. Even though I hadn't men-tioned anything about it to her, I knew she had pestered my parents to get family therapy for years. Grams would be all in.

I busied myself shuffling stacks of unopened mail off the table and restacking them on the nearby counter. The kitchen smelled of burned eggs, which my mother must have fried while I was at school. I grimaced. An unwashed frying pan filled with cloudy water and floating bits of eggshell rested in the sink. Ignoring that particular mess, I dampened a towel to wipe down the table. If I had time, I'd light a scented candle in the kitchen before Grams arrived.

"Why are you setting the table?" my mom asked from behind, startling me. She sat on the couch in the darkened living room.

"For dinner." I made an erratic grab for plates stacked on the counter and carried four to the table. Being caught off-guard by my mom rattled me. "Grams is coming. Dad's on his way."

"Lovely. All I need is that woman—" my mother said, a slight hint of slurred words. She tried to get up from the couch but plopped back down. "What time is it, again?"

"It's after six. You might want to get out of those pajamas." I pulled out silverware and slapped lines of knife, fork, spoon around the table. *And maybe take a shower, brush your teeth, get a life.*

The muted grating of the opening garage door signaled Dad was home, which meant Grams would be there any minute. I opened the fridge to grab a bag of salad mix and a bottle of Italian dressing. Mom lingered on the couch. Her oily hair stuck to the back of her head where she'd laid on it, but the top of it went vertical in a Marge Simpson spiral, but more tangled. I clenched my teeth as I regarded the mess who was my mother.

Dad walked into the kitchen. A forced smile was plastered on his face.

"Hey." He dropped keys on the counter. "How was school?"

"Fine," I said, clipped. I wasn't sure what rattled me most—talking to him or my mother's disheveled presence. But I needed to do this tonight.

If I didn't act soon, Ms. Poskey would make the call. I wanted to be the one to broach the subject.

My dad took off his glasses, massaged his temples and scalp. "God. This headache has been a killer today. Excruciating." He scrunched his entire face. "Too much caffeine, I think."

Perfect. Should I wait for a night when Mom at least bathed and Dad was less caffeinated? I pinched the bridge of my nose. The conditions for this discussion would never be quite right. I felt it in my gut. It had to be tonight.

My mom piped in from the living room. "You need a drink, Richard. That'll loosen you up." Dad flinched at the sound of her voice and turned around.

"Rosemary—I didn't know you were in there." He fumbled with his eyeglasses, then reached into the cabinet for a glass. The sound of running water drowned out her retort. He shook two aspirin out of the bottle and popped them in his mouth, then downed the glass of water in three loud gulps.

"Grams will be here any minute." I moved past him to pull out more glasses and filled them with ice, shouting over the grinding of the ice maker. "What do you want to drink?"

Dad waved his glass at me. "Water's good for me."

"I already have my drink, thank you," Mom gave an impish laugh. She was snockered.

I rolled my eyes and shot my father a dark look. He turned with a faraway, trapped expression, stared out the window over the sink, and kneaded the muscles where his shoulders and neck met. I filled another glass with water and poured myself milk. The doorbell rang, *Thank God*, and I rushed toward it, desperate to see Grams' face.

"Hello, beautiful," Grams chirped. She clutched a large casserole dish in two hands.

I pulled her into the entry hall and hugged her tightly, lasagna dish and all. The silky feel of her hair against my cheek was calming. I squeezed even tighter.

"Whoa—careful, sweetie." Grams chuckled. She wore chic sparkling hoop earrings that shimmered when she turned her head and a silk scarf tied around her neck. "I don't want to drop this thing."

"Sorry, Grams." I took the lasagna and led her into the kitchen. "Should I warm it up?"

"Maybe ten minutes or so." Grams immediately spied the dirty frying pan in the sink, and I silently thanked her for not commenting on the smell. Instead, she turned her attention to my dad. "How are you, Richard? How have things been at school?"

"Good. Kind of busy, but I'm good." My dad gave Grams a brief hug. "You?"

"Fine. I've been volunteering at the senior center this week. That activities director is a riot. You should hear some of—" She caught sight of her rumpled daughter on the couch and stopped in mid-sentence but covered her surprise. "Ah, Rosemary! I didn't know you were in there. How are you?"

"Nobody seems to know I'm here," Mom muttered. "I'm the same as I was the last time you asked, Mother." She saluted Grams with a highball glass in hand. My grandmother's smile faded.

"So, Grams," I butted in, "the hairstyle was a hit, just as you predicted!" I was determined to keep the evening on course. "Thanks for talking me into it."

"That's good, hon." Grams seemed grateful for the interruption. "Not surprised one bit. It shows off that gorgeous face, plain as day."

She eased into her seat at the kitchen table, and we continued with small talk until the timer buzzed and the lasagna was placed on the table. No one made lasagna as good as Grams. It overpowered the stench of burned eggs; the kitchen was suddenly filled with the aroma of mozzarella, garlic, oregano, and Italian sausage. My soul felt a little lighter.

I piled a large piece on my plate along with some salad. My movements were calm, but I felt spasms in my stomach. I shoveled a few quick bites into my mouth but knew I needed to relax. I laid the fork down on my plate and chewed more slowly, hoping the food would settle.

"Rosemary," Grams called, "come join us at the table. We should eat together as a family more—"

"Nope. Not hungry." My mother put down her now-empty glass but stayed planted on the couch.

"But it's your favorite," Grams countered. I hated hearing how pitiful she sounded.

"She said no," I said with more force than I'd intended. Having my mom at the table was the last thing I wanted. "We'll save a plate for you, Mom. For later." The crackle of disquiet rippled through the air. My head began throbbing just like it did before a severe storm hit, whenever the barometric pressure plunged. I said a silent prayer my mother would pass out. Of course, any other night she would, but right then it didn't look too promising.

Fork in hand and head down, Dad prodded at a torn lasagna noodle on his plate. Grams shifted in her seat to face me. After an awkward pause, she asked me about the first week of school. I told her about my classes and teachers.

My dad pretended to listen, but his eyes kept darting to my mother, who blurted out random, unintelligible comments from the living room. There would never be a perfect moment for this. Never. I took a deep breath, then dove into the meeting with Ms. Poskey, words forced through my now dry throat and lips.

"We talked for about an hour—you know, about my panic attacks and stuff." My hands balled into fists on my lap and sweat trickled down my lower back. A panic attack loomed, a whisper away. I sensed its biting presence in my quick, shallow breathing.

My mom snorted. "Panic attacks, my eye," she snapped from the living room.

I ignored her. "She suggested—well, there's this doctor who specializes in—I think it's post-traumatic stress disorder? Anyway, she thinks we should talk to him, that maybe he could—you know, help all of us with—"

"What? Slow down." My dad frowned and laid his glasses on the table. He worked at massaging his temples again. "Who is this woman again?"

"I think it's a fantastic idea," Grams said. She swallowed a bit of salad and dabbed at her lips. "And God knows, it's long overdue."

My dad glowered at her. "Dorothy, please. We've discussed this countless times."

"And countless times you've rejected the idea, Richard. Look where that's gotten us!" She circled a fork in the air, motioning to me and my parents. "This summer alone should be proof that this family needs help. Sheesh. It doesn't take Einstein to figure *that* out."

On cue, my adrenal glands kicked in at the mention of "this summer," and all the shame resurfaced. The acidic taste of it flooded my mouth. Casey's face appeared behind Grams' head, just above her left shoulder. My little sister, her shimmery gaze pleading, mouthed something to me. I squinted hard at her but couldn't make out what she said. I had the feeling she wanted me to keep speaking. I cleared my throat.

"Dad, I, uh, feel like I need to—" I said, as I tore my gaze away from her. When I looked past Grams' shoulder again, Casey was gone. The food I'd wolfed down minutes earlier felt lodged between my esophagus and stomach. I pressed against my breastbone and swallowed hard. "What I'm trying to say is, I think we should—it would—I need help. Grams is right. I think we all do." My voice was thin and wispy. "This doctor, he worked with families who lost loved ones on Nine-Eleven. He must be good."

My dad sat rod straight. Emotions—disbelief in raised eyebrows, anger in lips pressed together, and the ever-present sadness of his eyes—contradicted his usually hard-to-read face. Then, worst of all, it went blank. Just blinked out. I knew what that meant. He was disconnecting, mentally slipping away.

"Dad, it's just that I need to be able—" I started again just as a low cackle erupted from the living room, from my mother. It increased in volume from a low rumble to a full out, high-pitched shriek.

Who laughs at a time like this?

The sound confused me. The room tilted a few degrees. I struggled to regain a sense of balance.

"Oh, Lord. She thinks a shrink can fix us," Mom said between bouts of hysterical laughter. "What do you think, Richard? Can a shrink fix us?" The squawking continued, the harsh sound ricocheting off the walls. I dug my fingertips hard into my temples to keep myself from throwing up.

At that moment, my usual disdain of her turned into hatred. I wanted to hurt her. I held back, tempted to throw a plate at her to stop the deranged screeching. Before I could say or do anything, my dad slammed his fork down on the table—harsh and crisp, like the crack of a gunshot. I instinctively jerked away from the table.

"For the love, Rosemary. Shut. Up," Grams barked.

My mother grabbed a sofa pillow and buried her face in it. The muffled hysterics continued. I pressed the heels of my hands into my ears.

"Richard, just hear Emma out." Grams pressed her palms against the tabletop. Dad rose from his chair, plate in hand. "Your child needs—"

"Don't tell me what my child needs. Just stay out of this." He shoved his glasses back on his face; the light reflected off the lenses, masking his eyes. His sucked in a ragged breath. "Thank you for bringing dinner, Dorothy, but I'm not hungry."

He banged his untouched plate on the kitchen counter and grabbed his keys before he headed out. The door slammed. Within seconds, I heard the growl of the engine as he punched the accelerator. Like always, racing away.

My mom continued her crazed laughing, slightly muted by the pillow. Stunned, I bowed my head and watched tears drip onto my plate. I could barely swallow. It felt like I'd sucked down a piece of hard candy, and it was stuck. Grams gripped my shoulder.

Everything is stuck.

I glanced at Mom, the pillow covering her face, as her entire body shook with laughter. Or maybe she was sobbing. I couldn't really tell the difference. Casey stood next to our mother, her saucer-like eyes solemn. She pushed out with both arms, urging me to leave.

"Why does she act like that?" I asked Casey. My sister regarded me with miserable eyes, her arms waving more insistent for me to go. "I don't understand. Why does she do this?"

"Bipolar disorder—it's difficult to understand, hon. Gramps fought it, too." I froze at the sound of Grams' soft voice near my ear. She thought I had been speaking to her. She had no idea I was talking to—what?—a ghost? A vision? A figment of my imagination?

"She didn't show any serious signs until she was a freshman at college." Sadness emanated off Grams. "She needs to get back on meds, figure how to manage it. I wish I could do it for her," she said, her eyes welling, "but she has to be the one. She has to want it."

Grams stood up from the table, slowly and deliberately. Her face appeared frailer than it had an hour ago, and much older. The past few minutes seemed to have aged her. She reached for her purse on the counter.

"Come with me, Em. We're going to my house," She grabbed me around the forearm with firm but gentle fingers. "Don't worry. These spells come and go. It'll all be okay."

I allowed Grams to lead me outside, but I wasn't so sure about that. It didn't seem like my life would ever be okay.

***

It was almost ten o'clock that night when my dad pulled into Grams' driveway. Headlights filtered through the curtains of the darkened living room. I was on the couch, the television volume set low, its colored lights flickering rainbows across the walls. Grams slept in the rocking recliner next to the me. I heard him put his key in the front door lock and let himself in. His movements were hushed as he walked inside.

I feigned sleep, relaxing my eyelids and facial muscles as best I could. I heard him edge toward me, smelled the spicy cologne, felt him peering down at me. He tapped on my leg and then gently nudged it. I pretended to awaken, swinging my legs over the side of the couch as I sat up and stifled a fake yawn. He slumped down next to me.

We sat for a few minutes in uncomfortable silence. He coughed and cleared his throat.

"I'm sorry I ran out on you like that." His voice was so soft, I leaned in closer to hear him. He rested elbows on thighs and stared at steepled fingers. "I guess I just…I don't know. I figured we could get through this on our own. It appears I was wrong. Your grandmother tried to tell me many times before, but I've always wanted to handle it my way."

"I know." I ran hands through my messy hair. "I wish I could just put it all away somewhere, but that doesn't work for me."

He nodded, defeated. "Then I guess it's time we tried it your way." He leaned back against the couch and closed his eyes. "I just want you to be okay, Em. That's it. That's the most important thing to me."

"Thank you." I knew this decision had been difficult for him. "And I want you to be okay, too."

I glanced at Grams, who wore the faintest of grins but with eyelids still shut. Maybe I wasn't the only one who faked sleep in this family. A small hopeful smile of my own broke through.

Chapter 8

The cafeteria roared with noise as students clustered around tables, in constant motion as they shared food, gossip, and yelps of laughter. I sat alone and watched. During the first week of school, instead of sitting with Sophie and Tyler, I'd camped out in the library with an energy bar for lunch. I'd told Sophie I couldn't make it because I was already struggling to keep up in Advanced Literature. A lie, of course. But today I decided to join them, and my stomach growled its approval. I had missed eating real food. Besides, I had enough trouble without worrying about losing Sophie. Maybe I'd overreacted to the whole Sophie-Tyler thing, anyway.

"Glad you finally ventured out from your antisocial cave." Sophie side-eyed me and dropped her Spanish workbook on the table. "Save us seats? Gotta get pizza before the line gets too long."

"Got it covered," I said, pulling out a sandwich, an apple, yogurt, and two cookies from my lunch sack. It was a feast. I called after Sophie, "Hey, grab me an extra bottled water? I forgot mine."

"Sure." Seconds later, I saw a group of girls stop her. She broke into an animated story, her arms reaching at the air here and there. The girls giggled and elbowed each other as they hung on her every word. There was no doubt—my best friend could command an audience.

Then I noticed Sophie's eyes wander toward Ben, who sat on top of a nearby tabletop, surrounded by his football buddies. Ben was lanky but cut. He was the main reason I had decided not to worry so much about the Sophie-Tyler romance. Tyler wasn't going to take Sophie away from me, but there was a strong chance Ben might steal Sophie away from him.

I'd noticed she still ogled Ben in the hallways, and he returned the steamy glances, even as she walked next to Tyler. Maybe he was one of those guys who thought a girl was more attractive if she was unavailable. Or, more likely for Ben, it was the challenge of taking Sophie away from the good-looking new guy all the girls were whispering about. The way I figured it, maybe Sophie wasn't as into Tyler Herrera as she pretended.

Why Sophie had crushed on Ben since elementary school, I'd never get. Sure, he was handsome in the classic sense and definitely ripped, but Tyler was those things, too. Ben was a total turd, as far as I was concerned. I'd never forgotten what he'd done in the fifth grade. He and a group of his bonehead friends had made fun of a special-needs kid during recess. They'd been playing keep-away from a boy named Eddie, who kept trying to get the soccer ball back. Ben and his band of clueless dudes had mocked the boy, who played along at first, but then became more and more confused.

"Here you go, fat ass," Ben had sneered before slamming the ball hard into Eddie's doughy gut. "Don't be such a baby." His jerk-face friends had broken into laughter, fist-bumping each other as they left the kid crying, crumpled on his butt in the dirt by the swing set. I'd despised Ben since. Yes, it was years ago, and I should probably let it go, but as far as I could tell, he hadn't changed much since then.

Of course, Sophie had defended him. Ben had told her it was a big misunderstanding, that he'd been joking with Eddie. But I was there. I had seen it. There was no misunderstanding. I had been the one who led a hysterical Eddie to the nearest teacher. If I could redo that day, I would have clocked Ben right in the face with that stupid soccer ball. In fact, I'd fantasized about it the rest of fifth grade, and most of sixth. I once came close but never did it, mainly because of Fi, and, besides, I didn't have the energy to take him on at school when I was already buckling under my stressful home life.

Tyler, on the other hand, with his easy-going smile and mischievous eyes, seemed nicer than I first thought. Last week, as I was leaving Life Skills class, I'd dropped my unzipped backpack. Its entire contents—pens, books, papers, spirals, and tampons—had spilled onto the floor just outside the classroom door. My oh-so-helpful classmates had trampled over my stuff in a rush to get to their next class, but Tyler had stopped. He elbowed passers-by to keep them from stepping on my things and helped pick them up. He didn't even flinch as he tossed a tampon into the backpack.

"That's okay. I've got—" I'd said, stammering, of course, my face aflame.

"Not a problem," he'd said. After making sure everything was returned to the backpack, he had walked me to Algebra II, my least favorite class, and made me laugh along the way.

"So, what are your thoughts on boiling eggs?" he'd asked in reference to our first cooking chapter in Life Skills. He had a playful glint in his eyes as he dodged oncoming students so he could walk beside me. "Are you a fan of the hard-boiled or the soft-boiled?"

"What?" I raised an eyebrow and laughed. Maybe I'd misheard him. "You want to know my thoughts on *eggs*?"

"No pressure," he said, "but how you answer this question reveals *a lot* about your personality. So, think it over before you commit." A smile tugged at his lips.

"Hard-boiled. Definitely. I'm a hard-boiled-egg kind of girl," I said, a grin relaxing my face. "So, what does that say about me?"

Tyler didn't answer at first, just stared at my mouth. Again, I felt my face flush, I'm sure a brilliant pink. His tennis shoes squeaked against the glossy tile as he came to an abrupt stop in the hall. Other students bounced off him, then grumbled past.

"Right. Hard-boiled it is. Hold on." He slipped a phone out of his jeans pocket, his thumbs flying along the keypad as he pulled up the Internet.

"Okay. After much, *much* scientific study, researchers have determined that if you like hard-boiled eggs...." He paused, his eyebrows shooting up. "You're an athlete who's concerned about health. This, of course, drives your friends crazy because—" He took a spirited sidestep to keep me from grabbing the phone, and started reading again. His voice became softer. "—because you have a beautiful, toned body, and are never sick. Try to relax more. It'll do you good in the long run."

The heat seeping into my face was interfering with my brain function. I floundered for a funny comeback.

Nothing. I've got nothing.

"I'd say that's pretty accurate," Tyler said, his head bobbing in agreement. "Now, if you're like me, and prefer eggs scrambled—not too hard, but not runny goo either—it says: You take some time to warm up to."

I hooted. It was an unnatural sound. *Could I be any more awkward?*

Tyler's grin widened. He continued reading, "At first, you don't seem approachable, but as people get to know you, they fall in love. I repeat—They. Fall. In. Love. You are a hard worker, blah, blah, blah, but always elegant in whatever you do."

"That's not what it says." I grabbed the phone from him and reread the analysis of the Egg Personality Test. *Ridiculous.* "Who knew eggs revealed so much?"

"Eggs-actly!" said Tyler. "Okay. Gotta run before the bell rings. Maybe see you later?"

I nodded but paused at the open classroom door when I heard him shout: "Hey, Emma. Have an egg-cellent day!"

"Whatever!" I snorted. I wasn't sure which was more attractive. His eyes or that irresistible laugh. No, Tyler wasn't nearly as bad as I first thought. Not even close.

Snapping back to the present, I surveyed the cafeteria. Where had Fi gone? She wasn't with the group of girls anymore. Maybe she was still in line for that crappy pizza with the plastic cheese. Definitely not worth it.

"What are you thinking about?" Tyler interrupted my thoughts. He slid his tray to the seat across from mine. "You had a funny smile on your face. You keeping secrets?"

"Huh? No. I mean I don't know," I said, then motioned to his tray. "I was just thinking about the plastic cheese they put on that pizza. Blech!"

"Oh, that's right. You're a hard-boiled-egg kind of girl." He had that irresistible expression on his face again. "An athlete with an extraordinary...or wait, was it a perfectly toned...."

"Okay, okay!" I dipped my chin and covered my eyes. "Stop."

He chuckled and shook two small cartons of chocolate milk before he opened both. He finished the first one in three long swigs. I blushed again while recalling his description of my body and shifted in my seat. Tyler raised an eyebrow and continued to watch me as he held the second carton of milk.

"Uh, Sophie is sitting right here," I said, motioning to the chair next to me. "Want to change seats with me so you two can sit next to each other?"

"It's whatever," he said with a shrug. He didn't make a move.

A second later, Sophie carried a personal-size pizza box to the table and two bottles of water tucked under her arm. Ms. Poskey and another woman trailed behind.

"Hey." Sophie nodded at Tyler and put the bottles on the table. She slid her pizza box to the spot next to him, then motioned behind her and shot me a wide-eyed look.

"Ms. Poskey was looking for you," she said to me, "so I told her to follow me."

"Hi." I stood up. The stares of other students in the cafeteria who stopped to watch the exchange needled at my back.

"Hi, Emma," Ms. Poskey said. She patted my shoulder, then nodded at the woman standing next to her. "This is Coach Rodriguez. I've been telling her how much you love to run, and how you might be a great addition to our track team."

"Hey." Coach Rodriguez's handshake was as strong as the steeliness in her eyes—keen, intelligent, and alert. To me, they revealed a person who soaked up details in a glance and acted just as quick. *Decisive.* That's the word that popped into my mind. That, and maybe *badass.*

Coach Rodriguez wore black athletic joggers, a red-and-black shirt with a Roosevelt High Redhawks logo, and a pair of new-looking Nike running shoes. She was about the same height as me but seemed taller because of the way she carried herself, her back and shoulders straight. The coach had short, dark hair, khaki-colored skin, and a nose with the slightest bump just below the bridge. I also took note of her muscular frame. A hard-boiled-egg type, for sure.

"So, you like to run, huh?" Coach Rodriguez asked. "You run regularly?"

"Usually, every day before school." I shoved my hands in my pockets, not sure where to look.

"Tell you what. Come by Monday morning, meet me at the track, and we'll see how you handle yourself. Sound good?"

"Yeah. Sure. I guess." I wrinkled my brow, still uncertain what I was getting into. "Are you timing me? Am I, like, trying out or something?"

"No, nothing like that. You'll just be running. With me." The coach tapped my shoulder. "I'm late for a meeting. See you Monday, six-fifteen sharp. If you're late, I go without you."

I watched Coach Rodriguez and Ms. Poskey walk away, then plopped into my seat, open-mouthed.

"Fi, what just happened?" I whispered.

Sophie returned the bug-eyed face. "I think you just agreed to go for a 'friendly run' with a former soldier...who might secretly be Wonder Woman," she stage whispered back, hands on hips. Her face lit up. "Hey, do me a favor. Be on the lookout for those bullet-deflecting wristband thingys. I always wanted a pair of those."

"On the bright side," Tyler added, "if you can't keep up, maybe she'll let you follow behind on the invisible jet."

I reached for my apple and bit off a huge chunk.

"No, but nice try." I chomped, my mind racing. "She'd probably lasso me and drag me on my butt. 'No free rides,' I bet would be her line."

CHAPTER 9

I woke a few minutes before the five-thirty alarm sounded. It was Monday morning, and I had a run scheduled with the coach. Despite my predictable tiredness, I hopped out of bed. It'd been another night of restless sleep for me, one looping cycle of drifting into exhaustion, unable to move in my dreams, and waking to my own whimpered screams. I couldn't remember the last time I felt rested.

I stood up straight and shook my arms and legs to loosen my muscles, bent over and touched my toes ten times in rapid succession, five reps in all. It helped my blood start pumping and my head clear. I moved into sets of neck and shoulder rolls.

"I can't be late," I said out loud, my stomach jittery. I'd have about thirty minutes to get ready before meeting Coach Rodriguez at the track. Dad said he'd drop me off on his way to work. At first, he seemed puzzled I was running with her instead of him this morning. Except for my stay in Austin, I hadn't missed one of our runs in years. But once I'd explained I was considering joining the track team, he seemed content.

Dressed in running gear, I grabbed the small duffle bag I'd packed the night before with clothes and other stuff I'd need to get ready at school.

Dad came in from his run and tapped on my bedroom door.

"Come in."

"Just making sure you're up." His hair was pasted to his head with sweat, but he had that healthy after-run glow.

"I'm ready whenever you are."

"Won't take long." He leaned against the doorframe. "It was strange going without you this morning, but I'm glad you're doing this."

"Yeah. Me, too," I said before he nodded and closed the door.

I settled against the headboard and glanced at the framed family portrait on my nightstand. The photo represented a time when life had seemed normal. I picked it up and wiped a smudge off the glass with my unzipped hoodie, then studied each of the faces. Was this even our family or was this one of those fake families that come with the store-bought frames? These people were content: a beaming mother, a relaxed dad, a brighter version of myself, complete with a missing tooth and a blue bow in my hair, and the fiery eyes of Casey, who snuggled Bear in the crook of her arm. Casey most favored our mom, with dark features that contrasted the lighter ones of me and our dad. Except for the eyes. We both had our mother's eyes.

The portrait had been taken six months before Casey's death. I peered closely at it and tried for the thousandth time to spot any chinks in this family's armor. Could they have predicted what would happen, that one would die unexpectedly, much too soon, and the rest of the family would disintegrate? No. What was to come was nowhere to be seen. After Casey died, each of us had pulled in separate directions, spinning free of the familial bond, orbiting like specks of dust around the airy emptiness of its missing nucleus. We all needed Casey.

Her. Not me. I'm not enough for them.

It was another failure I could add to a rather long list. I returned the frame to the nightstand and leaned back. I shut my eyes and pulled out a specific memory—the day my parents had told me Mom was pregnant with Casey. It was surreal, the memory. I often wondered if I'd made that one up, too. But I hadn't. I'd been in first grade. My parents had sat me down at the kitchen table and said a new baby was on the way. They'd acted funny, all toothy grins and nervous giggles. I was filled with so much happiness at the news, I thought I might lift off the chair, float up into the sky like one of those massive hot-air balloons.

Then they encircled me in their embrace. Pressed against their chests, I could feel the vibration of their laughter, the recollection of it warming my skin so many years later. Maybe, at that moment, I *had* been enough.

A knock at the door. "Ready?" My father's face appeared through the crack.

"Ready." I lightly touched the framed photograph before leaving behind the warmth of the long-ago moment. I was off to see Wonder Woman.

***

Coach Rodriguez was sprawled on the dewy grass next to the track. She was bent over in hurdler stretches, but I saw the U.S. Navy emblem on the thigh of her old gray sweats. I wasn't sure what I was supposed to do, my stomach lurching as I stood there. Why had I agreed to it? What was the purpose of doing this? As I approached, my hands were shoved in my pockets.

Coach Rodriguez looked up. "Hey! You made it." Her face was scrubbed bare. She was probably in her early thirties, but without make-up on, she could pass for younger.

I cleared my throat. "Morning."

"You planning on warming-up?"

"Um—yeah. I guess."

I tossed my stuff on the ground and started my usual stretches. The fluid movements didn't relax me like usual. Instead, my heartbeat fluttered, and my body felt stiff and robotic. I forced myself to breathe in and out through the stretches. My muscles grudgingly yielded. Coach Rodriguez stood up and marched in place as she waited for me to finish.

"I figure we can get in a solid forty-five-minute run. You good with that?"

"Uh, yeah." My throat was dry and my movements jerky. What if I wasn't good enough? For Coach Rodriguez? Or for the team?

"Let's get moving then," she announced.

Starting at a light jog, I matched the coach's stride. Running on the track felt different with more give under my feet than the paved streets I traversed with my dad. The sound of my foot falls was muted, too, which took getting used to, but I found my rhythm about halfway through the first lap.

Coach Rodriguez spoke as we rounded the second curve.

"You have a nice stride." Her breathing was almost normal. "You sure you've never run track before?"

"No, but I run with my dad most mornings. I have for years."

"Why haven't you ever gone out for track?" she asked, focused straight ahead, a slight increase in her speed. I picked up my speed to match it.

"Well...." I coughed. How to explain everything? The circumstances of my sister's death. The issues with panic. The dysfunctional family. It was all so depressing. I didn't want to sound pathetic. "It's kind of a long story."

"I've got time. I like distractions when I'm working out." She shot me one of her laser-like, stare-into-your-soul glances, but softened it with a lopsided smile.

I kept quiet. Instead, I counted my steps, *inhale*, counted more steps, *exhale*. We moved in silence with only the sound of footfalls on the track.

"Okay—so don't tell me your long story." We had just finished the first warm-up lap and continued on. "But answer this. Why do you run every day? What's the payoff—besides staying in shape?"

I ran several yards before responding. I knew the answer immediately but was hesitant to share. "It's like when I run—I don't know—it's when I feel most free." I paused, then gave a strained laugh. "I know. That probably sounds strange."

"No, I can understand that." Coach Rodriguez increased her speed a little more. "Believe it or not, I get it completely."

"You do?" I asked.

"Sure." She still showed no signs of labored breathing. "But the real question is—it's a question most people have to ask themselves at some point in their lives—the real question is, are you running *from* something...or are you running *toward* something?" She sucked in air and blew it out. "There's a big difference. Something you might think about." Then she rocketed forward.

At that moment, I didn't have time to ponder the question. I was too busy giving everything I had just to trail her the rest of the way. Yep, Wonder Woman, I decided, and I breathlessly powered on.

If only I were a superhero. I would have protected Casey and saved our family from destruction. If only.

CHAPTER 10

I sat on the edge of the black leather couch in the therapist's waiting room and stared at the colorful blobbed abstracts that hung on the walls. The temperature in the office must have been single digits. Goose bumps traveled wave after wave from the base of my neck, down the length of each arm, and my teeth even chattered a little.

"It's freezing in here, right?" I asked Dad, shifting on the couch.

He glanced at me, shrugged, and hunched back over a clipboard on his lap that held a finger-thick packet of forms. Maybe it was just my nerves, but I was glad I'd grabbed my hoodie on the way out of the house this morning. We'd left my mother sleeping in my parents' room.

The night before, my parents had argued about the appointment. Of course, Mom had refused to go with us. Ever.

"Really, Richard? Let me guess. My mother finally got to you, didn't she? God—that woman never gives it a rest," she'd said as she twirled clear liquid around in a highball glass. Bits of crushed ice and vodka sloshed onto the table. "You're such a hypocrite. At least stand up for what you believe. How many times have you lectured me about 'the clueless masses' buying into psychology? You call yourself a scientist?" She paused, scanned him up and down pointedly. "What's next? An astrologer to diagram our sun and moon charts?" She downed the remaining contents of the glass, then slammed it on the table. She spit the final words as she stomped out of the room. "You're pathetic."

Accustomed to my mom's verbal abuse, my dad fixed his eyes into a thousand-yard stare. I'd read about it once—the detached gaze some soldiers wore during combat. They'd emotionally separate from the horrors around them. I suppose that's how he'd made it through these verbal blood baths.

Thank God she hadn't come today. I was skittish enough as it was.

I hugged the hoodie to my chest and leaned over to read my dad's responses written in perfect, tiny print. He tilted the clipboard away from my prying eyes. I'd answered the questionnaire online two nights before, but my dad had put it off. There were questions like "Have you ever felt so sad you couldn't function?" "If so, what did you do to cope?" "How do you express anger?" "Have you ever felt like harming yourself?" "Do you hear voices? Do you see things that aren't there?" "Do you believe in a higher power?" My dad shook his head and jotted something down. He didn't have to say a word. I knew what he thought of the questionnaire. I still couldn't believe he'd agreed to come.

The receptionist slid back the glass panel that separated her desk from the waiting room. I jolted at the sound.

"Settle down, Em." My dad stopped writing, catching my eyes with his and lowering his voice. "You sure you want to do this? Say the word, and we'll leave right now."

The receptionist peered at us through dark-red framed glasses perched on the tip of her nose. "Doctor Watters? Doctor Kapur will see you shortly." She looked at her wristwatch. "Will your wife be here soon? The doctor likes to meet the entire family before setting up individual meetings with each of you."

"No. She won't be coming at all," Dad said in a clipped tone. The receptionist pursed her lips and nodded, silver hoop earrings catching the fluorescent lighting above.

"Okay, sir. I'll let the doctor know." Her fingers clicked along the keyboard. "He should be with you in a few minutes." A slow *whoosh*, and the panel shut.

Dad returned to the paperwork and muttered under his breath. His eyes were bloodshot, as if he hadn't slept much last night. He had such a sadness hanging over him. *It's my fault. He hadn't always been this way.*

I closed my eyes and recalled another version of him, the dad he was when I was little, the one who told me knock-knock science jokes and mimicked the cartoon voices of Looney Tunes characters. His sarcastic impersonations of Sylvester and Daffy Duck always drew giddy laughter from Casey, Mom, and me. Where had that guy gone, the one with the silly voices and silver spark in his eyes? I had labeled that era as Pre-CD. Pre-Casey's Death. At that time, I had a family, the one captured in the portrait on my nightstand. The months and years that followed Casey's death I dubbed Post-CD—and that era sucked.

I looked at him again. "Can I ask you a question?" I blurted on impulse, before nipping at my thumb cuticle. The bitter nail polish had worn off the past few days, at least enough for me to stomach a nibble.

"What is it?" He kept writing, his head down. "I need to finish this."

"Remember when you used to do that Daffy Duck voice? When I was little? Remember how—remember how Casey would giggle so hard she'd make those snorting pig sounds?" I chuckled softly, hesitant, my fingers playing with the frayed cuticle. "When you did that voice, you'd always spray us with spit."

My dad winced, and his face drained of color. He squinted at the paperwork, making a final notation. "No," he said, just above a whisper, "I don't remember that." He abruptly stood up and carried the paperwork to the receptionist. The woman took the clipboard from him and closed the panel with another *whoosh*. When he returned to the couch, his face was blank, distant.

You may not remember, Dad, but I do. I remember silly voices and tickle fights and the smell of peppery cologne when I buried my face in the side of your neck and bear hugs so tight your heartbeat vibrated in my ears and feeling fearless when you'd lift me onto your shoulders, feeling like I could touch each star you'd name in the night sky above.

I couldn't say it aloud. I lacked the courage. Instead, I sucked in three deep breaths—I'd once read in a magazine article that the best way to keep from crying was to breathe deeply. I tore off more of the cuticle with my teeth and chewed the rubbery skin, the familiar copper taste again on my tongue. I grabbed a tissue from the box on the side table and wrapped it around my now-bleeding thumb. Grams would notice I'd been biting my cuticles again.

A side door opened, and a man with bronzed skin and near-black eyes entered the lobby. He was handsome for an older guy. Probably in his late thirties, he wore dark dress pants and a crisp, light-blue dress shirt, unbuttoned at the collar to reveal a white T-shirt underneath. We stood.

"You must be the Watters." He extended a hand. "Hello, Richard, Emma. I'm Aman Kapur. You can call me Dr. K, if you'd like. Most of my clients do."

I stared at him. His smooth voice matched his easy manner. His handshake was firm, but his hands felt soft, and his nails were buffed and manicured. Grams would approve. I shoved my left hand deeper into my pocket, hoping I wouldn't get blood on my favorite hoodie, and trailed my dad and Dr. K into a plush office.

Windows covered an entire wall, and downtown Dallas was visible below. Pieces of modern sculpture and antique books decorated his bookshelves. He motioned for us to sit, so we sunk into the soft, leather sectional and Dr. K took a chair in front of us. He crossed his legs, a notepad on his lap. His sharp eyes appeared to take in my hands stuffed in pockets, the uncontrollable fidgeting of my feet and legs, my father's arms crossed over his chest, and Dad's facial expression that read 'No Trespassing.'

"So, what brings you here today?" he asked. He scanned both our faces. I pulled my right hand out of my hoodie and plucked the side seam of my faded jeans. My chest tightened. My throat constricted, which would have made it tough to speak even if I'd wanted to. The silence was crushing me.

Finally, my dad spoke. "We've had a family tragedy that my daughter, my family," he cleared his throat, "has struggled with." He used his professorial voice, the one I'd hear him use when he rehearsed class lectures at home. More silence.

I summoned my voice, which sounded high-pitched and squeaky to my ears. "My counselor at school recommended you. Because of the Nine-Eleven stuff—how you helped those families who lost—people they loved. She thought maybe you could...maybe you could help us deal with—"

I gulped at air, determined not to cry, even though my eyes stung as if I had shampoo in them.

"I—well, a few months ago, I swallowed too much Tylenol." I continued to rhythmically pluck the side seam of my jeans. "I didn't want to die or anything. I thought maybe if I could just stop the pain...you know, for a little while." I sucked in more air before stumbling on. "Ms. Poskey, uh, that's my school counselor, she says I need to talk to someone. That it might help."

I heard my father's breathing quicken. He sat next to me, ramrod straight, arms wrapped tight around his chest. He stared at his loafers.

"I see." Dr. K jotted a few things down in the notepad. It made a scratching sound in the quiet room. "So—how recent was this family tragedy? Dr. Watters?"

"Casey died—well, it has been roughly six years ago now," he said, his voice flat.

"I'm sorry to hear that. And you all received counseling after it happened?" Dr. K asked. He wrote something else on the pad. Unhurried, Dr. K first studied my dad, and then me, all the while the question hung in the empty air.

"Uh, no, sir," I finally answered, shifting in my seat.

The tip of Dr. K's pen remained suspended above his open notebook. My dad had turned to focus on me. I balled my hand into a fist, rested it on my thigh, and silently begged it to stop trembling. My stomach was a tilt-a-whirl, roiling and swirling. If it didn't stop, I'd throw up. And I was downing so much air in my attempt not to cry, I felt light-headed, close to hyperventilating. The room took on a reddish-black hue.

"It's okay, Emma, really. Now, I'd like you to relax if you can. Just take your time," Dr. K said. His eyes teemed with concern. "This is a safe space."

I knew I looked wild-eyed right before a full-blown panic attack. I worked to collect myself. It took about five minutes before I could breathe regularly.

Dr. K uncrossed his knees slowly, like any quick movements might cause me and my dad to flee. The notes were face down on his lap. He focused on my dad. "No counseling after Casey's death? Not for any members of your family?"

Dad eventually responded, but not to Dr. K's question. His voice was shaky, almost whimsical, an odd sound for him in the Post-CD days. "I used to—I used to make my girls laugh."

I sought out the carpet, the ceiling, the walls. I looked anywhere but at my dad or Dr. K. Gasping sounds erupted beside me, then a soft, surprised whimper. My dad remained rigid, his body fighting the muffled sobs that escaped, resting his chin on his chest, a thumb and forefinger pinching the bridge of his nose. Stunned, I felt stinging in my eyes. I hadn't seen my father cry since Casey's funeral.

Unfazed, Dr. K passed me a box of tissues and motioned for me to hand it to my dad. I nudged it against his leg, and he grabbed a handful.

"Take your time," Dr. K said. "We'll talk when you're ready."

It took about ten minutes for my dad to stop crying. I grabbed a wad of tissues, too, and sopped up tears that leaked down my cheeks. Dad cleared his throat a couple of times and glanced at me with red-rimmed, glassy eyes.

"Well," he started, his voice hoarse. "Well, Doctor Ka...Doctor K. Our family has suffered.... You see, my wife.... My little girl...." He choked on air, on the verge of losing it. He paused, then tried again. "This summer, Emma tried to.... I almost lost her, too.... I'm having a difficult time...."

I couldn't take anymore. I reached for his hand and held it tightly. He squeezed back.

"I'm so sorry. The pain, I just wanted it to stop," I said between ragged breaths. He gripped my hand so hard, as if he'd never let go. I didn't care that it hurt. It was the first connection we'd made in years. Tears still funneled down my face.

"Our family is kind of…. messed up." My dad stared at my hand in his. Dr. K watched, then tossed the notepad on the table next to him. He leaned forward, elbows on knees.

"I understand," he said. "I'd like to help your family. But it's going to take time. Reopening old wounds can be quite painful. Frightening, even. Today's the first step. But it doesn't happen overnight. I need you to understand that it may take some time to learn to cope with your loss. There are no easy fixes to any of this."

I pulled my other hand out of my pocket, revealing the bloodied, tissue-wrapped thumb. I no longer felt the need to hide it from him.

You have no idea. You haven't even met Mom.

Chapter II

The afternoon sun filtered through gauzy clouds that strung across the North Texas sky. It created a magnificent, layered palette of pinks and oranges. I stared up in awe, as I stretched on the grass with the track team. A cool snap—temps in the high sixties—had blown in the night before, and my classmates and I were giddy with the slightest taste of autumn. Tomorrow would return to the usual high eighties but today was a gorgeous September day and a beautiful day to run.

It had taken two days of meeting with Ms. Poskey to change my schedule, but they were able to move me into off-season track. I wouldn't be in Life Skills class anymore because of the shift, but maybe that was a good thing. It was the only class I had with Tyler, and I'd been getting definite flirty vibes from California Dreamy. No way did I want to further complicate my relationship with Sophie. I sat with them at lunch but avoided being alone with him. It wasn't that I didn't like his flirting. It was the opposite. I liked it *a lot*. But I loved Fi, and I'd never let a boy—dreamy or otherwise—get in between the two of us.

Earlier today, when I'd walked into the locker room for the first time the entire room had gone silent. The girls, in various states of dressing out for practice, blatantly stared. I'd held my school workout gear bundled in a clump pressed to my chest, almost like a shield, and followed

Coach, who showed me to my locker. Then she'd turned to face the group.

"Good afternoon, ladies," Coach Rodriguez yelled. Her voice had the succinct drill-sergeant quality I'd heard in movies, but never in real life. She gripped me by the shoulder. "This is Emma Watters. Some of you may already know her. If you don't, introduce yourselves. I know you'll make her feel part of the team."

Heads bobbed up and down. She gave me another squeeze on the shoulder and left. As she vanished through the door, she yelled behind her, "See you on the track in five minutes. Let's hustle!" The girls burst into action, shimmying into compression running pants, tying shoelaces, pulling back hair. Locker doors slammed, and the girls filed out, a few stopping to say a quick hello on their way out. Then the locker room was empty.

I undressed, a feeling of dread coiling in the small of my intestines. I finished changing, then stood frozen, chewing the top of my knuckle—the only thing available to gnaw on because I had the *No Bite* crap on my nails. I can do this, I told myself over and over.

But what if I can't? What if I let everyone down, including Coach?

I hadn't been on a team since third grade when Sophie's dad coached us for soccer. That had been Pre-CD. In the fallout of Post-CD, I'd quit the team and avoided expectations from anyone. If no one expected anything from me, I couldn't let them down.

Get a grip. Focus on what I know. Just like Dr. K says, it's all about baby steps. All I need to know right now is this—I can run.

I threw on the rest of my clothes, tied back my hair, opened the gymnasium door, and walked into the sunlight. The team was broken into partners on the grass, one teammate holding the other's feet and shouting the number of completed sit-ups. I dropped down at the edge of the group and folded over to touch my toes. I held the stretch. A calmness came over me.

"Miss Watters," Coach Rodriguez said in her no-nonsense voice, "I know you're new with us, so I'll cut you slack today." She stood with hands on hips. "I expect each of you to be out here ready to warm up exactly ten minutes after the second bell rings, no exceptions. Next time you're late, you run extra laps."

My mouth sprung open. My calmness—*poof*—gone. "Yes, ma'am," I managed to get out, as my shoulder muscles stiffened.

Crap. My first day, and I'd already been called out. In front of every-one. My heartbeat skittered hard within my chest.

"Good. We understand each other." Her voice was neutral. "All right. Let's do leg stretches. Warm 'em up, ladies! We'll start running lad-ders, beginning with the hundred-meter. Work our way up to the four hundred meter, then go in reverse." She clapped her hands together. "Everybody got that?"

The other girls nodded. I did, too, even though I had no clue what she was talking about. I looked and was surprised to spot Lacy, who waved and moved next to me, performing the series of stretches with ease. I followed her lead.

"Don't worry," Lacy murmured. "It takes a little while to get used to her style." Leaning into a long stretch, she added, "She's like a *real* badass, but exceptionally cool once you get to know her. She talks like that to all of us, like we're in the military or something."

"Thanks for letting me know," I whispered back, afraid she'd catch us talking.

The team lined up at the starting line on the track. I fell in next to Lacy in the middle of the pack. A whistle sounded, and we took off. The coach ran with us. She'd speed up to say something to a runner at the front, then fall back to assist another.

"Nice heel-toe strikes, Watters." Coach Rodriguez appeared out of nowhere next to me. "Unclench those fists, though. Loose hands. Keep'em loose so you don't cut off circulation. Yeah, that's it. And thumbs pointed toward the sky when you pump those arms." She moved on, weaving in and out of the pack without effort, offering suggestions. "Everyone—breathe!"

I listened to every word she said and tried to incorporate the advice. We walked a hundred meters once we finished, then started the two-hundred-meter run. The team alternated between running and walking each distance up to the four-hundred-meter, then reversed the order back down to the hundred-meter.

By the time we finished, my body was flying on endorphins. The other girls grumbled and groaned all around, but I found myself grinning. I *loved* it. I reveled in the freedom of every labored breath that filled my lungs and every push that extended me forward. Even at the end, when Coach Rodriguez announced we'd finish the day by running bleachers, I took to the stands with zeal, my thighs on fire. I'd be exhausted tonight, but in a good way.

"Hey, slow down, Emma!" Lacy said, as she came up next to me. She elbowed me playfully. "You're making the rest of us look bad."

I heard other girls echoing the same sentiments behind us, only their voices were much chillier than Lacy's. At that moment, though, I couldn't have cared less.

Some people didn't appreciate freedom, I thought, as I pounded up the bleachers, my feet springing off the aluminum seats, blood singing a rhythm in my ears. But I did. I understood the weight of a life lived without it.

Chapter 12

What a killer day. I was physically beat but mentally exhilarated after practice. I'd returned a call to Sophie as soon as I arrived home.

"So? How'd it go?" she asked as soon as she came onscreen to video chat. "Is she a *beast* like everyone says?"

"Total beast," I said, sinking onto my bed and shifting to find a comfortable position. I groaned with each movement. My quads were tightening up, probably from running the bleachers. She snickered from the screen. "I'm glad you find this humorous, Fi. I'm not sure I can feel my legs."

"Speaking of legs, Coach Rodriguez is known for hers. So, trust me, it'll pay off. I heard that all the senior guys are dying to take her AP Government class—even though they're scared of her, and her class is like insanely tough—just so they can ogle her." She shook her head. "Boys are so sadly predictable, right?" Sophie answered her own question with a superior laugh.

Propping the phone against the dresser mirror, she worked her hair into a thick side braid. She paused and looked directly into the camera with pouty lips and half-closed eyes. "What do you think? Too Katniss Everdeen?"

"No—too Kardashian." I snorted at my own joke, then tried to hide a yawn. It had been a long day. "But seriously. You're gorgeous, Fi." Before I crashed, I needed to study for a science quiz and tackle five chapters in my novel for English.

"Wanna hear the latest?" Sophie leaned in close to the screen.

"What's up?"

"Well," she said, "I've heard it from a good source that Ben may be on the market again. That *someone* may be interested in a guy on the junior varsity football team."

"So, Ben's interested in a guy on the junior varsity squad?" I gave Sophie my best wide-eyed-and-innocent.

"Yeah. Funny. Ha, ha." Sophie rolled her eyes. She unwound the braid and worked it into a bun on top of her head. "Try to keep up with me, Em. So, I heard Kiley met this junior at a party last weekend. Can't think of the dude's name, but it doesn't matter. Anyway, the important thing is it sounds like she's probably not into Ben anymore!"

"That's great." I kept my voice neutral. "What does that mean for Tyler?"

"Nothing." Sophie glared at me. "It just means that Kiley isn't into Ben anymore. That's all it means."

I heard Ms. Zohar's voice in the background.

"Okay," Sophie yelled to her mom. She turned back toward the screen. "Gotta go. See you in the morning."

"Yeah. See you." I was glad the conversation ended before it turned uncomfortable. I leaned against the pillows and stared at the ceiling. Was Sophie going to string Tyler along even though she obviously still had a thing for Ben? And even if Fi did, why should I care?

I did care, though, even if I couldn't explain it. I cared a lot.

My dad had texted earlier to say he was bringing dinner home. I knew if I lied here contemplating Sophie's love triangle, I'd drift off, or stiffen up more, so I forced myself from the bed. I moved to my desk and dug through my backpack, locating my science binder. My homework was to refamiliarize myself with photosynthesis, the most essential chemical process on the planet. It was incredible how plants took in water and carbon dioxide, and then through an interaction between sunlight and chlorophyll, managed to grow and release oxygen into the atmosphere. It truly amazed me. Yet, what mostly held my attention was the photo of a lush, deep green tropical plant on the study site that I'd pulled up on my laptop. Its leaves almost matched the color of a certain *somebody's* eyes.

***

I munched on the take-out pizza Dad brought home and the microwaved broccoli I'd thrown together so we'd have something green with our dinner. There it was. The color green again! I'd almost spit out the gob of chewed vegetable in my mouth. *Chill, you dweeb.* I was acting ridiculous. My dad had brought our favorite types of pizza home: his was a thin-crust veggie with extra olives, and mine was the Hawaiian. For the first time in a while, my mom sat down at the table on her own and nibbled a slice, too. Maybe she was coming out of her most recent funk.

"So how was your first track practice?" Dad asked, as he wolfed down a hefty wedge that he folded like a taco.

"Awesome," I said between bites. "But it kicked my butt."

"Are we still on for our morning runs?" he asked. I could tell my answer mattered even if he acted like it didn't.

"Sure. I can handle both."

I noticed the sauce smudged under his upturned mouth. I *could* handle it. And I'd be in great condition by the time track season rolled around.

"I ran track when I was in middle school," my mom blurted out while fiddling with a piece of crust. "I was fast, too. A sprinter. Ran the four hundred."

"I never knew that about you," Dad said, his voice soft. Both of us stopped chewing to listen. My mom rarely joined in a conversation—in a customary way, anyway—but every now and then she'd surprise me.

"Why didn't you run in high school?" my dad asked, his hands still, as if any sudden movement might frighten her away or, worse, provoke an attack.

My mom squinted at the pile of pineapple chunks on her plate that she had scraped off a Hawaiian slice. She seemed confused by his question.

"I don't remember why I gave it up," she said with a half shrug. It looked like she had washed her hair. Maybe even used a hair dryer. I smelled the flowery scent of shower soap. "Maybe something else caught my attention. Boys, probably. I always liked the boys."

My dad and I nodded as if she had offered some thought-provoking bit of wisdom. Without notice, she pushed away from the table and headed down the hall to her darkroom. Her plate with half of a pizza slice was left behind.

Before disappearing into her darkroom, she stopped in the hall and called out, "Good luck with track."

Wow. I raised an eyebrow at my dad, who mirrored it before shrugging. "So, back to this track coach," he said. "What's she like?"

"About my height, but strong—like muscular—you know. Used to be military. The Navy, I think. She's smart and super-tough," I said.

"Intimidating, too. She called me out for being a couple minutes late today, but I think she was trying to let me know how it is. Not in a bad way."

"She sounds intriguing." He wiped his mouth with a napkin.

"I know, right?" I took a sip of milk. "Even though she's strict, I think I'll like her."

Not long after dinner, I headed for bed. It was nine o'clock, early for me, but I was wiped. I grabbed Bear and snuggled him close under the blankets as my body relaxed and my mind faded into peaceful darkness.

That night I dreamed of running in an endless field of fresh-cut grass, which cushioned my bare feet and tickled the skin between my toes. The gauzy clouds I'd admired earlier spread across the sky. I glided next to an older version of Casey, who looked almost identical to our mother, but much happier and brighter. We chatted in a casual manner, just two sisters hanging out. The conversation made zero sense, but in the dream it all seemed so normal. It was beautiful there, in that ethereal realm, and I didn't want it to end. There were so many things I wanted to share with her. Just before my alarm erupted, I woke to the sound of Casey's elated laughter. The sound of it filled me with joy. But on the edge of that happiness, a deep longing circled, like it always did. A yearning for what had been but could never be again.

Chapter 13

More than a month of school had passed in a blur with homework and track workouts filling my days. It was a blustery fall morning, and we were headed to school, excited it was Friday. Ms. Zohar—at Sophie's now regular command—dropped us about a block away, and we trudged against what felt like hurricane-force winds to get to the building. Pigheaded Fi was more concerned that someone might see her mom letting us off than she was about the relentless whipping wind that battered us.

Despite reservations, Ms. Zohar had stopped to let us out. "Do you need help, Fi? The weather's—"

"Nope. Got it, Mom," Sophie raised her hand to silence her mom. "See ya."

"Sweetie, you look like Piglet, ready to sail away on a kite," Ms. Zohar had joked. She watched as her daughter stepped out of the minivan and teetered in the blasts of wind. "Fi!"

"No, really, we got it, Ma," Sophie had yelled. Fighting to keep her wrap-around skirt from splaying up to her waist, she wrestled to close the door. I whooped loudly into the gusts, then turned to see her still fighting with it—long, dark coils of hair thrashing about her face like the mythical snakes of Medusa.

Sophie, who didn't find the situation humorous, appeared to also have fire shooting out of her eyes like Medusa. She screeched, "Mother…. *freaking unbelievable*…YES, someone help!" I bolted over to help with the door.

"Thank, God," she huffed as we waved away her mom and leaned into the headwind. Leaf debris and blowing dirt pummeled our faces.

Yeah, this was way cooler than her mom dropping us off at the front door. *Pigheaded Fi.* I crunched on grit that had blown into the back of my mouth. Miserable, we plodded on for what seemed like days, before arriving at the school entrance.

"Gotta see my teacher about an essay," Sophie told me as she veered left to my right. She was oblivious that her normally perfect hair stood out in all directions, like she'd stuck all ten fingers into an electric outlet.

"Hey, Fi, you might wanna do something with your hair. It's —"

"Can't talk. Gotta run," Sophie interrupted, all business. "I told her I'd be there early. I'm desperate to get her input on it."

"First, brush your—" I tried, only to be interrupted again.

"B'bye, Em. Talk later, 'kay?" Sophie strutted off toward the class-rooms, oblivious to the stares and giggles.

"Fi!" I yelled after her. "Do something with your hair!"

She must not have heard me because she kept walking. I shook my head and headed to the girls' restroom. I had some damage control to do before first period, too. I brushed my hair into a ponytail, dabbed at watery eyes, reapplied lip gloss, straightened my clothes, then entered a stall to pee. While in there, I heard the voices of two girls entering the restroom.

"Yeah, tell me about it. *Total freak*," one girl said to the other. "Have you seen the way she, like, *smiles* when we're running our asses off? I mean, who *does* that, right? That's some crazy shit. Like she gets that dorky look on her face. You know what I'm talking about, right?" The faucet turned on and then off. "Major kiss-ass." Something clanked on the sink. "You know, I bet she has the hots for Coach."

I recognized the voice but couldn't place it. I still hadn't peed, choosing to hold it instead. My gut told me to keep as quiet as possible. There was a *swish-swish*. One of the girls had sprayed perfume. My nostrils flared as the fragrance hit me. A blend of citrus and ginger. I concentrated hard, trying to remember where I'd smelled it before. I could almost taste it on my tongue—the fragrance and the name of the girl who used it. I remained frozen on the toilet seat; my chest hunched to my knees. Despite my screaming bladder, I didn't want to make noise. I shouldn't be eavesdropping, but my instinct said otherwise.

"Yeah, I know what you mean," another familiar voice said, "but I sort of feel sorry for her, you know?"

"Seriously? *Why?*" the other girl shot back. The smacking I heard sounded like she was blotting lipstick.

One of them turned the water on again, so I couldn't make out the first part of the response, "...and I think she either killed her sister, or she let her die. Something like that. It was all over the news. Can't remember all the details, but I do remember my mom and her friends talking about it. I was, like, ten or something," the second girl said. "My mom said the whole scenario was really messed up."

They're talking about me and Casey. My heartbeat pinged around my chest. Panic at first. Anger quickly replacing it. A rage rumbled inside that wanted out.

Don't talk about my *sister. Or me. Your mom doesn't know* crap. *You don't know anything!*

I squeezed my eyes against the burn of tears. I couldn't risk taking deep breaths without being heard. My intestines constricted, and I tasted a soured version of the brown sugar and oatmeal I'd had at breakfast, seeping up into my mouth, making me want to gag.

"Okay. So, that *is* messed up," the first girl acknowledged. I heard the rustle of backpacks and purses. They were getting ready to leave. "But sorry—not sorry. She's still a total freak."

"Yeah, I guess," the other girl said.

The bathroom door opened and then closed with a soft thump. I was alone.

I heard the class bell ring, and the warning bell that followed a few minutes later. I didn't care. Maybe I was a freak. I remained on the toilet, gasping between sobs, desperate to stave off the rushing blood whooshing in my ears, the distinct fragrance still wafting in the bathroom.

I remembered name of the perfume—Jo Malone. It was a custom blend fragrance. Expensive. Unique. There was only one person I knew who wore that scent. *Aliah*. Aliah Knight was on my team. She was a junior and had been the school's top runner the previous year. Aliah, who didn't know anything about me, had called me a freak. The other girl, though I wasn't positive, was probably another teammate.

Still struggling to take in air and fighting off a lightheadedness that threatened to topple me over, I finally peed. My insides were shaking. I walked to the sink; my hands trembled as I washed them under icy water for much longer than needed. I glimpsed at the mirror—my makeup was smeared, face blotchy. I didn't feel like doing damage control. Instead, I gathered my stuff and walked out on shaky feet. I moved down the corridor, not sure what I should do. I couldn't face anyone right now. I just couldn't.

The compulsion to run pushed at my brain. I wanted to bolt out of the school's large, front double-doors, and let them slam shut behind me. I wanted to flee, to surrender myself into the fierce tailwind blowing that October day and let it push me through the neighborhood streets that surrounded the school, far past them, past my neighborhood and my miserable house and the memories of what happened there. I wished my legs would carry me far from this town.

I reached the end of the hall and veered left toward the double doors—they led to my freedom. I swayed before grabbing onto the wall to steady myself. Casey stood in front of the doors, about eight feet from me, blocking the way. Her legs were shoulder-width apart and her arms were extended on either side. Her jaw was squared, determined. She stared at me with pleading eyes. I gasped, my watery gaze on Casey.

I can't, Case. Don't you see? They'll always see me as the freak. The one responsible for my little sister's death.

Casey, silent like always, pinned me with that look. I fought it, but I knew why she stood there. I closed my eyes and leaned my head against the wall. She was gone when I opened my eyes, but her presence lingered, barring my escape. It didn't matter what anyone else thought about me. I couldn't leave. Not now. Outdistancing the memories, the guilt, which trailed my every movement, was impossible anyway. Casey had kept me from running for a reason. She wanted to help.

I turned around, my back to the doors. At the hallway intersection, I veered right, toward Ms. Poskey's office. I needed someone to talk to, someone who'd listen.

Chapter 14

I'd miss first period, chemistry, but I didn't care. I made my way to the counselor's office on autopilot. The elderly office assistant said Ms. Poskey was at an off-campus meeting but should return soon. I slumped into a seat and studied my hands in a trance-like state, occasionally looking up to catch a nervous glance the older woman threw my way.

After hearing the girls in the bathroom, I felt beaten up, pummeled. They were just words, but words could cut as deeply as knives. Would I ever recover from Casey's death? I'd asked Dr. K something similar at our last session. For most people, he'd said, the hardest part of conquering a tragedy was facing it. He made it sound so simple, like a message in a fortune cookie.

Face your past and you shall see the fortunes of your future unfold, or some cheesy crap like that. Yeah. Whatever.

I closed my eyes, leaned back in the chair and rested my head. I needed a place where I could just sit and *be*. I drifted in and out with my thoughts, as other students came and went from the office. About forty-five minutes later, Ms. Poskey strode in, heels clacking on the shiny white tiled floor.

"Hey, Emma." The smell of coffee hung in the air. "What brings you here? Hope you weren't waiting too long. Those district meetings are a beating."

I looked up and blinked at her. Ms. Poskey's smile tightened. I knew my face was streaked with black mascara, my eyes puffy and red.

"Go in, Emma. Sit, please." Ms. Poskey unlocked her office while holding folders under her arm and a jumbo paper coffee cup in her hand, the white plastic lid smudged with berry-colored lipstick. "Give me a second to check messages. It'll just take a sec."

She closed the door behind me. After a couple of minutes, I heard Ms. Poskey issuing instructions to the office assistant. She joined me then, snapping the door shut firmly before sinking into the chair next to mine.

"You don't look well. What happened?"

I opened my mouth, the words trickling out hesitant at first, then springing forth faster and faster. Once I started sharing the story, I couldn't stop. I recounted the bathroom scene and the conversation I'd overheard, not leaving anything out. I also told her how it made me feel, something Dr. K constantly harped on.

"I wanted to hurt them," I said through gritted teeth. My hands balled into fists. "I felt this rage, you know? Like in my stomach. I wanted to shove them, or kick them, or do whatever it took to stop them from talking about me. About Casey. Because—why would they say those things when they don't even know me? They don't even know what happened to my sister."

Just saying it aloud made me feel better. Releasing the words trapped in my head, stringing them into sentences, was cathartic. Some of the anger and anxiety slipped from my tense body and rushed out through my story, my words.

I went on to share some of what I remembered of the accident, which wasn't much. The packed funeral afterward, sitting between Grams and my mom, trying to catch my mother's eye to see if she had forgiven me, if she still loved me, painfully aware that she refused to even look at me. As if I didn't exist anymore. How Grams had hugged me close and whispered repeatedly that it wasn't my fault, that Casey was an angel who would watch over us now. How I felt guilty for Casey's death, and if I could change places with her, if I could be the angel watching over them instead, I would. I'd give my life, no regrets, if my little sister could have hers back.

I talked for almost an hour. Ms. Poskey gave an occasional nod, encouraging me to sift through my memories, my story. Tears welled in her eyes when I finished speaking. It took several minutes before she spoke, her voice husky.

"People can be cruel, Emma. Sometimes it's intentional, and sometimes just plain ignorance." She wiped at her cheeks with a frown. "I'm sorry you had to hear those girls today."

"Yeah. Me, too." I mopped my face with a tissue. I didn't tell Ms. Poskey that my first instinct had been to run or that Casey had stopped me. I also didn't tell Ms. Poskey I suspected Aliah Knight instigated the conversation.

"Mostly, I'm sorry about what you went through—losing your sister—and everything you've dealt with since," Ms. Poskey said. "You're an amazing girl, Emma. I hope you realize that."

I ducked my head. Grams and Ms. Zohar had been the only ones who ever complimented me like that. Mostly, it made me uncomfortable because I knew I wasn't amazing, even if I'd like to be.

"Um, thanks for listening. It helps to have someone to talk to." I stood to leave but decided last minute to give the counselor an awkward hug.

"Well, I'm glad to help, Emma. Anytime."

I promised to tell Dr. K about what had happened in the bathroom and to come to Ms. Poskey if anything like that happened again in school. I felt a lot less heavy than when I'd arrived. And I hadn't run away today, even though it hurt. I was glad I stuck it out. Later, even though it wouldn't be easy either, I'd deal with Aliah my own way. Just not now. Not today.

***

At lunch, Sophie knew something was up.

"You okay? You looked wrecked," she said, across from me at the lunch table. She looked like Ms. Zohar when she went into Mother Hen mode. "Hannah from first period checked in late. She saw you in the office. She told me you were zoned out in a chair and maybe you'd been crying. What happened? Would they not let you go home? What the hell?"

"Good afternoon, mademoiselles." Tyler slid into the seat next to Sophie with his lunch tray. He glanced at me. "Everything cool?" He squinted and leaned closer. "Tired, Em?"

I decided I wouldn't tell Sophie about what I'd heard Aliah say in the bathroom. I didn't want her getting overprotective—she was known for a thunderous temper, and I knew she wouldn't hesitate confronting Aliah, even if she were an upperclassman and the star on the girl's track team.

"Yeah, I'm feeling better now. It was weird. My stomach hurt, and I felt sort of nauseated, so I skipped a couple classes," I said. I tore off a piece of crust from my sandwich and nibbled at it. "It came on kinda sudden, but I feel better now. It's all good."

"Girl stuff?" Sophie asked. Tyler cut his eyes away.

"Yeah, probably." I sipped my water. "What's the day been like for you two?"

"Well, it took me about thirty minutes to get my hair under control this morning," Sophie said with a laugh. "Why didn't you tell me I had an Einstein thing going on?"

I snorted. "I tried to, but you were obsessing over your English essay."

"Speaking of Einstein, I made an 'A' in Life Skills today." Tyler bit off a large chunk of his hamburger and washed it down with chocolate milk. Sophie and I clapped, and he dabbed at his lips with a napkin. "That's right, ladies. Ms. Devon said nobody...and I must stress *nobody*... can boil an egg quite like me."

Tyler gave me a sly eyebrow wiggle, and I burst into giggles. Fi laughed, too, but her bemused expression made it clear she didn't get the joke.

Chapter 15

The next day, while on our Saturday morning run, I glanced over at Dad. Since we'd been seeing Dr. K individually, he'd been hanging back more often when we ran together. I'd noticed he'd tried to talk to me more, too, even if it still felt unnatural. *Baby steps*, I reminded myself, but he was preoccupied, like something was tumbling around inside his head that needed working out.

"Hey, do you mind if I pace myself a little faster? I need to burn off a few work hassles I'm facing." He rubbed the back of his neck. "It was particularly hellish this week."

"Sure. Meet you back at the house?"

"Yep." He waved and took off. "See you there."

I hoped Dr. K could help my dad. I wanted to see him happy again, or at least less miserable. I wondered how he'd managed to hold our lives together as well as he had—or at least the public perception of our life. He wasn't perfect, that's for sure, but at least he tried. He was chair of the physics department at the university—an important position with weighty research responsibilities—and basically operated as a single parent. All the while he had to contend with a child's death, as well as take care of my mom, who'd stopped functioning the day Casey died.

And there were me and my issues. It was no wonder he always seemed weighed down, his shoulders slumping with the immensity of it all.

Nowadays, with me being older, it was probably easier for him. I couldn't imagine how difficult it had been for him in the days, weeks, and months following Casey's death. How had he managed to stay with my mom all this time?

I'd read online about how couples who faced the death of a child struggled to stay together. When my mom hibernated in their darkened bedroom for days, or raged at anything that moved, he had stuck around. I wanted more for both of my parents. I wanted to see them living again.

It worked out well that my dad decided to run ahead of me. I had some thinking of my own to do. I had to figure out how I should confront Aliah, if at all. Yesterday afternoon, I had ignored it and gave all I had at practice. The mean remarks and snickering behind my back only fueled my decision to teach Aliah and her sidekick, Caroline, a lesson. I'd figured out Caroline was the other girl in the bathroom, but she was only a follower. Aliah was the real problem. She stood about six feet tall and had the graceful limbs of a runway model. People at school, even teachers, said she looked like Rihanna. And she was wicked fast. Until I came along, she had led the runners, but now she shared the spotlight with me. I often tied with her or came in a hair behind.

Aliah moved like a cheetah on the track, her stride effortless, supple. She had stunning eyes that ranged in color from a green hazel to golden amber, depending on the colors she wore.

I thought I could take Aliah on the track, though. Sure, I'd have to push myself, but I knew I could do it. She relied too much on her natural ability. If I followed Coach's workout and outworked Alia, I'd be stronger in no time. And faster. Then I'd snatch the title of star runner, which would be the best way to give payback to someone like her. I'd show her what a *freak* I was when it came to running.

I took a couple of twists and turns down streets away from my usual route, not paying attention to where I was going. I curved down a street with houses sitting back on larger lots. I'd gone north instead of south, which put me in the older section of the neighborhood. It was prettier here. Each house was custom-designed, not the cookie-cutter sort near mine. Established trees in the area, their branches meeting overhead to form one long leafy arch, made it even more welcoming. I should run this way more often, I thought.

The sound of rolling composite wheels scraping pavement interrupted my thoughts. It sounded weird cutting into the calmness of the early Saturday morning. I looked back and almost jumped. Tyler had cruised up beside me on a skateboard. He wore flannel pajama bottoms, a ratty blue Rolling Stones T-shirt, and bedhead hair stuck up around his ears. I swear, he couldn't have been more adorable if he tried. I grinned at him, my neck burning.

"Hey." He still had sleep in the corners of his eyes. "Fancy meeting you here."

Seeing him on the street, dressed like he had just hopped out of bed, disoriented me. "Wait, what? You're skateboarding at the crack of dawn?"

"My mom sent me out to get the newspaper. We're like the only people who still buy it, but they always throw it in our neighbor's yard." He ruffled his hair with both hands without stopping on his board. "I didn't know you ran right by my street. I wasn't sure it was you. I called out but guess you couldn't hear me. Thought I'd use my board to catch up, find out who it was, the mysterious hot chick running in my hood."

I chuckled. He had that effect on me. I didn't even care he was seeing me all sweaty and gross.

"Do you ever *not* run?" Tyler asked. He used his left foot to propel the skateboard along the street before coasting a while.

"Huh?" I slowed my pace a bit so that he could keep up. "What do you mean?"

"I mean, what else do you do?" he asked. "For fun, I mean."

"I read." I tugged at the ear buds dangling on a cord around my neck. "Listen to music. Watch movies."

He mulled that over as he grinned to himself.

"Okay. We'll come back to your favorite book, musician, and film. Cause I wanna know the answers. But first I need to ask you something. Has Sophie mentioned anything to you about us?"

"What?" My heart slammed hard against my chest. "What do you mean *about us*?"

Tyler kicked off with his foot again and steered his skateboard around a stick lying in the road. "Well, she has asked me about—you know—she says I talk too much to you at lunch. Or it's more like she thinks maybe I *flirt* too much with you. Those were her actual words."

"What?" I said again, abruptly halting as Tyler rolled forward.

He stopped, did some fancy maneuver where he popped the skateboard up and grabbed it in mid-air. He squared his shoulders to face me. "Look, maybe I shouldn't have said anything." He pulled on the front of his shirt, looking away. "I, uh, I didn't know what to tell her when she said that."

"You tell her you're *not* flirting with me. That's what you tell her," I blustered, my face heated with anger. How could boys be so dumb? I didn't want Sophie getting the wrong idea. I never wanted to hurt

Sophie. Ever. And I didn't want to fight over a guy, that's for sure. "You tell her the truth. That you and I are *just friends*. That's it. Simple."

Tyler blinked several times as he fidgeted with one of the wheels on his board. I stood with my hip jutted out and waited for him to speak.

"But maybe I have been," he said finally. Tyler caught my eyes. His voice was so soft that I had to lean forward to hear him.

"Maybe you have been?" I asked. It was my turn to be thick-headed. "Maybe you have been *what*?"

"Flirting." He maintained eye contact. My heart vaulted into my throat as my stomach plunged, as if I were dropping fast in an elevator, like ten floors in two seconds. "Not that you'd notice."

Oh, I'd noticed but hoped Sophie hadn't. Maybe Tyler was one of those guys who flirted with everyone. My lips froze in a perfectly formed "o" as I stood speechless. I needed time to process. Tyler placed his board on the ground. We stared at each other, the silence broken only by songbirds in the trees overhead.

"So?" His voice was nervous, husky.

"So?" I don't know what my voice was.

"Please stop repeating everything I say." He lifted his hands, palms up. His eyes begged me to respond.

I shook my head. I wished I could tell him I liked it when he flirted with me, liked it way too much. That with every ridiculous pun and every lopsided grin, my insides lit up like a string of Christmas lights. But I couldn't tell him any of my feelings without betraying Fi.

"Right." I nodded. Abrupt. "I need to go. My dad—he'll be worried." I dragged my eyes away from his.

"We need to talk about this, don't we?" Tyler asked, dark brows knitted. "Maybe I shouldn't have said what I just did. I don't want to scare you off, Em."

Em.

My knees almost buckled when he shortened my name. I wanted so much to tell him everything I felt.

Hello. Hey, EM-MA, wake-up call. This is your best friend's boyfriend. Fi. Remember her?

It figured. The one guy I truly liked would be taken—and by my best friend, no less. There would be no future conversations about this or maybe about anything.

"Look—we have nothing to talk about," I said as I focused on the ground. "You're Fi's *boy*friend. I'm Fi's *best* friend." I kicked a pebble at my feet. "Nothing more to say."

"But you don't understand. I don't feel—"

"Stop." I put both hands up. "Don't say anything else. I don't want to hear anything about Sophie, or anything about the two of you. Maybe you two need to talk some things over, but I need to stay out of it. She and I, well, we don't do the girl drama thing. Never have."

"Just let me explain."

"No. I mean it." My voice quivered. My heart was breaking as I moved away from him. "We're still friends, but *just friends*, okay? I gotta go."

I could feel his eyes on my back as I jogged away. I looked over my shoulder once and saw him still standing there. I blinked back the sting in my eyes and started my mantra.

One. Two. Three. Inhale.

As I neared the end of the street, my father rounded the corner running hard, his face flushed, his hair springing up in all directions. I came to another abrupt stop.

"Thank God!" He gripped both my arms and his fingers dug into my biceps. "I was so worried. A neighbor told me he spotted you running this way, or I wouldn't have known where you were. "Dad's voice switched from concern to irritation. "You should have been back half an hour ago. You didn't answer my texts. What happened?" He released me and bent over, hands on knees. He gulped mouthfuls of air. His soaked t-shirt stuck to his chest. My dad stood up straight then, hands on his hips and squinted behind me. I turned and saw Tyler in the middle of the street right where I'd left him, one foot on his board.

"Everything okay?" Tyler called to me, worry in his voice, his hands on hips mirroring my father's. It looked as if he was ready to hop on the board and skate to my rescue.

I cupped my hands and hollered back. "It's okay. It's my dad."

Tyler's stance relaxed. "Oh. Nice to meet you, Mr. Watters!" he yelled. "See you later, Em." He waved, then leaped on his skateboard, and rolled off in the opposite direction.

My dad lifted his hand in a half-hearted wave and watched Tyler glide away.

"So, who's the guy in pajamas with a skateboard?" he asked.

It pained me, but I followed my dad's gaze. I wanted to tell him the truth. That Tyler made me feel seen, something I hadn't felt in so many years. That he thought I was talented and funny and maybe even pretty. I wished I could tell my dad that Tyler caused my heart to race faster than a 40-meter sprint. That he gave me hope I might someday have a shot at happier times—hope that I could reclaim my life. But none of that came to my lips. Because they were words I could never utter aloud.

"Oh, him?" I watched him riding away, almost out of sight. "That's just Tyler." I tried to keep the sadness from my voice as he disappeared around a corner. "That's Fi's boyfriend."

CHAPTER 16

Thanksgiving break was a day away, and Coach was determined to work us hard before we stuffed ourselves for a week. I was Lacy's partner and anchored her feet as she counted her sit-ups aloud. Coach didn't believe in weight circuit conditioning. She was old-school. She used interval running drills and military-style sit-ups and push-ups. The techniques had paid off. After almost three months of it, I was stronger, my long muscles sculpted and defined.

I could see Lacy struggling.

"Thirty-five," I counted with her, as she barely gasped the number out. "C'mon, Lace. You got this!"

"Oh, my lord," Lacy huffed. She was bright red and glazed in sweat. Her chin had just reached her bent knees before she sagged back to the ground. "This. Is. Killing. Me."

"Let's go, people. I want *controlled* movements—control up, control down. No flopping. Give me one set of fifty sit-ups, each of you—no less." Coach Rodriguez said as she paced among the runners paired on the grassy middle of the track. The girls groaned in response. "No whining. If you want to *be* strong, *think* strong. You got me, ladies?"

I glanced at Aliah and Caroline, who were nearby. Aliah glistened with sweat and muttered curse words with each lift, with Caroline anchoring her feet. Catching my eye, Aliah scowled at me. "Such...a...*freak*," she said through gritted teeth.

"*Shhhhhhh*," Caroline told Aliah, nodding toward Coach. "She'll hear you."

Coach Rodriguez hadn't heard them, but I had. A burning anger seeped into my chest. I'd had about enough of Aliah. She elbowed me whenever we were bunched together in a pack of runners and constantly whispered to Caroline or mocked me whenever I walked by. About a week ago, Aliah had gone out of her way to push me during a practice race. I'd stumbled and fallen. Coach, on the other side of the track, hadn't seen it happen. But I had refused to react. Instead, I'd bounced up, dropped my chin and dug in, putting everything I had into passing Aliah. We tied at the finish line.

Today, I made a silent stand. I wouldn't back down, wouldn't give Aliah the satisfaction. Adrenaline spiked in my gut. I hated girl drama or whatever, but this was different. I hadn't felt important and needed, a part of something, in a long time. I wasn't letting anyone rob me of this satisfaction. Not without a fight.

I pinned her with a hard stare and telegraphed the message. She didn't look away, staring right back. A stalemate. Caroline darted her eyes between us, a worried knot forming on her forehead.

"Emma," Lacy mewed like a newborn kitten. "I...."

I ended the staring contest to check on my friend. She lay still on her back, her face a greenish hue as she clutched her stomach.

"What's wrong, Lace?"

"I think...I might...throw up." Lacy's eyes widened, and she struggled to her feet. I helped her make it to the side of the group where she puked the contents of her lunch. A sour smell hit my nose and my stomach curdled. I held my breath and patted Lacy's back. When there seemed to be nothing left in her stomach, the dry heaving began. The sound of her retching and the long strands of saliva that dangled from her mouth almost pushed me over the edge. I didn't have a strong stomach when it came to vomit, especially after my ER visit over the summer.

Coach jogged over to us, and a few girls gathered around to help.

"What's going on, O'Neil?" Coach asked. She spoke in a hushed voice, her arm around Lacy's back. "Did you drink enough water today?"

"Not sure, Coach," Lacy got out before retching again.

"That smell is so disgusting." It was Aliah's voice in the group behind them. "Oh, my God," she shrieked with laughter, "I'm gagging!"

A few other girls laughed nervously, but most remained somber. Lacy's shoulders sagged even more, and her ears turned a bright red. Then her back started to shudder with sobs.

"It's okay, Lace. Just ignore her," I whispered. Then I turned to Aliah, who stood taller than the rest. My hands balled into fists. "Way to be helpful," I said, the growl in my voice jarring even my own ears. The others exchanged surprise looks. Aliah stood her ground, her eyes mirroring my fury. I continued, "There's something seriously wrong with you. That's your *teammate*. Not that you would care."

A sneer was on her face, as Aliah moved through the group, her muscled body tense. She stepped up to me. "Shut the fuck up, Freak," she said in a cold voice, looking ready to strike. I'd struck a nerve. The other girls murmured to each other, confused by the turn of events. Coach looked over her shoulder, a deep frown etched in her face.

"I need a volunteer. Someone to help O'Neil to the nurse. Someone other than these two," she called out in a clipped tone. Caroline stepped forward, her hand raised as she ducked past Aliah. She helped Lacy walk back toward the gym.

"Thanks to Watters and Knight, you *all* stay late today. Give me another set of fifty sit-ups," Coach yelled. The group groaned in unison. Many of them shot daggers at Aliah and me. "We stand together as a team and fall together as a team. Understood?"

I bowed my head. Making the others suffer wasn't right. I shot a look at Aliah, who still held her head high, arrogant and apathetic.

"Coach?" Aliah said, her voice tinged with its usual haughtiness. "Would you please count for me? I need a partner."

Coach paused, her jaw muscles moving under her skin. She narrowed her eyes disbelievingly at Aliah and linked her hands behind her back. "No—I won't." Her lips turned up into a hard curve. "You're in luck, though. Watters, here, needs a partner. Get to it, ladies."

I wanted to puke now. I should have kept quiet. I mouthed "sorry" to the girls who could stand to look at me, then locked gazes with Aliah again. My face felt as stony as Aliah's appeared. A few moments passed, and we continued to stare each other down

"Well? What are you waiting for?" The harshness of Coach's tone startled me. "That means *now*!"

***

I held Aliah's feet and watched my unwilling partner struggle to finish the last ten of the required sit-ups. I had completed the additional set of sit-ups with ease—I'd been doing extras most nights in front of the TV. But Aliah was falling apart. I took enormous pleasure in that fact. She wasn't so perfect right now— the blotchiness of her skin, the way her cheeks ballooned when she strained to lift her torso, her face scrunched like a prune. It made me smile. Aliah managed enough energy to whisper, "Fuck you, *Freak*."

I laughed. The girl had a thing for 'F' words. She needed to expand her vocabulary. Instead of saying anything, I gave her the most crazed, freakish grin I could muster. Yep. I'd show her. A freak, indeed.

Chapter 17

Thanksgiving morning was here and life wasn't quite as sucky. I worked alongside Grams in her kitchen as we prepared the feast. I sliced celery into thin pieces, breathing in the crisp freshness of the cut stalks. Grams stuffed the turkey, my least favorite part. I loved smelling turkey while it roasted and I loved eating it, but watching Grams manhandle its raw flesh, shoving herbs, cornbread dressing, butter, and who-knew-what-else inside the bird agitated my stomach.

I turned away and forced myself to focus on my life seeming a bit better these days. It had been more than two months since I'd had a full-throttle panic attack, probably the longest stretch I could remember in Post-CD, and I hadn't gnawed my fingernails or cuticles much either. I still nibbled from time to time when nerves got ahold of me, so I painted my nails regularly with that ear-wax-tasting polish, especially when I knew I had a stressful week ahead.

Dr. K had taught me a few coping techniques to control my panic using mental imagery, biofeedback, and deep breathing. And any time I felt overly anxious at school, I headed to Ms. Poskey's office and we talked it out. I almost always felt better afterwards. The intense practices in off-season track helped, too. I hadn't had as many nightmares, and I was often so exhausted by the time I went to bed that I fell asleep as soon as I closed my eyes.

Maybe things were looking up in the Watters' abode. Dad even joked occasionally these days, his face settling into more relaxed lines. Maybe he had gained a newfound respect for psychology, thanks to Dr. K. Last week I even heard him practicing his Daffy Duck voice in the shower. I hadn't said anything to him about it, figured he'd use it on me when he was ready. Even my mom's behavior was a bit more stable, although the word "stable" was relative where she was concerned. She still refused to see Dr. K, but the number of mornings I found her sprawled on the couch after pulling all-nighters doing God-knows-what were fewer. Still, I found myself always on alert around her. Things might appear normal one minute, but the next might shift into total irrationality with a wrong word or perceived slight. I just never knew.

"Now what was I about to ask you, Em? Too many cobwebs in the attic this morning." Grams pressed knuckles against her forehead. "Oh! Do you mind peeling those sweet potatoes? My hands are weak as kittens." She returned to slowly stuffing the turkey.

"No problem." I dug around a drawer for a paring knife. "I can't wait to eat the sweet potato casserole. My favorite."

"I thought pumpkin pie was your favorite? And what about the cornbread dressing?" Grams gave a shaky laugh and wiped the back of her hand against her temple. "And the homemade banana pudding?"

I shot her a quick look. Her cheeriness sounded forced. "Okay. You got me. *All of it* is my favorite," I said with a snort. I had spent the night at Grams' house, and we woke up at five in the morning to start meal prep. We'd been working for almost two hours. My parents wouldn't be over until later in the day, which meant I had Grams all to myself without the usual tension. I loved listening to her hum tunes as she bustled around the kitchen. This morning she was dressed in a long velour leopard-print housecoat coat she'd had for as long as I could remember. Grams promised to teach me how to make the sweet potato casserole and cornbread dressing, both old family recipes. I don't recall my mom ever making them, but maybe she had Pre-CD.

I looked up and spotted Casey just as she appeared in the kitchen nook next to the breakfast table. She was older, closer to the age she would have been if she had lived. I paused, struck by how exquisite she was. I smiled at her, but she didn't return it. Instead, her facial expression was blank, her eyes hooded, focusing on a spot just over my shoulder. She pointed past me. Puzzled, I twisted around. Grams stood by the cabinets like a statue, her white-knuckled hands gripping the countertop.

"Casey? My dear angel, is that you?" Grams whispered, looking past me, her face wistful. She peered past me into the kitchen nook. "I've missed you so, child." Her words were breathy. My mouth opened. She could *see* Casey? Then Grams' body crumpled in slow motion. Without thought, I lunged at her, barely catching her before she hit the ground.

"No! No, Grams, no!" I said over and over again.

I held her frail body and gently lowered her to the floor. My heart fluttered in my chest; goose bumps rippled across my arms and legs. Grams was lying on the cold floor. I couldn't bear that, so I ripped off the bathrobe I was wearing—a girly, pink fuzzy thing Grams always made me use when I stayed the night—and covered her. I felt for a pulse. It beat faintly, almost undetectable, and her chest rose and fell in short measures. I balled-up a dishtowel, wedged it under her head, and scrambled for my phone. With shaky fingers, I dialed 9-1-1, and once I was told they were on their way, I called my dad. He picked up on the first ring.

"Happy Turkey Day!" he sang into the phone, his voice warm. "What time you want us over there?"

"Something's happened to Grams, Dad," I fired out quickly. I gripped her hand in mine. "Something bad. You need to come now—I'm scared. She fainted. I don't know what's wrong. I called an ambulance, and it's on the way."

"I'll be right there." He hung up. I was alone. I checked the room for Casey in hopes that she was still with me, but she had vanished.

One of Grams' eyelids peeled back, but the other refused to open all the way, sagging like a half-drawn shade. Grams' body trembled, and it took a while for her to focus on me. She stared into my eyes and gave a weak half-smile, as if awakened from a pleasant dream, part of her mouth drooping. She tried to whisper something. I leaned closer, my nose almost touching hers. "A-gelll. Cas. No...deh. No...deh." Her words were slurred and her eyes bright with tears.

"Yes, Grams. Casey's an angel." I nodded through stinging tears of my own. I tried to warm her chilled hand with mine, placing it next to my heart. "She's our angel. Just like you always say, Grams."

***

The emergency room physicians said Grams had suffered a mild stroke. They administered drugs right away to keep her from experiencing brain damage and admitted her into the hospital for three days, where they would put her through a battery of tests. It took a full day before she was able to speak. My parents and I had spent Thanksgiving dinner in the hospital cafeteria, not speaking to one another, each toying with cold pressed turkey meat and flavorless instant mashed potatoes. Mom had slipped away after that initial visit and hadn't returned.

"It was Casey, Richard, I swear. She held me, kept me warm. I felt her heartbeat. Told me I'd be okay," Grams said the following day. Her words were slow and mushy, but emphatic. My dad gave me a look. I swallowed back the choking sensation that grabbed me when I realized how close I'd been to losing Grams. If I hadn't been there, Grams would have been alone on the kitchen floor for hours. If Casey hadn't motioned to her, would I have reacted in time?

Please, God, don't take her from me, too.

As she got better, Grams told everyone about seeing Casey. Anyone who would listen. Doctors. Nurses. Her friends who visited from church and the senior center. She told Ms. Zohar and Sophie, who brought flowers for Grams and pumpkin pie for me and my dad.

"She's been through a lot," Dad said as we walked them out of the hospital after their visit. "The brain's complicated. Neurons can backfire—it produces bizarre reactions. A scientific phenomenon. The same parts of the brain that spark up when we dream sometimes do the same when those neurons go haywire."

"How do you know what she saw? You can't prove it, one way or the other," I said quietly. "Maybe she really *did* see Casey. Ever consider that?" I wanted to defend my grandmother, tell him that I had seen her too. That I saw her often. That professorial tone of his pissed me off. It was condescending, and it reinforced my decision to keep quiet about my own visions.

"I'm sure she truly believes an angel came to her." He gave a short laugh. "And it would be logical if it were to come in the form of a loved one. The brain can create its own reality."

"Oh, I don't know, Richard. Anything's possible," Ms. Zohar said with a shrug. She hugged me close and whispered in my ear, "My money's on Grams. I bet she did see Casey."

I gave her a small smile and lowered my face. I knew the reality—it wasn't a case of failing neurons that saved my grandmother. Maybe one day soon, I could let Grams know the truth. Maybe one day I'd tell her, *Yes, Grams, Casey was there. She always is.*

CHAPTER 18

Hesitant, I eyed Tyler over my lunch bag. "So, where's Fi?" I scanned the cafeteria.

"Some cheer thing, I think," Tyler said. He casually chewed pizza. That explained where Lacy was today, too. "Looks like you're stuck with me." He ducked his head under the table and brought it back up with a smile. "It appears you're wearing chunky boots. You can't make a run for it."

Crap.

I hadn't been alone with Tyler since that morning he spotted me out running. We had hung out with the group, but never alone. As if by some unspoken code, or maybe shared awkwardness, neither of us had brought it up either. Sophie, who wasn't known for discretion, hadn't said anything unusual to me about Tyler. Of course, Grams had been in the hospital, so maybe she hadn't felt right about bringing it up. The whole thing gave me a headache. I rubbed my temples and sore jaw muscles.

"You okay?" Tyler asked. He had lost the smile. "Sophie told me about your grandmother, what happened over Thanksgiving."

"Yeah. I'm fine." I avoided eye contact, reaching into my lunch bag and pulling out a sandwich, bottle of water, and an apple.

"You get my texts?"

I inched the sandwich out of the baggie, my head still bent. "Yeah. I got them. I meant to reply—I just didn't know what to say." I picked at the crust, dusted crumbs off the tabletop.

"But she's doing better now, right?" He shifted in his chair and an awkward silence followed.

"She is," I said as I tore off a small corner of the sandwich.

"That must have been scary, huh?" Tyler tried again.

"Yeah. It was." I pushed the small bite into my mouth, forcing myself to chew. It would be difficult to put into words exactly how scared I had been. "Sorry I didn't text back. I—uh—thanks for checking on Grams and me. I've been kind of out of it. I figured Sophie would keep you posted on everything."

"She did."

"Grams is in a place for physical therapy," I said, "but the doctors say she should be getting out, like, any day. She's speaking a lot clearer, too."

"Good." He leaned in, elbows on either side of his tray. "I asked my mom about it. She's a nurse, you know. Your grandmother was lucky you were there. Mom said the earlier the treatment, the better the outcome." Tyler leaned back and toyed with the fork on his tray.

"Yeah." I nodded. "My whole family was lucky. I don't know what we would do without Grams. She's—like the only normal person—" I choked on the words as a flood of unexpected emotion smacked me in the face, a rogue wave that surged over me and took me under. I blinked back tears.

Just like that, the Earth could have opened up, swallowed her whole, and she would have been gone. Like Casey.

"Hey...it's okay," Tyler whispered. "She's okay now." He reached over to dab my cheeks with a napkin.

Then he gently reached for my hands. I stiffened at first and looked around to make sure no one noticed us, then I allowed myself to relax. No one in the cafeteria paid us any attention. "Hey, I'm sorry. I didn't mean to upset you. I just—"

"No, it's not you." I shook my head, not sure whether my insides were zinging from the flood of emotion or the touch of his hands. "It just hit me again how...absolutely lost...I'd be without her. She's just...I don't know. She's like a mother, a big sister, an aunt, and a grandmother all wrapped up into one, you know?"

Tyler squeezed my hands. His fingers were long, and his wrists large and knobby. Double-jointed, Grams would say. He wore a sand-colored, rope-knot bracelet on his left wrist.

"You're lucky to be so close to her," he said. His thumbs rubbed the top of my knuckles in a circular motion, causing my heart to flutter, not in a panic-attack way, but in a slight-dip-on-a-roller-coaster way. "My grandmother, my dad's mom, died when I was a baby, so I never got the chance to know her, and my mom's mom still lives in California. In Bakersfield. Where my mom's from."

The rest of the cafeteria—trays slamming on the return counter, the clattering of silverware, the ebb and flow of students' voices— all of it faded away, and it was only Tyler and me. His deep voice, his eyes, his hands wrapped around mine.

"Anyway, her mom, let's just say she's hell on wheels, from what I've heard. Not that I'd know because I've never spent any time with her. She and my mom have a complicated relationship—they only speak on holidays."

I listened to Tyler's story, his soothing voice. I knew I was lucky to have the relationship I had with Grams, but I fully appreciated it after listening to him. I wanted to know more about his life. Even after hanging out for three months, there was so much I didn't know. "So where does your dad live? Do you see him much?"

"He's a doctor in San Diego. My parents' divorce was final this past summer, but he already has a girlfriend living with him. Or maybe he had her while he was still married to my mom." He shrugged. "She's a nurses' assistant he works with. No one says anything about it, but I found some, um, *revealing* photos on his phone once when I was visiting. I shouldn't have been snooping, but, whatever." He shook his head in disgust. "She's young. Like college-age, I think. It's kinda weird that she's not much older than me."

"Gross. That sucks."

"Yeah, well, we'll see if I ever meet her." Something caught his eye over my shoulder, and he released my hands like they were two fistfuls of hot coals. I flinched at the distance he put between us. What? Had I said something wrong? He turned his full attention to whoever was coming up behind me. I fumbled with the apple to have something to do with myself. I bit down hard on it and chomped loudly.

"Hey, Sophie! Hey, Lacy!" Tyler called. "Looks like you almost finished your thing, huh? How'd it go?"

I sucked in bits of apple and coughed as I turned to watch them walk up.

Please God, please God, please God. I prayed they hadn't seen Tyler holding my hands.

Sophie held a neon-yellow poster board promoting an upcoming school dance. Lacy trailed her with a huge packing tape dispenser.

Sophie shrugged and the decorated poster board flopped in half. "We still have about ten more to go. We need someone who's tall to help us hang them over by the gym. You done eating?" she asked Tyler. "If you're busy, I can ask Ben. He's tall, too."

"No. That's cool. I can help." He shoved the last of pizza into his mouth in one bite and chased it down with chocolate milk. "Just a sec."

"I was updating him on Grams, and on how everything else is going." I crunched more apple and tried hard to swallow without choking. Guilt nagged at me. I had enjoyed Tyler's full attention a few minutes ago, even if he was just comforting me. "I'm about finished. I can help, too, Fi."

"Nope. That's okay. But thanks." She avoided my eyes. "Just meet us outside of the boys' gym, Tyler. And hurry. They gotta be up before next class period."

"Bye, Emma," Lacy called over her shoulder and trailed Sophie again. Both swished away in their cheer uniforms.

"See you at track," I called back, then breathed a relieved sigh. If Fi had seen us, she would have said something. At least, that's what I told myself.

Tyler returned his empty tray and walked back to the table. He hovered, as if he wanted to say something more. Finally, he shrugged and rubbed his hands together. "Okay, I'll see you later. Maybe we can finish this conversation tonight? Like I could call you?"

"Maybe." I watched him walk away.

What am I going to do about him? About Fi? And why does life have to be so complicated?

CHAPTER 19

Me: *Where are you? All OK? We don't wanna be late!*

I hit 'send' on my phone, making it the fifth text I'd sent Sophie that day. So far, no response. Something was wrong. We were supposed to go to the movies today, just the two of us, to watch the new rom-com with Tom Holland. Nothing stood between Sophie and Tom Holland—the hottest guy on the planet, a fact we both agreed on. Dad wanted to know which showing we were seeing since he was driving us.

Me: *Fi! Tom is WAITING!*

I hit 'send' again.

Maybe Sophie had seen Tyler holding my hands yesterday in the cafeteria, after all. Maybe she was ghosting me. Sophie hadn't mentioned anything last night when we texted about seeing the movie. If she had seen anything, she would have confronted me, for sure. Sophie had spent the night at her dad's house. Maybe something was up there. Maybe he'd introduced her to yet another new and much-younger girlfriend or had done something else to upset her.

I didn't like Sophie's dad. Every time he was around me, he acted strange. He never spoke, just stole wary glances at me from under thick black lashes. It was kind of creepy and uncomfortable. He'd always been that way, acting weird around me, even when Sophie and I were younger.

Maybe he didn't want his daughter associated with the girl who was involved in her own sister's death. Was that it?

Once, during the summer before fourth grade, I'd asked Sophie about it. "Is it just me? Or does your dad not like me?" At the time, Sophie's parents had been divorced for less than a year. "He never says anything to me. Not one word. I don't think he even knows my name."

"Of course, he knows your name, silly," Sophie had laughed. "I don't know why he's so weird with you. He's basically a loudmouth around most people."

I'd never told Sophie I didn't like him. In fact, whenever he was around, I'd clam up, too. There was something about him, from his dodgy glances to the rasp of his voice, that didn't sit right with me. Perhaps it was because I was loyal to Ms. Zohar. The fact he had left his wife, Sophie, and Jacob for another woman was a major strike against him. Not to mention the parade of girlfriends he'd had since, along with a new sports car every six months. He smelled of midlife-crisis to me. Such a loser.

I checked my phone again, then restarted it in case something was screwy with it. I stretched out on the bed, my head propped on Bear, and dangled my bare feet over the edge. I put my phone down next to me and considered chewing the cuticle of my left thumbnail, but, instead, chose to thump my fingers to the beat of a Taylor Swift song that played. I liked her older music best, but the newer pop songs were catchy, too.

Maybe it something else keeping her? What if Sophie is with Tyler and doesn't want to be disturbed?

I pushed away the sting of jealousy at the thought of them together and instead picked up my phone and scrolled through social media, on the hunt for clues of where Sophie could be. Nothing. I spotted an older selfie of her, Tyler and me making silly faces in front of school.

Sophie had her eyes crossed while I stuck my tongue to my nose, and Tyler, squeezed between us with his head against mine, cocked an eyebrow. He had great hair. And great eyes. Good combo. Not only was he good-looking but witty, too, making him even more attractive. I didn't get Sophie sometimes. It was no contest between Ben and him. Was it a crime to think your best friend's boyfriend is incredibly hot if you never acted on it?

I continued staring at him, a touch of a smile on my lips. So. Yes, I liked him, even if I could never like-like him because of Sophie. He listened to me, made me laugh when I got too heavy. I ran a finger over the screen shot of the three of us. It reminded me of that *Sesame Street* song I used to sing when I was little, "One of These Things (Is Not Like the Others)." In the song, kids had to identify which object didn't belong in the group. Sophie and Tyler might pass for brother and sister, both with gorgeous eyes and similar olive complexions. Even in this goofy photo, they easily could be "Most Beautiful" and "Most Handsome." Then there was me, fair-skinned with a dusting of freckles I tried to hide with foundation. My almost invisible blonde eyebrows looked washed out compared with their striking features.

The phone vibrated in my hand with an incoming text.

Sophie: *At front door.*

Strange. She knew I avoided using our front door. She always came around to the back. I shrugged.

Me: *Just a sec.*

I jumped off the bed and bounded down the hallway where I heard my dad's science documentary on television in the living room. It was about black holes. Big surprise. The commentator droned on about angular momentum, whatever the hell that was. It made my head hurt.

"Fi's here," I announced to my parents. Dad lounged comfortably with his sock-covered feet on the sofa, engrossed in his show. He raised a hand in silent acknowledgement. My mother sat on the chair staring out of the French doors that led to the back yard. She ignored me. Again, big surprise.

I flung open the front door, confused but happy to see Sophie. "Hey. Everything okay? Where have you—" I stopped mid-sentence. One glance told me something was way wrong. She wore a stony face, her eyelids pink and puffy. It looked like her makeup had been scrubbed off. Very un-Sophie-like if we were going to see a movie.

"What's going on? You okay?" I opened the storm door wide and motioned for her to come inside. "Did you have a fight with your dad? I had a feeling something was."

Sophie took a step inside the house, almost grudgingly. She halted, one hand on her hip, which jutted slightly out. My phone, which I'd shoved in my pocket, began vibrating. Finally, it stopped then buzzed once, indicating someone had left a voicemail. I ignored it, totally focused on Sophie. She looked rumpled in a T-shirt with a rip at the bottom and worn sweats. Also, extremely un-Sophie-like.

She squinted at me. Then she bent forward, her hair pulled back into a messy bun and covered her face with her hands. I touched her shoulder and felt her flinch. I yanked my hand back, frightened and surprised.

"Hey, what's—I've been texting all day. You're full-on scaring me now, Fi." A churning began deep in my gut.

Finally, she uncovered her face, her intense stare pinning me where I stood. I knew the look. I'd witnessed others get the withering glare, but I'd never been on the receiving end. It was an unfiltered look of disgust.

"And who else have you been texting lately?" she asked in a bitter voice, her top lip curled.

"Wait. What?" I asked, baffled and afraid all at once. "What's going on, Fi?" I had no clue, but it was something major. As if on cue, the phone vibrated again in my pocket. It buzzed repeatedly as more texts rolled in.

"I saw you and Tyler yesterday. You two were...*together*...holding hands at lunch. So, wanna explain why you're making moves on my boyfriend, Em?"

Oh, God. So that was it.

"No, wait, Fi, it's not like that. Not even close. We were talking about Grams, about how close I came to losing her. Then I kind of lost it." I shook my head emphatically, as my hands flew about. "And Tyler, he was just, you know, comforting me." I took a step back. "That's *it*. Nothing more, Fi. I swear."

"Nothing more, huh?" Sophie said, then smirked. "Tell me why I should believe anything you say, huh? I've always been there for you. Even when you fucking tried to off yourself without even telling me anything was wrong. Without even giving me—your best friend since forever—a chance to help, to stop you from being such a *fucking idiot*. You were just going to kill yourself like that—*WHAM*," she said as she clapped her hands together, "and leave the rest of us behind. Now this."

I winced. Sophie never raged at me. We'd never fought like this. Usually, our mild disagreements ended with us laughing together at how stupid we were acting. This was different. Her glaring anger had blindsided me. I *was* ashamed I'd never confided in her about that horrible night in July, but she'd been at camp for two weeks and wasn't around to talk to. I'd felt so isolated, so alone. When we finally started talking again, after I'd come home and school began, I just wanted to move forward, start fresh. I figured she had wanted that, too.

"Fi, I'm sorry. I shouldn't have ever done that. I don't know—"

"Save it," Sophie said. "I'm not interested in your sob story right now. The rest of us have sad stories, too. Does that ever even occur to you? *I* have sob stories. It's not always about *you,* Em." She hugged her chest tight. "I don't want to hear about Tyler comforting you. He's just a stupid boy. You can have each other for all I care."

She stepped forward and placed her hands on her hips. "No...what I want to know is why you kept something so important from me for all these years. Me, your supposed *best friend,* who stuck by you all this time, dealing with your problems and always covering when you had one of your weird attacks in front of all our friends—or when you were trying to hide those god-awful bloody fingernails!"

She leaned in closer, her eyes slits, her voice menacingly calm, and uttered the next words with the force of a hammer, each word a nail driven into my flesh. "What pisses me off more than anything is why you never bothered to tell me about *your mother* and *my father.*"

My mind froze. "Wait." I managed to squeak. I wasn't sure I'd heard her correctly. "What are you saying?" A vice tightened around my chest. "Fi—I'm—I'm so confused. I honestly don't know what you're talking about."

"*I honestly don't know what you're talking about,*" Sophie mimicked my squeaky voice, almost hysterical. "Right. Always the victim. Well, guess what? You *lie.* You had to know because you were there. You know how I know? I found this strange letter your mom wrote to my dad shoved in the back of one of his drawers. He wouldn't explain anything to me. Just his usual asshole self, but it makes so much sense now why he always acted weird around you."

She continued glaring at me. "He wouldn't say anything about any-thing, so I asked Mom. She didn't want to say anything either—but I made her. She finally told me the real reason she and Dad split up." She snorted in disgust. "Your mom and my dad *were having an affair*, Emma. Your mom was on her way to see my dad the day Casey died. But you knew that, right? You knew because *you were there*. You answered the fucking phone when he called your house."

"What?" I saw Sophie's mouth form the words but couldn't quite connect the meaning. Like listening to a foreign language and sluggishly translating it into English, the gist of the conversation was getting lost in the process. It seemed as if I should know what Sophie was referring to, but a fog had slipped in, like it always did, making remembering that particular day almost impossible.

"Fi, stop. I just don't—" I shook my head harder, but it wouldn't shake free. I was trapped. I clenched my teeth as adrenaline coursed through my body, my nerves in hyper-drive, my senses overloading. "I really—"

"Emma, your mother destroyed my family. She destroyed *my life*," Sophie yelled. "Do you get that? You should have told me instead of keeping it from me. I deserved to know. We were best friends—sisters."

She waited for me to say something, but I had no words. All I could offer was a shocked silence, and the noiseless opening and closing of my mouth, a hooked fish dying at the end of a line. I didn't remember anything about my mom and Sophie's dad. *Nothing.* My mom was selfish and lots of other things, but surely even she wasn't capable of what Fi was accusing her of. If so, that would make Casey's death even more senseless. I was desperate to stop the conversation and where it would lead. My throat constricted, and instinctively I gulped saliva, cradling the side of my neck.

"What? Are we having another panic attack?" Sophie rolled her eyes and threw her hands into the air. "Sure, we are!" Her words sliced into me, like knives that targeted my critical organs. The world tilted.

"Whenever things go to hell, we have an attack, right, Em? Then you don't have to deal with a damn thing, and you just get a free pass." She grunted in frustration. "Not this time. No free pass today." Sophie's finger stabbed the air in front of my nose. "I deserve better than that after putting up with all your crap year after year. All the while you knew the reason behind my parents' divorce." Her voice cracked, but she quickly recovered. "You knew I always blamed myself for it. How could you keep the truth from me?"

I took a few steps backward, as my heart hammered fast and dangerous. I groped for answers. I hardly remembered anything from the day Casey died. Even when Dr. K tried to draw it out in our sessions, I came up blank. Just bits and pieces. The fog in my memory banks revealed little, just shadow figures in the distance. I heard the clock *tick, tick, tick* on the wall in the dining room, but otherwise, silence.

"Nothing? It figures," she spat at me. Her arms thrashed at the air. "Why would I expect anything else from you?" She paused and drew herself up. Her entire face contorted as she fired at me, "You should have done yourself a favor and finished the job this summer. It's not like you've got the courage to live an actual life."

I stood still, but it felt like I'd been slammed to the floor, the wind knocked out of me.

Sophie waited for some kind of response, but I could barely breathe, much less speak. "That's it. Like—whatever. I'm so over you." Angry tears welled in her eyes. "Don't call me. Ever." The windows in the dining room rattled when she slammed the door behind her.

I remained still for some time—I wasn't sure how long—absorbing what had just happened. I concentrated on my breath, forcing myself to inhale through my nose, holding it, then pushing a long exhale through my mouth like Dr. K had taught me. I squeezed my eyes shut and tried to imagine the calm waters of a lake, the rays of sun skipping across its surface, but I couldn't hold onto the image for long. No mental imagery could help. The television had been switched off at some point. I realized how quiet the house was; silence hung heavy within its walls, like always.

Then it hit me. My parents had heard the argument. I marched to the living room where I saw Dad first, the raw agony in his eyes causing my stomach to drop. It shook me. He looked away, his brows bunched together. When he finally met my eyes, he had shuttered it all, a faraway look now locked in place. Full armor engaged, ready to deflect. He blinked at me, then abruptly rose from the sofa, grabbed shoes off the floor and hurried through the utility room to the garage. I heard his car start, then the rumble of the garage door opening and closing. I was left alone with my mother.

She sat motionless in the chair, regal, her proud profile as perfect as the statue of a Roman goddess. Distant like a goddess, too, like she refused to grace such weak mortals with any explanations.

Was she drugged or just delusional? Maybe she was drunk again. How could someone not react to what just happened?

Another feeling overtook me. Silent rage. The flames of it flickered within and licked through my veins in a flash fire that heated my finger-tips and blotched my cheeks. A desire to spew it toward the motionless goddess burned on my tongue.

Did she really have an affair with Fi's dad? How could she?

I fought back a wave of nausea—the idea was despicable on so many levels. If it were true, it had damaged so many people I loved. Had my mother's reckless behavior caused Casey's death?

I couldn't be certain Sophie was right. Besides, I was the one to blame for Casey's death, not my mom. I was the one who had taken my eyes off

Casey that day, hadn't reacted fast enough once I realized she had slipped outside. I had failed to protect her. It was my fault.

"You heard all that. You heard what Fi told me." It wasn't a question, but a statement. My voice was ragged and harsh to my ears. "So. Is it true?"

The ugly scowl Mom aimed at me mirrored my own rage. But where mine was burning, hers was subzero. *With a hint of hatred, too?* My mother gripped the arms of the chair as if she were ready to spring forward.

"Do not speak to me that way. *Ever.*" Her voice was soft but threatening, her eyes unflinching. "I don't have to explain anything, especially not to you."

"Is it true?" I asked, this time less forceful, less accusing.

She didn't answer. Just stared me down. It was unnerving to see her eyes so alive, so focused on me, like a big cat staring down its prey—cold and calculating. The familiar fear rose again, the fire within sputtering out from lack of oxygen, dying inside my belly. I was scared but stood my ground. If it came down to it, I could outrun her.

"You still haven't answered the question," I said. "What Fi just told me.... *Is it true?*"

"And I won't answer the question," my mother shot back. Her voice matched the disdain I saw on her face. "And you won't ask me again. Understand?"

Mom slowly rose from the chair, her fixed stare never leaving me. I fought the urge to flee, even though danger bells clanged inside my head. But if I were to take off now, I'd be running forever.

"Go, Emma. Scurry along. That's what you're best at, isn't it?" my mother said. An indifferent smile touched her lips. "Your so-called friend even said as much."

I wanted to scream. *Why do you hate me so much? I'm your daughter. Doesn't that count for anything?* Instead, I worked to keep my voice level.

"Maybe. But I'm not running from this. Not anymore," I said through stiff lips. Fear fluttered inside me as I worked to compose my features and steady trembling limbs. I returned the stare for a few beats, then mustered all my remaining courage and walked out of the house.

I deliberately stepped over the threshold of the front door, the same spot where I had stood frozen years ago and watched Casey die. I squared my shoulders and held my head high, knowing my mom was waiting for me to bolt. *I will not run. I will not run. I will not run.* As much as I wanted to take flight, I refused to give her the pleasure. I gulped in air as soon as I cleared the driveway and glanced back to see if she had followed. She hadn't.

I pulled out my phone and checked text messages. They were from Tyler—warnings that Fi was pissed and headed to my house.

Tyler: *DO NOT ANSWER THE DOOR.*

God. How I wished I had checked my phone earlier before everything went to hell. But then again, maybe it was best I hadn't.

I headed to the stop sign at the corner and paused before going right. I needed time to process what had just happened. Dad had left me to face my mother alone, and my best friend was done with me. Somehow my life had nosedived right back into Suckville. *Would I ever have the chance to leave Suckville for good or was I stuck here forever?*

The cool evening air helped clear my muddled thoughts. Sophie was right about one thing. If I wanted to live—not just exist, but *live*—I had to face my little sister's death, and the time leading up to it, even if it meant uncovering ugly truths. I needed resolution. As I ambled on, my legs automatically moved me in the direction of Grams' house, a safe haven where I could regroup. But I didn't run there. Not this time. Instead, I took my time walking the five-and-a-half blocks as I revisited what little I remembered about that tragic day. I didn't see Casey anywhere but knew she was near.

Grams' small brick house was set back from the street, a warm glow in almost every room, a beacon that guided me in the darkness. I wanted all the intangible things that thrived inside that home—light, laughter, love, but most of all forgiveness. I tried the doorknob, but it was locked, and I didn't have my key on me. I rang the doorbell, and Grams answered with a puzzled smile on her face. I stepped inside and closed the door tight against the relentless shadows that nipped at my heels.

Chapter 20

I rubbed gunk from my eyes as I slogged into consciousness. *It's Sunday, right?* Disoriented, I jackknifed into a sitting position.

I shook the fog from my brain, then yawned. *Ouch.* I had forgotten to wear my night guard—my stiff jaw bones creaked, and an aching gripped my temples. The fresh smell of laundry softener on the pillowcase reminded me I was at Grams' house. The memory of why I'd spent the night there seeped into my brain—the horrible argument with Sophie, the shocking accusations of tawdry secrets.

The insides of my lids scraped against my eyeballs with each blink. I had cried most of the night. The faintest glow of dawn filtered through the bedroom window's white curtains, the darkness mingling with the mere hope of the light to come. My body automatically woke at this time. At home, my dad would have made his coffee and bacon and soon would be dressed for his run. Would he come by here this morning? Was he as stunned as I was by Sophie's revelation?

I eased back against the pillows and let the events of the night before return in slow, measured visuals, like scrolling through a series of photos on my phone, studying each one before moving to the next. My mother's cold face. I flinched at the memory of the loathing in her eyes.

She'll never forgive me for Casey's death.

I blinked away the image. Next, it was Dad. I recoiled as I recalled his ashen face, the way his eyes had retreated, the way he used to look before Dr. K had started helping him. If Sophie's accusation was true, could he recover from the betrayals and the devastation it had caused?

I closed and reopened my eyes, another image appearing. Sophie's fierce burning gaze, nostrils flared, her mouth a sneer. Her words ricocheted inside my brain. I covered my face with a pillow to try to stop the sound of them *buzzing, buzzing,* like a swarm of yellow jackets gathering for an attack.

Sophie's dad? My mom? Disgusting.

I pressed my face harder into the pillow and tried to make sense of it. No way. Nausea hit again.

How could Fi ever believe I would intentionally keep something like that *from her? She had to know I'd never do that to her.*

One thing Sophie had said stung the most and reverberated inside my head: *It's not like you've got the courage to actually live a life.* It did take courage to live. I was discovering that. Did I have enough of it? I had tried to stop the pain this summer, but all that did was bring me more guilt, more shame. Maybe part of living was to feel the pain and continue moving on, despite it.

I pushed away the pillow, shoved back the blankets and kicked my legs over the side of the bed. *The courage.* I knew I had it, and if I didn't have enough, I'd find more of it. I glanced over my shoulder, and there she sat on the corner of the bed. She was the younger Casey, beaming up at me.

"Have you been here this whole time?" I asked with a croaky voice. I cleared my throat and smiled at her. I longed to touch her translucent face, to stroke the gleaming curls that framed it, but I'd tried doing that a few times before and it always ended with Casey disappearing. Perhaps it was against the rules of whatever allowed this to happen—me getting to see my little sister. "I wish you would speak to me. I miss hearing your voice." Casey's dimples deepened.

"Emma.... Honey?" Grams called as she rapped lightly on the bedroom door. "You okay? Did you say something?"

I watched Casey. I wanted Grams to come in, to see her there with me. Maybe this was the moment Casey would appear to Grams again. I wanted my grandmother to know she *had* seen Casey the day of her stroke, that she hadn't imagined it. But Casey flickered away as soon as the door pushed open.

"Feeling any better?" Grams peeked in. The smell of coffee drifted through the cracked door. "I've been so worried. You wouldn't tell me what upset you last night." She opened the door wider. "You ready to talk about it?"

"Sorry, Grams. I didn't mean to worry you." I got out of bed and reached for the athletic leggings I'd balled up and thrown on the floor last night. "It was just another fight at the house. With Mom. It's okay."

Grams was regaining her strength, but she still wasn't completely back to herself. If for nothing else, I had to find courage for Grams. My grandmother had found it for me all these years. I owed her that.

"I thought I'd go for a run, maybe meet up with Dad, make sure he's okay, then come back, make you breakfast?" I gathered socks and shoes off the floor, then walked to Grams and pecked her on the cheek. "How about pancakes?"

I hadn't told Grams what Sophie had said last night, or how my dad took off, or the scary way Mom reacted. She had been through too much from the stroke, and she didn't need to deal with the continued craziness of the Watters family. The insanity that kept on giving.

"That sounds lovely, Em." Grams cupped my cheek in the palm of her soft hand and peered at me with knowing eyes. "You really okay, sweetie?"

"I am, Grams. I promise." I latched onto her gaze. Those eyes were the same color as my mother's and mine, yet I was struck by how much more vibrant Grams' seemed to be. She was made of tough stock. She'd endured her daughter's challenging illness and the losses of her husband and granddaughter, but she had never stopped living her life to the fullest. Never gave up. I hoped someday I could have the same lively eyes as my grandmother, but I'd have to earn them.

I wanted all of us—my dad, and, yes, even my mom—to have a chance at living again. If I had to, which it looked like I would, I'd fight to make things right again in our family, or as right as they could be. No more running from the past, no more secrets. I had the courage within me. I just had to remember where I'd hidden it all this time.

Chapter 21

S weat dripped down my face despite the cool temperature outside. My muscles burned, my sides hurt, but I pressed on. I rounded the last bend of the track with Aliah a hair's width behind. I'd managed to keep the inside lane, but she crowded me, even bumped my elbow as she pumped her arms. I heard her ragged breathing to my right, along with the determined thud of her steps.

I'm not giving up either. Focus.

"Woo! Go, Emma!" I heard girls call out as I neared the finish. Coach waited just ahead, her stopwatch extended, her clipboard cradled in her other arm. Ever since Aliah had made fun of Lacy being sick in the fall, I'd been on a mission, training like a madwoman. I *would* outrun her—become the fastest on the team—just to make a point. During the past couple weeks, we had tied on our running times, but I had yet to beat her.

Just as I flew past the finish line, Aliah lunged into my peripheral vision with a loud grunt.

"Dead even—again!" Coach shouted as we blew past her. I slowed, bent over and sucked in as much air as my burning lungs would hold. Aliah stayed right next to me, also folded over, her hands on her knees.

"You...will never...beat me, Watters. Never."

"Whatever," I said between puffed exhales and a roll of the eyes. I was done exchanging insults. My actions would be my words. I wiped the perspiration off the back of my neck.

"You know, I'm getting sick of your—" Aliah started. She straightened, took a menacing move toward me but stopped short when Coach Rodriguez jogged over. Some of the girls ran over and slapped us on the backs.

"Great race!" Coach beamed. "You two push each other. That's what I want to see out there—both of you giving it your all." She waved the stopwatch, her face animated. "You each topped your best time by two seconds. You came in at fifty-four-forty-five."

"Cool." My breathing had begun to level out.

"Yeah, cool," Aliah chimed in, her arms stretched above her head. The look she gave me screamed otherwise.

Coach blew her whistle and motioned for the team to gather around. "We have tryouts coming up next week, so sign up for the events you're interested in." She waited a beat and clapped her hands once. "If anyone has questions, talk to me. If not, hit the showers. See you next practice."

I watched the other girls cluster together and heard the excited chatter about what events they planned to try for. A couple of girls stood in line to ask Coach a question.

Lacy sidled up to me. "What are you going for?"

"The four hundred. I'm not sure what else," I said. "What about you? The hurdles, for sure, right?" Lacy had beautiful form and never broke her stride on the leaps. We headed toward the locker room.

"Yep. My favorite. I'll probably try for long jump, too." Lacy leaned in close. "Maybe you should think about the sixteen-hundred-meter relay, Em. With the way you and Aliah are tearing it up, we'd have a shot at dominating in that event."

"No way." I dabbed my face with the hem of my shirt. "Relays aren't my thing. I don't wanna let anyone down. I feel better if it's just me. What if, you know, I had a panic attack, dropped the baton or whatever in the middle of a race—"

"Panic attack? That'd be about right, wouldn't it?" Aliah butted in from behind. I hadn't known she and her posse were there. She released a snarky laugh, then lifted her face to the sky, cupped her hands around her mouth, and shouted, "Watch out! It's a freak attack!"

No one laughed except for Aliah. Such a joke. *At least get some new material.* I was so over her snark.

"Maybe you shouldn't compete at all," she said. "I've heard about your freak attacks. Save us all the embarrassment."

Lacy put her arm around my waist. "Just ignore her," she whispered.

I gritted my teeth, looking at Aliah over my shoulder, about to succumb to slinging a return insult. But I luckily swallowed my words when I spotted Coach on Aliah's heels. Her mouth puckered and her eyes narrowed into slits.

"Knight, you're not finished. I need five more laps from you." Yep. There was no doubt. She was *pissed.* "Let's run those legs of yours instead of that mouth."

Aliah halted at the sound of the coach's voice. She rolled her eyes and huffed, then faced Coach Rodriguez with a small smile. "But, Coach—it was a joke—"

Coach stopped her with a scowl and a flick of her hand. "Five laps. Now." She scanned the group. "Anyone else care to share a joke? No? Then hit the showers. Watters, my office when you're finished. I need a word."

"Yes, ma'am." I hung my head and moved along with the others. No one uttered a peep as we filed into the locker room. I grabbed my stuff and headed for the showers, where I stood under the spray and let the warm water stream through my hair, down my face and body. I needed to watch my temper. If I hadn't noticed the coach when I had, I'd be doing extra laps right now, too. I did not want to get sideways with Coach. That was for sure.

The Sophie drama was stressful enough—she hadn't spoken to me since that night, had ignored me in the hallways, and sat at Ben's table during lunch. Dr. K had been working with me to help retrieve my memories about Casey's death, but I still didn't recall much. He urged me to be patient; my mind would allow the memories to return when it was ready to handle them. But it was frustrating. I couldn't fix things with Fi until I remembered everything.

I wasn't sure what Coach wanted to talk about, but my mind slipped into catastrophic mode. *It can't be good, right? Why would she want to speak to me alone?* I quickly shampooed and rinsed my hair and rushed to dry off and slip into clean clothes. I passed a stone-faced Aliah, when I was leaving. She looked right through me. Like I even cared. I gathered my stuff and headed to Coach's office. I wanted to get it over with, whatever *it* was.

CHAPTER 22

Perched on the edge of her desk, Coach Rodriguez jotted notes on the clipboard in her lap. She glanced up when I knocked on the open door. "Come in. Shut that, will you?"

I swallowed hard and closed it behind me. My hands were damp with sweat despite the recent shower. Something about Coach, the way she filled the room with her presence, made me shy, especially trapped in the tiny, cramped office with her.

"Take a seat, Watters." She returned her attention to the clipboard.

"Yes, ma'am." I sat down on a hard, plastic chair and tried to get comfortable. I leaned forward with elbows on my knees, my clammy hands clasped together. I bobbed my right knee up and down, nerves whizzing. I watched Coach finish scribbling before tossing the clipboard aside.

"So, how're you doing, Watters?" she asked from her perch. "Still enjoying track?"

"Yes, ma'am." No hesitation. It was the one thing that made sense in my life. That—and Grams. The rest of my life seemed mired in chaos or teetering on the verge of it.

"That's good to hear. You're a natural." Coach grabbed a water bottle off her desk, took a long swig, then set it down. She crossed her arms and let her fist support her chin, as if she were considering the best way to say something difficult.

God. This cannot be good. I bounced my knee even faster.

"I'll cut to the chase. I've noticed the tension between you and Knight." Coach paused. "Am I correct?"

I hesitated, gritting my teeth again, about to hold back, then decided against it. "Yeah. I guess so."

"Can you tell me what the problem is?" Her face was unreadable.

I shifted in the chair. I didn't want to discuss it with Coach, but I was trapped in her office.

Wonder Woman and her stupid golden lasso of truth.

I shrugged. "No. Not really. I don't—it's like I don't know what it is other than—well, she's rude to people, and some of them are my friends." I studied the tops of my shoes. "I don't like it. I guess that's all there is to it." I concentrated on the gray scuff mark that marred the toe of my left sneaker.

"Hmmm—I see." She was silent. I peeked up to see her brow furrowed. "So, she rubs you the wrong way, huh? That it? Maybe too aggressive?"

"Yeah. Aggressive is one way you could put it." I laced my fingers together even tighter. More silence.

"Have you ever thought maybe you two aren't so different?"

A soft surprised laugh escaped my lips. She must be joking, right?

But one look at Coach showed she was serious. That stung. I shook my head. No way could I be compared to Aliah. *No way.*

"Absolutely not. I don't treat people like she does. Not even close. She enjoys making people feel bad about themselves. She bullies everyone." I recalled how cruel she'd been in the bathroom that day before school, how she constantly made fun of others, how she seemed to look down on everybody, as if she were superior to everyone. I had *nothing* in common with Aliah.

"Hmmm."

That annoyed me. I frowned at her. Dr. K sometimes did that to me, too, when he was listening to me but didn't agree with what I'd said. When he wanted me to see things from a different perspective.

"So, tell me, other than her being 'rude' sometimes, what else do you know about Aliah?" Coach asked.

I scratched a spot behind my ear. "I don't know. Not much, I guess."

"Well, it seems to me if you're going to judge someone, call 'em rude or mean or whatever, first you better know who they are, where they're coming from, right?" Coach hopped off the desk and moved to the chair next to me. "So, tell me—who is Aliah?"

I contemplated the question. I didn't know many details about Aliah other than I'd heard the girl aced all her classes and would probably graduate at the top of her class. "I haven't tried to talk to her much. I think I heard her dad's a doctor?"

"Yes, he's a cardiologist, a renowned surgeon in Dallas. He's one of the top in the country, in fact," Coach said with a nod. "You know, I had a dad like that, too. He was uber-successful, and he demanded the same from me." She tucked loose strands of hair behind her ear. "It can put a lot of pressure on you. I spent most of my childhood, and part of my adulthood, trying to please the man. Guess what? I had to deal with his constant disappointment." A wry laugh escaped her. "And I guess he had to deal with mine."

Where was she going with this? What did this have to do with Aliah and me? Sometimes adults made zero sense. I didn't attempt to hide my confusion.

"What I'm getting at, Emma, is that Aliah has *always* been the fastest runner, wherever she has been. Her father expects her to be the fastest runner just like *he* was the fastest when he was in high school." She cocked her head. "Then you came along. Now, maybe she isn't number one anymore, which is something she expects of herself. Now maybe she's not as good as her dad demands her to be either. Do you understand what I'm saying?"

"Yeah. She's threatened. I get it," I said, "but my dad isn't like hers. I still don't see how we're anything alike."

"Okay. Who is hardest on you?" Coach leaned forward in the chair and bit the bottom of her lip. "Who pressures you when you don't meet expectations?"

I massaged my temples to stall an oncoming headache—a distant, thudding drum beat in the back of my head. "No one pressures me, not for anything like that. Most of the time it's just me, how I feel about it, not my dad."

"Exactly," Coach Rodriguez said, as she gestured with both arms. "You see. You're hardest on yourself because you know you can do even better, run even faster, right? You're a competitor. You keep pushing yourself. You don't do it for anyone else but yourself."

I struggled to make the connection.

"Aliah pushes herself because she's a competitor, too. She also pushes against others—gets aggressive—because, ultimately, she doesn't want to let her father down, either. You know, lose his approval. It doesn't excuse her behavior, but for her, the stakes are high, so she lashes out at whoever is in the way."

It was difficult to understand. I knew what it was like to live in the shadows of something—maybe not of an overachieving, demanding father—but I did encounter the shadows cast by Casey's death and my mother's illness. Still, I couldn't wrap my mind around the reason Aliah treated others so horribly.

"You're both competitors. You are alike in that one way, Emma. Maybe not in other ways, but in the end, you both want to be the fastest, and you both push yourselves to do it." Coach leaned back with a satisfied grin. As if everything made perfect sense.

"I guess I see what you mean," I said. "Maybe we're alike in that one area. But—"

"I know you don't like her tactics, and I'll help her with that, but I need you to find a way to work with Aliah, find the common ground you *do* share. Sometimes you have to do that when you're on a team," she said, "because if you two can find a way to do that, you'd push each other in a positive way. You'd both excel individually, and especially together on the sixteen-hundred-meter relay team."

The relay? Coach wanted me to run the relay? I couldn't do that. "Coach...I don't do relays." The hammering of drums in my head increased in volume as the headache closed in, my hands sweaty again.

"Why?"

Coach pinned me to the chair with her intense gaze. I swallowed before answering. "Well, the idea of...well, they make me nervous. Remember, I told you I have panic attacks. Since I was young. I never know when one will hit." I studied the clasped hands in front of me as if they belonged to someone else. "I don't want to let the team down."

Coach reached over and placed her hand over my clasped ones. She was quiet. I risked a quick glance to gauge what she was thinking. "If the fear of having a panic attack is holding you back from running a relay, I can help you with that," she said. "Trust me."

"You don't understand. You don't know what it's like." I didn't want to ruin everything for the others, face their disappointment. I'd let too many people down in my life already. I'd let Casey down. No one could rely on me.

"I *do* know what it's like." It was spoken quietly. I studied Coach's face, which had taken on a hard, determined look while staring at the hand resting on top of mine. "To feel like you can't breathe, like your heart might tear through your chest, like the world is turning sideways, and you have nothing to hold onto."

My eyes widened. How could she know what I felt, what I went through? "How would you—"

"I *know*," Coach continued, "because I have them myself. I *know* because I was diagnosed with PTSD after Iraq." A small, grim smile pulled at her lips. "Trust me, Emma—I 100 percent *know* what a panic attack feels like."

Every superhero has at least one weakness, I thought. That's what makes them more human.

Chapter 23

Late the next day, I found myself standing in front of Grams, who was getting ready for a Bingo Night date at the senior center. She had refused to call it a date, but a gentleman was taking Grams to an early dinner before the event began.

She walked past me in a gorgeous teal dress, which brought out her eyes and complimented the silver of her hair. "Wow! You look like a movie star! You're going to bingo, not a gala."

"So—I'm gussied up a smidge. What of it?"

"Yeah. What of it?" I leveled Grams with a knowing look. "Oh, c'mon, Grams! Admit it. You're crushing on this guy. What's his name again?"

"Edward," Grams said, a smile toying at the corners of her mouth, "and what's 'crushing' anyway? Sounds awful dangerous. Besides, I've known Edward forever and a day. I worked with his late wife, Gracie, at the center." She smoothed the folds of the skirt, her smile fading. "She died about a year ago from lung cancer—God rest her soul." Grams glanced out the window just as his car pulled up front. She brightened. "Since then, he and I, well, we've become good, er, close friends."

"Hmmm. Well, have a good time with your *close friend*. And make sure you're home by ten o'clock, so I don't worry." I winked. "I'll be waiting up to hear all the details."

Grams leaned in to kiss my cheek. Filled with sudden emotion, I embraced her, squeezing tightly, inhaling her perfume, and reveling in the softness of her cheek pressed against mine.

I couldn't make it without you, Grams.

When Edward came through the door, I heard him murmur, "Dorothy, you are a vision to behold," in an affectionate voice. Grams' cheeks flushed a beautiful pink, almost the same color of the bouquet of roses he handed her. He introduced himself to me and clasped my hand between his own. He was a charmer. I couldn't blame Grams for blushing around this man.

Good for her. She deserves happiness.

I took the roses, promising to put them in a vase, then stood on the front porch watching them head for the car. Grams beamed like a beauty contestant as Edward held the car door open for her and waited until she was settled in the passenger's seat before closing it. He was like one of the gallant movie stars in the old black-and-white films I sometimes watched with her. Grams blew a kiss to me out the window before they took off. I stood on the porch long after Edward's car had disappeared around the corner.

***

In the kitchen, I filled a vase with water and arranged the flowers. Then I rummaged through the pantry for something to munch on. Sweet or salty? Or both? I settled for a bag of trail mix and walked to the guest room, which was my bedroom when I stayed here. The room—with light green walls and floral bedding—exuded tranquility and smelled of honeysuckle thanks to the plug-in air freshener in the adjacent bathroom. I switched on a playlist from my phone and dove belly-first onto the huge fluffy, bed pillows, crossing my legs at the ankles as I crunched on the trail mix. I picked out the sesame sticks, my favorite, and ate all of them first.

Since Fi had dropped the bomb on me, I'd stayed at Grams' house. I still couldn't face my mother, Sophie, or Ms. Zohar, for that matter. I'd seen my dad, but we weren't able to discuss that night yet, either; it was like a silent, unspoken agreement we'd reached. Eventually, I'd told Grams about some of it—that Sophie thought I was interested in Tyler—because I had to explain why my best friend was missing. Bringing myself to explain everything else, the thing that was so much worse, remained too tough. If I said it aloud, it would make it more real, and I *really* didn't want it to be true.

I glanced at the stuffed backpack on a nearby chair. There was homework to be done this weekend, but I had no desire to tackle it. Not right now. I had other things to contend with. My mind wandered back to the day before and my talk with Coach. I couldn't get it out of my head. We'd spent an hour after practice yesterday, with me mostly listening as Coach shared stories about her tours in Iraq, some of what she had seen and gone through over there, including a tragic situation that led to her fellow soldiers' deaths. A PTSD diagnosis had eventually followed.

"There are things that happened over there—things I'm not proud of," Coach Rodriguez had said, the back of her head leaning against the wall, with a faraway gaze directed at the ceiling. "Things I wish I could go back and do over, you know?"

Yeah. I *did* know. I'd lost count of the number of times I'd told myself just that. If only I had a do-over. But early on I'd realized life wasn't interested in do-overs. So, like a priest in a confessional, I had remained perfectly still as I listened, although I wasn't sure I wanted to hear what haunted one of the most put-together people I'd ever met. My nerves had fired off in random parts of my body again and again, and my stomach tightened, braced for the unknown. It seemed everyone—even Wonder Woman—carried baggage.

The idea was both depressing and liberating. Depressing because no one was free of it but liberating because I wasn't the only one who hauled it around. I bet even Dr. K had baggage.

Coach Rodriguez had told me how she'd been stationed at a place called Camp Fallujah in Iraq when the war first started. She was ex-Naval intelligence but hadn't given much detail about what her duties were during the war. Later, I had looked up Camp Fallujah on the Internet because I'd never heard of it before.

"I'm responsible for the deaths of twelve soldiers," Coach had told the ceiling, as if I weren't sitting inches away. "I should have known better. Should have listened to my gut, fought my captain on the intel we had, forced him to take the threat—*and me*—more seriously. He dismissed it, dismissed me, and I was afraid to push back." She'd raked fingers through her hair. "I was afraid it would affect my military career, embarrass my father. He'd spent a lifetime building the perfect officer's career." Her voice had become husky and raw. "Those men died because of that—because of me."

I had tried to follow along. From what I could gather, Coach had received information about a rebel stronghold in a village south of Fallujah. She'd relayed to her captain what the source had told her, but the captain shrugged off the warning and sent a recognizance team anyway. The American soldiers had been ambushed, their vehicles blasted off the road and set ablaze. The few who were able had dragged the wounded to whatever cover they managed to find. Later, Coach had watched footage from the Humvee cams, which showed what they had suffered. It haunted her most nights, she told me.

It sounded like a scene from one of those bloody war movies Dad enjoyed. To lug those images around...to feel responsible for so many deaths.

I had swallowed hard and concentrated on the hands in my lap. Tears welled in my eyes as I absorbed the anguish in Coach's voice.

"I still see a therapist for PTSD." With the heels of her hands, Coach massaged her temples. "It does get better. I promise." She straightened in the chair and regarded me with kind eyes. "My therapist, well, she has done a lot to help me cope with my anger—and grief." She cracked a derisive laugh. "Yep. Apparently, I had lots of grief to work through. Anyway, it helped. I still have occasional panic attacks, you know, when life gets too intense, but they're not nearly as extreme as they were."

I nodded, my head still bowed. How long would it take for me to get past my attacks? Another six years? Twenty? A lifetime? Would I ever get past them? I stole a quick peek at Coach. I would have never guessed we had that in common. Not in a million years. She seemed so together all the time. Unlike me.

"I'm sorry about everything. About all that you went through," I whispered.

I meant it, too. I wouldn't wish PTSD or whatever horrific events that spurred it on anyone. I knew the words were empty, probably meaning-less, to Coach. They couldn't erase what had happened. They wouldn't bring back twelve lives plucked away.

"Thanks," Coach said with a half-smile, half-grimace on her lips. "I'm sorry, too. I don't usually talk about it, especially not with my students. But I hope it'll help you." She leaned her elbows on her knees. "So, what about you? Are you seeing someone about yours?"

"Yeah." I rubbed my hands against the tops of my thighs. "I just started a couple of months ago. I think it's helping some." I debated whether I should share my story, mindful I couldn't recall all the details of the day

Casey died. Only that I was supposed to watch her but had taken my eyes off her for a few seconds. Long enough for Casey to die. Long enough for me to shatter my life, and the lives of my parents, too. Just a few seconds I could never get back and lives I could never give back.

Finally, I had spoken. I'd forced out every word, each as bitter tasting as an aspirin dissolving on the tongue. I'd known Coach might think less of me once I'd uttered them. "Um. I'm—uh—my little sister is dead—because of me." Air came out in ragged bursts. "She was three, would have been four in a few days. I was supposed to watch her, but…."

There, for whatever reason, I'd said it. The tightness in my chest hadn't gone away nor the sensation of hands squeezing my throat, but my heart hadn't raced like it usually did, and I hadn't felt any vertigo coming on. *Baby steps*, like Dr. K always told me.

Coach had remained silent. Strong fingers had covered my hand, but I hadn't been able to look at her. There was no need. I'd known what Coach was thinking—there were no words. I already knew that about death, just like I knew it about life. There were no do-overs. No words existed that could erase those excruciating seconds, rub out their permanence, not for people like me and Coach. Not for those of us who revisited those painful moments over and over in our minds.

Chapter 24

The sound of locker doors slamming and the undulating hum of students' conversations—peppered with peals of laughter—filled the hallways. Before I saw him out of the corner of my eye, I felt his presence behind me. Tyler hovered over my left shoulder and watched as I shoved binders and folders into my locker. I struggled to concentrate on what I needed for my next class.

His woodsy cologne taunted me, and seized by the scent, I inhaled deeply without being too obvious. This was the reason I'd been avoiding him. We were both silent. He managed a half smile. I reached in my locker, grabbed a science folder, then fumbled a book and watched as it tumbled to the ground and smacked the speckled tile below. Moving faster than I could, Tyler picked it up and held it out to me. Still, he didn't say anything.

"Thanks," I mumbled without meeting his eyes. My face was probably a splotchy crimson as I grabbed it from him and chucked it inside. Slowly, I closed the locker door and turned to face him.

"What's up?" I asked in a shaky voice. Over his shoulder, I scanned the crowds of students moving in opposite directions down the hall, checking to make sure Sophie wasn't nearby. Since the Sophie incident, I had stayed away from Tyler and the lunch table, reverting to solitary lunches in the library. Each day I snuck a peanut butter and jelly sandwich in and would steal bites when the librarians weren't watching. I had to eat but couldn't go to the cafeteria, couldn't face Tyler after Fi's accusations. I couldn't face either one of them.

God. Everything is so screwed up.

Maybe what Sophie had said about Tyler was true. Maybe I *had* flirted with him because, if I were honest with myself, I found him attractive. So, I decided to keep my distance by riding with my dad to school and getting Grams to pick me up after practice.

Tyler broke into my thoughts. "Well, you haven't responded to any of my texts. I don't know, I think I've sent fifty maybe? Or was it seventy-eight?" He rapped a knuckle against his forehead for effect. "That's right. Yeah. Exactly seventy-eight texts." He placed a hand on the locker next to mine and leaned in. "Okay, so I'm exaggerating for effect here. But seriously, I've lost count of how many times I've called, how many messages I've left you."

Managing eye contact was impossible, so instead, I stared at his mouth as he spoke. *Big mistake.* I looked around again and willed myself not to think about how his navy-blue polo hugged the width of his shoulders or how it made the color of his eyes darken to jade. I checked the groups of people who moved past us again. Sophie might walk this way any second. She usually did on her way to sixth period.

"I wanted to make sure you're okay," Tyler said. He searched my face. "I heard Sophie got a hold of you the day she was so pissed. She unloaded on me, too—told me some seriously messed up stuff about her dad, and—uh—your mom." Silence. "Emma?" With gentle fingers, he guided my face, so our eyes met. My heart bobbed inside my chest. "Please, talk to me."

I shrugged, my voice nowhere to be found. I didn't know what to do. I liked Tyler, liked him as more than a friend, but I knew I wouldn't do anything about that. I couldn't hurt Sophie anymore. Especially if my mom had done what Sophie claimed.

"Listen, I don't know what all's going on, Em," he said softly, "but I miss you. I need to talk to you about...things. I tried to that morning, but you ran off. You need to know Sophie and I were basically never more than friends. Or we haven't been for a long time."

"What?"

"Yeah." He brushed the back of a hand over his forehead before moving in closer and lowering his voice. "Okay, yes, she's beautiful and funny and all that. This summer I thought maybe.... then we kissed, and it was like...it was like kissing my sister or something. It just wasn't there, the chemistry, you know?"

No, I didn't know. I hadn't officially kissed a boy. Not *really*. Okay, so there was that party in seventh grade when I'd pecked lips with Alex Martinez, but that had abruptly ended when I had seized with panic as he leaned in for more. *Ugh.* The memory still made me cringe all these years later.

Tyler continued. "When I met you—no, I think it was the first time I saw you smile—well, I just knew it wasn't going to work with Sophie. Ever."

I stood motionless. His eyes were fixed on mine. My stomach flip-flopped, and I struggled to get words out. "But—" I sifted through sludge-like thoughts, unable to hold onto to any single one. "I thought.... Fi said.... You two have been dating since summer."

"Not really. That's what I've been trying to tell you." Tyler pushed away a lock of dark hair that dangled in eyes. "It was more like good friends who held hands. I think Sophie just wanted people to think she had a boyfriend, you know? I think we both know I'm not the guy she wants." He shrugged. "And she's not the girl I want."

"Oh." I swallowed hard.

He must have known Fi still had a thing for Ben. If he didn't want Fi as a girlfriend, who did he want? I wanted it to be me. *I* wanted to be that girl. The simple fact hit me hard and everything inside my head shifted and tilted, like an internal walk through a house of mirrors. I thought about the times he made me laugh. How he always seemed to lighten my spirits with a stupid pun or the lift of an eyebrow. How he stopped to help pick up my books off the floor. How he always searched for me at lunch, a satisfied grin spreading across his face when he'd spot me, and how he *always* asked about my day.

"Emma, can we talk later?" Tyler interrupted my thoughts. "Like maybe over ice cream or coffee?" He hesitated before he grinned. "Or maybe at Mickey's Diner? I hear they make great eggs."

Even with the stupid egg jokes, he's irresistible. I barely met his eyes. I didn't want him reading my thoughts. Maybe that's how Fi knew even before I had. She'd read it on my face. I had a lot to figure out, and I knew I needed to discuss it with him.

"Okay," I managed. "Sure. I think—that'd be great."

"Really?" His eyes opened wide as his smiled broadened. "I wasn't sure you'd say yes." Happy, he leaned in for a quick hug, and I placed an awkward hand on his shoulder. "I'll text you to work out a time, okay?"

As if on cue, Sophie glided down the hallway in the middle of a small group. She was laughing as she turned and spotted us. Her eyes widened at first but then narrowed as she took in my semi-embrace with Tyler. Startled, I backed away from him and bumped into the lockers. Sophie appeared more disgusted than angry. She turned toward Ben, who draped an arm over her shoulders, and intertwined her fingers with his. He nuzzled the side of her face. She glanced back at me—and then Tyler, who turned to see what I was gaping at—and gave us both a victorious smirk.

I watched my best friend drift away. I knew I needed to fix our relationship. But not now. Not today. Fi finally had the boy she wanted. Maybe I could finally have the one I wanted, too.

Chapter 25

I yelped happily as I crossed the finish line, the wind whipping my loosened ponytail against the tops of my shoulders. It was exhilarating. I'd beaten Aliah. Finally!

Aliah, less than a step behind, loudly sucked in air as we both slowed to a stop.

"Dammit, Frea—Watters," she said, struggling to catch her breath. "You win...this time."

Her practice T-shirt was drenched and clung to her just like mine, both our faces lacquered in sweat. We'd run two consecutive four-hundred-meter sprints to determine who had the fastest times.

"Well done, ladies!" Coach yelled as she jogged toward us. We both stood with our hands on hips, faces to the sky and mouths wide open. I heard scattered applause and cheers from the other girls. Most of them had watched on the sidelines while Aliah and I battled on the track.

"I *love* how you two push each other." Coach moved between the two of us, lightly draping her arms around our shoulders. "If you two were to run like that in every race, we'll be tough to beat."

"Thanks, Coach," I said and nodded at Aliah. "Good race."

"Yeah. You too," Aliah said begrudgingly, then veered her eyes away.

I walked away on wobbly legs, my muscles quivering, but my heart full. Had that been the tiniest look of respect on Aliah's face? Maybe? I couldn't believe it. I had done it. I'd beaten her not once, but *twice*. When I glanced back, Coach still had her hand on Aliah's shoulder, speaking in a hushed voice. I knew it wasn't easy for Aliah to lose, but she was far from giving up. She'd keep pushing me. And I would do the same.

I slapped at my thighs as the muscles tightened like overstretched rubber bands not quite ready to snap back into form. I made my way to Lacy and plopped down on the grass next to her. Stretching, I felt resistance at first, then a pleasant give as I gently reached beyond my toes. I was physically exhausted, but my mind raced as fast as I had moved on the track.

"Great run out there," Lacy said. She bumped fists with me. "You were incredible! So was Aliah, even though I was pulling for you."

"Thanks." I couldn't stop beaming. I was proud of myself, something I didn't experience often. All the extra hours of training had paid off. The coveted anchor leg on the relay team was mine.

In the first race, I'd outrun Aliah by less than a hundredth of a second. We had come in almost nose-to-nose. "Let's do it again, Watters," Aliah had growled through gritted teeth. The second time I crossed the finish line by at least half a stride. I'd been fueled by a resolve I couldn't name, something powerful charging inside, refusing to back down. I'd earned the fourth leg of the race, the spot traditionally designated for the fastest runner.

It wasn't about getting back at Aliah anymore. It'd become more about beating a worthy challenger. I had reflected on what Coach Rodriguez had told me about Aliah's dad. I think I better understood Aliah's aggressive behavior. I didn't agree with it, but I got the reasons behind it. Coach had been right about another thing, too. Aliah and I did push each other to be stronger runners. For the first time I could remember, I wasn't using it as a way to escape the past. Instead, I was running toward something within my grasp, something better.

Lately, Aliah had been slightly nicer to me, too. Well, less hostile might be a better way of putting it. It wasn't as if we were besties or anything, but she hadn't called me a freak in at least two weeks, and she seemed less vicious, overall. Maybe Coach was helping her with that. One day after practice, I had seen them sitting together on the bleachers, deep in conversation. At first, Aliah's face was hard, her lip curled, but after a few minutes, it looked like she'd started crying. I couldn't tell from where I stood. Coach had patted her on the back as Aliah folded over, her hands shielding her face. I had wondered about their conversation. Maybe Coach had given Aliah the same speech I'd heard. Maybe she had taken it to heart, too.

"I guess this means you're running the last leg of the relay, right?" Lacy interrupted my thoughts.

"Yeah!" I pumped my arm in the air. "Crazy, right?"

"You deserve it. You're a rock star." Lacy released her stretch, twisted in the other direction and held the position. "It's tough being the last leg. Sometimes your team's so far behind, there's a lot of pressure to try to make up the distance, you know?" She finished the stretch and moved into a new one, her eyes squeezed in concentration. "But with the way you run, girl, it shouldn't be a problem."

"Yeah. You think?" The smile on my face wilted. I'd been so focused on beating Aliah, I hadn't thought about the pressure that an anchor faces.

What if I stumble? What if I can't make up the distance? What if I lose a lead? What if I choke and let everyone down?

My team would be relying on me. The familiar tang of stomach acid coated the back of my throat. What if I had a panic attack during a relay? The humiliation? It would be Suckville again, bigtime.

Lacy stopped stretching, cocked her head at me and scrunched her face. "Hey. It's all good. I didn't mean to scare you." Her voice was confident as she rose to her feet. "You'll do great. You really will, okay?"

I blinked back at her, my mind sprinting away into images of humiliating scenarios.

"Em, I've watched you run. Trust me. You're going to kill it!"

Or it'll kill me.

"Yeah, sure. Thanks." I ducked my head and tugged at blades of grass. "I'm not crazy-worried or anything like that. Just a little nervous. Nothing major." But maybe I was just a little lying. Nothing major.

Chapter 26

On Monday, I half-walked, half-sprinted to athletics, my last class of the day. It was a cool but cloudless afternoon in early March. I pulled on thick athletic leggings and a school-issued hoodie as fast as possible. As other girls trickled into the locker room, I headed to the track. The relay team was supposed to run drills today, and I hoped to jog off nervous energy before the rest of the team came outside. I tried to calm my stomach. But the knots intensified when I spotted Coach approaching with aluminum batons tucked under her arm.

"What's up, Watters? Getting an early jump?" She tossed the clipboard and batons onto the track, then dug around inside the pocket of her athletic pants and pulled out a stopwatch. She flung it onto the pile. "Ready to get down to business?"

"Sure," I managed in a voice more confident than I felt.

Trini and Anne, two other girls on the mile relay, jogged up. I didn't know them well, but they seemed nice enough. Aliah lumbered behind.

"Hey," both girls called in unison.

"Hey." I waved a hand. Nerves spurred my stomach into a cacophony of gurgles. I knew my smile looked forced.

"It's a great day for relay drills, right?" Coach moved to her pile of stuff. Whistling under her breath, she picked up the items.

"Ready for this?" Trini asked me softly. She was petite with shoulder-length straight black hair twisted into a messy bun, and huge, brown childlike eyes lined in black. Her long mascara'd lashes, button nose, and high-pitched voice gave off a cartoon air about her. As she spoke, Trini rubbed her hands up and down the front of her thin but defined thigh muscles. "I'm not as fast as the rest of you," she said with a tight laugh. "I'm way nervous. Like, there's a high possibility I might puke."

"Shut up. You're *way* faster than me," Anne said. She was tall with thin red hair pulled taut by a black headband. It emphasized her pale, freckled face. She spoke with an East Texas accent, her words drawn out longer than typical of other parts of Texas. "Y'all are gonna leave me in the dust."

"What?" Trini playfully punched Anne's shoulder. "I don't think so, chica."

Watching the two of them banter eased the tension from my muscles. "No worries. You'll both do great."

Anne raised a thin ginger eyebrow at me. "That's easy for you to say," she said, "because you're *you*. Compared to the rest of us, well, you're just a passing blur."

"I wish."

"Okay. First things, first," said Coach as she approached. "Let's do some basic work on hand-offs. Has everyone done this before?" she asked. I was the only one who hadn't. Aliah, who had just ambled up to the group, crossed her arms, shifted her hip to one side and rolled her eyes. A touch of panic pushed at my chest.

"It's something all of you must work on, so let's partner up. Anne and Emma, you two take this." Coach tossed us a baton, then pitched the other to Trini and Aliah, who snatched it out of the air.

"We'll go over passing-off techniques. Lots of coaches don't focus on exchanges in this event, but a bad baton pass can be the difference between a win or loss on the clock." She took off her aviator sunglasses and tucked them inside the collar of her sweatshirt. "Be aware of your teammate. Sync with her pace as she's about to pass off. When she makes it to the exchange zone—pay attention. Is she coming in too fast? Speed up so she doesn't run into you! Is she dragging? About to fall over? Then slow down!" She surveyed us. "In other words, adapt to her. Think of her as your dance partner. Your goal is to get that baton into your hand—make that move smooth and easy, *graceful*—without ever slowing down."

Of course, I suck at dancing.

Coach first worked on us visually gauging each other's pacing. "Looking good, ladies. Now work on making a smooth handoff with the batons. Repetition, repetition."

Anne and I ran through the drill repeatedly. It was rough. I was too keyed up and calculating Anne's stride was difficult. Sometimes I'd take off before she completed the hand-off. And when I managed to sync our steps, I'd accidentally bobble the baton or watch it slip through my sweaty fingers. I was a mess.

"I'm so sorry." I covered my face with my hands. I'd just hesitated and caused Anne to lurch into me as she dropped the baton. "I suck at graceful." I wished I could curl up under the bleachers and hide.

"It's okay. It's our first time doing this together." Anne patted my back. "Relax! It'll come!"

We spent the entire practice working on the drill. At the end, Coach had us run segments of the relay. Aliah and Trini were up first. Coach stood on the sidelines and yelled instructions as she made notes. Trini was a head shorter than Aliah, but the two adjusted and passed the baton on the first try, although I wouldn't have called it seamless.

"Do it again, ladies," Coach yelled. "Smooth and easy. Knight, let go of the stick when handing off! Gutierrez shouldn't have to fight you for it." Their next exchange was seamless.

Trini and Anne had run together on the same school team for years; they executed their hand-off perfectly. Anne and I were up next.

My mouth was dry, and I clenched and unclenched my fists, unable to stand still. As Anne entered the exchange zone and zoomed toward me, I faltered.

Should I take off? Or maybe wait a sec?

The others stared at me. I gulped and counted Anne's strides in my head—nine, ten, eleven, twelve.

Oh, crap.

Thirteen, fourteen, fifteen. I began a slow walk, my torso rotated sideways and my left arm extended.

"She's coming in faster than that, Watters!" Coach yelled. "Sync up!"

I took off a second too late. I heard Anne grunt, saw her arm extended, just before the baton rammed into my shoulder. We tussled a bit before I finally grabbed the baton.

Crap!

It slid momentarily from my sweaty fingers, but I grabbed it back again. I willed myself to grip it, to focus on the feel of the smooth aluminum in my palm.

"No. No. No!" Coach shouted from the side. The heels of her hands were pressed against the sides of her head. I struggled to calm down, sucking in several gulps of air. Anne and I tried the exchange two more times without luck.

"We'll keep working on it," Coach said on the walk to the locker room. Her voice lacked the usual enthusiasm.

"Don't worry. We'll get there," Anne said to me as we trailed behind. "You'll get used to it—just takes practice."

I nodded, eyes downcast. I wasn't sure I'd ever get the hang of it. Awkward and gangly—that's what I was. My fingers sought out my thumbnail, pressed against the cuticle. What had I signed up for? What was I thinking when I'd agreed to this? I appreciated my teammates staying positive, but I had a private message echoing through my brain—*They can't rely on me.*

Chapter 27

My three relay teammates were huddled together when I slipped into the locker room after practice. It looked like they were talking about me based on the guilty glances shot my way. Like they wanted me off the team. I couldn't blame them. They'd been working with me all week without success. It didn't matter how fast I was. I couldn't win a relay if I couldn't grab the baton without causing a pile-up. Or keep hold of it. Pretty basic.

Our first meet was in two weeks. If I couldn't get a handle on my anxiety, the entire relay team would suffer. Just as I had feared from the beginning. My head throbbed.

Coach needs to replace me on the relay. I'm not ready. I'll run solo, like always.

I pressed my forehead against the cold metal of the locker door and felt the abrupt shutter of metal bump against my flesh as someone down the line slammed a locker shut. I closed my eyes and breathed in the fine mist of fruity body sprays that lingered in the room, never quite masking the ever-present musky scent of sweaty socks and damp towels.

A hand tentatively tapped my shoulder. "Hey, Emma." I glanced sideways at Anne. Aliah and Trini trailed behind.

"Yeah?"

"So. We've been thinking," Anne said, as she wrung her long-fingered hands in front of her.

Here it goes. I clenched my jaw, bracing for the inevitable, and pushed away from the locker. The least I could do was face them when they told me to get lost.

"We want to...well, we think you need some extra help. You know, more practice," she drawled out. Anne didn't seem to know what to do with her hands but finally stuck them behind her back. "And we were thinking maybe we could all get together, you know, like maybe tomorrow morning? If you're free?" She continued as I stood openmouthed. "We could, like, meet first thing in the morning, practice super hard. Like Coach says, 'Repetition! Repetition!'"

Wait. What? They wanted me to stay?

She gestured behind her. "We know you can do it, that you'll get it, I mean. You just need to do it again and again. Muscle memory and all that." Over Anne's shoulder, Trini nodded with enthusiasm. Aliah stood next to her nonchalantly studying her manicured nails. "If we finish up in time, we could get some fraps at the coffee shop. Maybe do some team bonding."

I gaped at them, unable to speak.

"Well? We don't have all day," Aliah finally spoke, impatient as ever. "Do you want our help or not?"

"Yes," I choked out. "Sure."

"Great!" Anne clapped her hands and looked at everyone. "Y'all, let's meet on the track tomorrow morning, say around seven-thirty? Sound good?" Trini and Aliah agreed and headed to their lockers.

"Hey," I said, stopping Anne from turning away. "I just wanna say thanks. I mean, I appreciate your—everyone's help."

"That's what we do as a team, right, girl?" Anne said. "We help each other!" She playfully slapped my shoulder. "Tell you what. You teach me to run as fast as you, and I'll teach you how to hold a baton!" She wrinkled her lightly freckled nose and laughed. "I think I've got it easier."

Yep. That's what you did when you were on a team. It'd been so long since I'd belonged to one, I'd almost forgotten how it worked.

***

It had taken lots of deep breathing to settle my nerves and more than thirty tries before I began feeling slightly more confident with the hand-offs. The girls were right. Repetition helped. And Aliah, who had anchored relays on other teams, gave me some tips on syncing my pace with Anne's right before she hit the exchange zone so that neither of us had to slow down. The private practice with the girls proved a success.

I sat at the table in the coffee shop and laughed along with the others as Trini performed a Coach impression.

"All right, ladies, let's see some *burn* in that," Trini said, hands on hips. "No whining, ladies, or we'll go another ten miles, and this time, we'll run it backward, hands tied behind our backs. *You got me*?" We cackled together. Anne snorted, and accidentally sprayed Trini with a mouthful of vanilla Frappuccino. We erupted into louder peals of laughter. I was amazed by how relaxed Aliah was today. She acted so different, less guarded.

"Okay, I have to pee. Got me, ladies?" Trini said. She dabbed at her shirt with a napkin, still laughing, and trotted to the restroom.

"I gotta go, too," Anne giggled as she followed.

That left me and Aliah sitting alone together. "So," I started awkwardly but continued despite the quickening in my stomach, "thanks for your help today."

Aliah shrugged. "No problem."

"Can I ask you something?" I drummed my fingers on the table, noticing how decent my cuticles looked these days. I glanced up at Aliah's wary face.

"Ask away."

"Why are you being so nice? To me, I mean." I flattened my hands on the tabletop. "You used to call me 'Freak.' Like on a daily basis."

"Yeah. About that...." Aliah said with a groan. "Look, I'm sorry, okay?" She shifted in her chair. "That was juvenile."

I noticed that Aliah twisted a ring with a silver and gold heart on her index finger. She stared at it, unable to stop the twisting, it seemed. Eventually, she spoke.

"Look, I get it." She raised her eyes at me. "I didn't know, okay? I didn't get it then, when I first met you. But I do now."

"What are you talking about?"

"Okay." Aliah continued fidgeting with the ring. "After I talked to Coach a couple of weeks ago, I searched for your name on the Internet."

"Oh." I wasn't sure where this conversation was going.

Aliah sighed impatiently. "Look, I found the obituary online. Then I found other stuff, follow-up articles. I found your family's name and read about everything that happened." She swallowed a few times before speaking. "I'm sorry about your sister. The whole thing was messed up."

The lightness of the day suddenly transformed into something heavy and gray, like a thunderhead crowding out the sun. "Thanks," I said. My voice sounded flat, lifeless. I wanted to cry. The compassion in Aliah's voice caught me off-guard. I was vulnerable every time Casey came up, but even more so coming from her.

"I mean that." She reached across the table and clumsily flicked my forearm. "I understand what it's like to lose someone. I mean, I don't know what you went through. I just know what I went through." She started twisting the ring again. Silence followed, and a faraway glaze crept into her eyes.

"She died when I was six, my mother. It was breast cancer. An aggressive kind." Aliah kept her gaze averted. "My father, he's a doctor. He tried to save her, thought he could. Took her to the best oncologists, got her the best treatments, but...." She shrugged. "They thought she had it beat, you know, but it came back. Ten months later, she was gone." She looked down at the ring again. "I'm not sure I've ever gotten over it. Not sure I ever will."

I nodded, solemn. I understood that kind of pain.

"Anyway, I'm sorry. I don't know...sometimes, I just get so angry about everything, about her not being here. I miss her." Aliah's voice was husky. "She would have been ashamed of the way I treated you." She gulped and shook her head, casting her eyes downward. "I'm ashamed."

"I understand. I do. Really." Another silence followed. I motioned to her hand. "Is that her ring?"

"Yeah." A sadness tinged the beauty of Aliah's eyes, something I had never noticed before. "My dad gave this to her when he found out she was pregnant with me."

"It's beautiful." I paused. "Aliah?"

"Yeah?"

"I'm truly sorry about your mom."

Aliah nodded. We shared a look just as the others returned to the table. We'd most likely never be close, but at least we understood each other now. As usual, Coach had nailed it. We did share a couple of traits, but one was stronger than the rest: It didn't matter how fast we ran, outrunning the tragic circumstances of our pasts was something neither of us had mastered.

Chapter 28

It was time to confront my mother. Sophie's accusation still rang in my head. I choked down mouthfuls of dread with each step across the driveway and steered myself toward the front porch. I'd told Grams I was going out for fresh air and had walked the five blocks home. I hadn't been there in weeks, instead relying on Dad or Grams to pick up things I needed. My dad, who was due back from a conference tonight, had told me over the phone last week that he missed me and wanted me home. The house was too quiet with me gone, he'd said.

He'd also asked me to check on my mom while he was at his physics conference in Switzerland for two weeks, but I hadn't. Instead, Grams had done it. Each time, she came home more tired and strained than when she left, which reinforced my decision to confront Mom, and, more importantly, the past. I needed to know the truth. I deserved to know it. I wanted to know exactly what happened before Casey died, and since my mind had locked down that information, my mom was the only one who knew, my only hope for the truth.

I'd tried, with Dr. K's help, to remember on my own, but we came up with nothing, session after session. Post-CD had created a void inside me, like a black hole that had sucked those memories from me and pulled apart all our lives. It haunted me, how I couldn't remember what happened.

With determination, I climbed the few steps to the front porch. I wasn't using the back door. Not today. I'd avoided this spot for years, but I made myself stand there and study the place where it had happened. Where it had all gone so wrong. I steeled myself to open the storm door and put the key into the lock. The front door still stuck when I turned the knob. Just like everything around here, it had needed repair for far too long. I left it ajar as I entered the house.

"Mom?" I called out, cautious but focused. My voice cracked, and my heartbeat quickened. I hadn't laid eyes on her since that horrible night three weeks prior. I stayed in the entryway as I gathered myself, wiping clammy palms against my jeans. I yanked at the hoodie, which stuck to my body, and tugged at the armpits. I had no idea what to expect. One thing was clear, though. I wasn't leaving until she gave me answers.

I headed toward the kitchen and paused at the doorway. "Mom? You home?" Empty cereal boxes and dirty soup cans lay scattered across the counter. I tossed a crushed Pop Tarts box in the overflowing recycling bin. The room smelled like week-old garbage. I took quick inventory of the pantry and found it almost empty. I stuck my head inside the refrigerator; it was bare, too. I'd text my dad to let him know he'd need to pick up groceries on his way home tonight. Or maybe Grams would drive me to the store. The kitchen was wrecked. How hard was it to rinse off a dish?

The plates, bowls, and cups that were piled in and around the sink reeked. I rinsed out one side of the sink, squirted a hefty amount of dish soap, and filled it with hot water. One by one, I put the crusty dishes in. They'd need to soak for a few hours.

Where the hell is she?

Usually around this time, my mom either sat in the backyard with a cocktail or parked herself in front of the television, typically a news channel, a statue with empty eyes watching bombs going off. I wasn't sure what she did during the day, but it didn't seem like much. Sometimes her bicycle lay on its side in the front yard when I'd come home from school or went for a run in the morning, so I knew she left occasionally for fresh air. If I sat in this house all day, every day, I'd lose it. In Post-CD days, the house seemed dark, cluttered, musty, and unloved, as if it needed its windows pushed open wide, and a stiff wind to blow through to knock away the dust bunnies and sad memories taking space in every corner.

"Hey, Mom. You up?" I yelled again. I peered out into the backyard. No one there. I grabbed the single clean glass from the cabinet and filled it with water from the fridge. I gulped it down and headed toward the bedrooms, peeking in the office along the way. I tried her darkroom, but it was locked, as usual. I couldn't hear anyone moving around inside.

"Mom! You here?" I walked into my parents' dark bedroom. No mom, just an unmade bed, dirty clothes on the floor, and stacks of scientific books on the nightstand and the floor next to my father's side. I scanned my room, then headed for Casey's, which remained locked in time from more than six years ago.

My parents had moved a twin bed in there when Casey was about eight months old so one of them would be near her if she had bad dreams. The bedspread was yellow with green jungle print, which matched the rest of her room, including the small quilt lying on Casey's toddler bed. Grams had made that quilt. It still amazed me that the room remained unchanged, but I understood. I hadn't wanted to change it either. Sometimes I'd sit in here and think about my sister—what she would be like now, how she would act, what music she'd listen to, what books she'd love. Would we still be as close as we'd been, or would we squabble over who left the toothpaste glob on the bathroom counter?

Cartoon jungle animals decorated the walls, bright yellows and brilliant greens. It was the brightest room in the house. Childish crayon drawings of zebras, and tigers, and lions, and elephants—big loopy circle-bodies and stick legs—hung in random spots, tacked on the walls, yellowed from age and curled at the edges. Casey loved animals. Her favorite picture book was *Where's My Mom* by Julia Donaldson, a story about a baby monkey who can't locate its mother, and all the other animals in the jungle help the little one find its way back to her. How many times I'd read that book to Casey, I couldn't say. We'd gone over the same pages repeatedly as she studied each animal and mimicked their noises. Her favorite animal sound was the lion's roar, even though there wasn't a lion in the book. She'd run around the house roaring, her dark ringlets a precursor to the mane of curls she'd have grown had she lived, hair just like our mom's. Her roars had earned Casey the nickname Lion Girl from my parents. In Post-CD, I'd sometimes find Mom in my sister's room, an unlit cigarette dangling from her lips. She'd be vigorously cleaning the windows, or dusting the dresser and bookcase, either mumbling to herself or humming a sad tune. Casey's room was the cleanest room in our house.

Today, I didn't see my mom in there. Not immediately. I paused by the door for a few moments before a peculiar odor hit me—one incompatible with the bright airiness of the jungle room. The medicinal smell of vodka mixed with the sour stench of vomit. Something was wrong. Had my mom gotten sick in here and left it? I moved farther inside, on the balls of my feet, ready for flight.

"Mom?" I whispered just as I spotted the soles of her sneakers sticking up perpendicular to the floor. She was flat on her back, parallel to the twin bed, a large, empty blue bottle cradled in the crook of her arm. Bear, which she must have taken from my room, lay next to her head, turned so that she faced the stuffed animal almost nose-to-nose, her eyelids closed, like maybe she'd been conversing with it before fading out. Her pale face was partially covered by dark curls. Bits of ocher-colored sick matted her hair and covered her chin and neck. It also plastered most of her favorite flannel. Three empty pill bottles lay nearby.

I sucked in a mouthful of sour air and recoiled. A dry heave hit. One wave, then another. My legs quivered as I took a step back, then fled from the room, just making it to the bathroom where I threw up streams of vinegary-tasting bile. I splashed cold water on my face, not bothering to dry it, then moved in a daze back to Casey's room. I held onto to the walls for support, trying to stave off the topsy-turvy sensation of vertigo. I grabbed for the doorframe and leaned against it, then inched forward and swayed over my mother's lifeless form. Fear froze most of my brain function, and I struggled to process what I saw. My muscles screamed to run, to leave it all behind, but my limbs wouldn't respond. Nothing inside me responded. Minutes went by, but maybe it was seconds, I don't know. I couldn't grasp time.

Then I heard it. A buzzing started inside my brain, transforming into a rambling fuzzy sound, like white static on a radio when it's not tuned to a frequency. I heard her voice—determined and strong—at first bubbling up from underwater, its volume increasing, then breaking the surface, then blasting my eardrums at full-force.

"*Move, Em, move!*" Casey bellowed inside my head.

I jumped from the force. Every nerve ending in my body sparked to life. My scalp, arms, and legs puckered in goose bumps. I shook my head again, unbelieving, droplets of water still dripping down my face. I squinted hard at my mother, and blinked once, twice, three times. *Is this real?* The glimmering form of my sister crouched over our mom. Casey held me with a knowing stare.

I'm losing it this time. I must be.

In Post-CD, Casey had *never* spoken to me. Not one word. I squeezed my eyes shut, gave my head a severe shake, and the noise inside my brain finally stopped. No static. Just silence. When I eased open my eyelids, the vision of my sister was gone. Mom still lay lifeless on the floor before me. I forced myself closer, hedging, as if she might suddenly spring at me. Trembling, I made it to her, reached down and felt the side of her neck. Her skin was cool and smooth. A slight pulse vibrated, almost nonexistent, but there. On some level, I had always known I'd find her like this one day.

"*MOVE, EMMA*!" My sister's voice again surged at me from behind, frightening me, throwing me off-balance for a second and jarring me from the dreamlike state. I looked again for Casey but didn't see anything. "*MOVE!*" Charged air surrounded me and electrified me, like tiny pin pricks on every inch of my skin. My sister wasn't visible, but she was there.

"Case, I know, I know—I'll get help," I said before staggering to the kitchen in a sprint. I grabbed my phone off the table and dialed 9-1-1.

The EMTs were on their way, the dispatcher's calm voice assured me, and the woman insisted on keeping me on the line until they arrived. I knew the drill since I'd gone through this with Grams. I grabbed ice cubes from the freezer and pressed them against the back of my neck, something Dr. K had taught me to help cope with anxiety. With great effort, I trudged back to Casey's room and pleaded with myself to calm down. I tossed the ice cubes on the floor and put the phone on speaker while I checked Mom's pulse. It still beat faintly, but she wasn't breathing.

"Oh, God. I don't think she's—" A sob broke free. "She's not breathing."

"Okay, sweetheart. Stay calm and listen to me carefully," the dispatcher said.

The woman talked me through the steps of administering rescue breathing, something I vaguely remembered from swim lessons years ago. I gently moved my mother's face toward mine; the closeness felt awkward. It had been years since I'd touched my mom, held her hand, hugged her close, kissed her cheek. I wiped away the sick from her mouth with the edge of my hoodie. I tilted her head back, opened her jaws wider and pinched her nose. The acrid taste when I put my mouth on hers almost made me heave. I gagged but willed myself not to throw up. Instead, I focused on the dispatcher's instructions. On expanding my mother's lungs with air. On watching her chest rise. Simple. No panic allowed, I told myself, as I blew short bursts of air into her lungs again and again and again. That and compressing her chest, one—two—three.

The EMTs arrived in a few minutes. They hustled into the room and shooed me out of the way. Someone wrapped a warm blanket around my shoulders and guided me to the living room, where he placed me on the couch. I was vaguely aware of chattering teeth, looking around for the source of the sound before realizing it was me.

"Is there someone we should call? An adult?" an EMT asked.

Everything swirled in slow motion, but I knew I had to make the calls. My dad didn't answer his cell—he was probably boarding a plane—so I left a quick message on voicemail and hoped I didn't freak him out too badly. Then I dialed Grams. As soon as I heard her voice, I started to cry, barely able to get out what had happened.

"Oh, my baby…. Oh, please, not my baby," Grams choked through tears of her own. I heard the shuffle of her grabbing her purse and the jangle of car keys in the background. "I'll be right there, Em."

I hung up and wandered back toward Casey's room. It was crowded in the hallway. The EMTs—three men and a woman—used a board to transport my mother down the narrow hall to the gurney outside the front door. I followed, the storm door slamming behind us. They loaded her onto the gurney and secured her with straps. One of the EMTs repeatedly asked questions directly into her ear, while another one spoke into a handheld radio. Mom was unresponsive but appeared oddly at peace, I thought, as I watched them place her in the ambulance.

It was a rare and beautiful sight to see my mom's face this serene, this vulnerable, so childlike and innocent. So much like Casey's. The EMTs had wiped away most of the vomit and a shock of dark hair against the white sheet perfectly framed the fragility of her face. She looked relaxed—none of the usual worries lining her brow, her long, black lashes splayed across her cheeks, just above the oxygen mask covering her face.

Free. She looks free.

A police officer—a short, muscular man probably in his late twenties—approached. He guided me away from the group of EMTs, my mother, and the ambulance.

"Hey, kid. How are you doing?" He had earnest brown eyes.

I hugged the blanket closer to my body. I couldn't get warm enough.

"We need to call someone for you?"

"My grandmother will be here any minute." I was lightheaded. Like Earth's gravity had let me go, and I was a balloon floating at the mercy of a grim, swirling wind.

"Listen." He tapped a clipboard against the palm of his hand. "It's Emma, right?"

I bobbed my head, zombie-like. Nothing seemed real. It was as if I were watching someone else's life. Like a two-dimensional movie played out on a flat screen before me.

"Listen, Emma, we can take a statement at the hospital a little later, okay? I know this must have been difficult for you, finding your mom like that. You're probably in shock right now." He paused, putting his other hand on my shoulder and bent his head so we were eye-to-eye. "But I want you to understand something here, okay? What you did to-day—calling like you did—the EMTs told me you saved your mom's life. That's a good thing, Emma—a *brave* thing." He squeezed my shoulder. "So, someday down the road, when you think back on this crappy day, you remember *that*, okay? Not the bad stuff. You focus on how brave you were, how you saved her."

I nodded with tears welling in my eyes. Not because of the kind police officer's words, but because, as I had stared at my mother's tranquil face moments earlier, a nagging thought surfaced in the back of my brain, like a drop of black India ink spreading through a glass of clear water, muddying it with a cloudy cast. Before I was able to fully face the thought, Grams burst through the door, frantic. I knew she had seen them putting my mom in the ambulance. She rushed to me and pulled me into a fierce hug. I started shaking harder.

"It's okay, child," Grams whispered into the side of my head and pressed me close. "She'll be right as rain soon enough. We'll all be okay, you hear?" I breathed her in and relaxed against the familiarity of her em-brace, her soft bosom, the faint scent of laundry softener intermingled with perfume.

Yet the inky thought continued to spread, swirling its darkness about. God help me, I couldn't shake that image of my mother at peace.

Did I do the right thing? Or would it have been better for every-one—Dad, Grams, me, but mostly, Mom—if I had let her go? Let her be free. Forever.

I chewed hard on my lip and allowed Grams to hold me upright as I struggled with the enormity of the thought.

What's wrong with me? How can I even think something like this?

I buried my head against Grams, listening to her strong, steady heartbeat, acutely aware it was the first sound my mother had ever heard inside my grandmother's womb.

I was relieved Grams couldn't read my mind. She continued to rub my back and whisper comforting words. I kept my face hidden so she couldn't read it in my eyes. She'd never know that for a few seconds, I'd considered the possibility of my mother's death as a potential blessing for us all.

Chapter 29

Grams and I clung to each other as we watched the EMT slam the back double-doors of the ambulance closed with my mom inside. I took the blanket from my shoulders and wrapped it around Grams, who was trembling. Neighbors I didn't really know—who had come out of their houses when the emergency vehicles arrived—slowly drifted back inside as the ambulance pulled away. Just one more episode in the Watters' Family Freak Show. How many episodes of "crazy" had these people witnessed? The numbness I felt outweighed any of my usual embarrassment.

As the ambulance siren's intermittent shrieks faded, I heard my name called and the scraping of resin wheels on pavement. Tyler leaped off his skateboard and ran toward us, wild-eyed.

"What happened?" He was breathless and red-faced when reached us at the porch and stood with his skateboard under his arm. "What's going on? Are you okay, Emma? Is everything okay?"

Seeing the concern on his face caused tears to well again. "My mom—" I whispered. That's all I could get out.

He took a step closer, his arm reaching toward me. "Is she going to be okay?"

A sad, harsh laugh escaped my mouth. "I don't know." I looked down to avoid his eyes. Vomit speckled the sleeve of my hoodie, and the rancid odor coated the inside of my nostrils. Wasn't there any way out of this mess? It was all too much. My sobs deepened, tears spilling out like the overflow of a swollen river. "I don't know." I took in a ragged breath; my heart exhausted inside my chest. "I don't know if she's ever going to be—okay." Grams pulled me closer.

"How can I help? What can I do?" Tyler asked. His voice sounded desperate. He moved even closer and touched my arm. "Please. I'll do anything."

It took a moment, but I pulled myself together. I blew my nose on a wad of tissue Grams pushed at me.

"We need to get to the hospital," I said, motioning toward Grams. "I don't want her driving when she's this upset. And my dad won't be home for hours." The driver would only allow one person to ride with Mom, but both of us had refused to leave the other behind.

"But I can drive," Grams said, her voice soft and strained.

"No, you can't, Grams. Not like this."

"I'm on it." Tyler pulled his phone out of his pocket and moved a short distance away. A few minutes passed and he walked back. "I couldn't get hold of my mom. She must still be in class. But I called Ms. Zohar, and she's on her way."

Ms. Zo! Great! Would this day ever end? I reminded myself Tyler was just trying to help. He didn't understand.

"She's the only person I could think of."

"That's wonderful." Grams' voice sounded as haggard as her face appeared. "Thank you, Tyler. I'm Emma's grandmother. You probably figured that part out. We haven't met officially, but I've heard wonderful things about you."

"Same here, ma'am."

Instead of shaking his outstretched hand, Grams pulled Tyler into a quick hug. She still held me with her other arm.

"I hope your daughter is—I hope everything's okay," Tyler said when she released him.

Grams pressed her lips together, forced a small smile. Gently, she touched my shoulder. "Hon, why don't you run inside and change out of that." She waved a hand at the soiled front of the hoodie. "I'll stay here with Tyler."

"Oh. Yeah. Be right back." I reentered the musty house I called home. The stillness within its walls contradicted the flurry of activity only minutes ago. My legs moved on autopilot to my bedroom closet, and I pulled a sweatshirt off the top shelf. I threw the hoodie and the shirt underneath into the dirty clothes hamper.

Compelled by a feeling I couldn't explain, I moved toward Casey's room. I walked in to pick Bear off the floor. Surprisingly, he had remained unsoiled.

"I'm sorry, Case. I wish none of this had ever happened," I said to the empty room. I squeezed Bear to my chest and buried my face in his soft fuzz. I couldn't shake the shame of those dark thoughts about letting my mother die. Trying to save her was the only thing I could have done. It would have haunted me forever if I hadn't. "Thank you for snapping me out of it, Case. For helping me do the right thing. You're the best sister anyone could ask for."

I waited to see if Casey might reappear, but she didn't. The only things I saw were remnants of my mom's overdose and the eyes of my sister's hand-drawn lions, zebras, and tigers that stared back at me from the walls.

I retraced my steps to the front door and locked it behind me. Ms. Zohar's minivan had arrived, and Tyler was helping Grams into the front seat, so I climbed into the back.

"Thanks for coming," I told Ms. Zohar. Sophie's absence was palpable for me.

"I'm so sorry about your mom." She dabbed at red eyes reflected in the rearview mirror. I nodded, an exhaustion seeping into my bones. Tyler climbed into the backseat next to me and closed the door.

"Wait. What are you doing?" I asked.

"I'm going with you," he said. He lightly touched my arm, which rested on the armrest between us.

"You don't have to. It's—I don't know what's going to happen." I didn't want his pity. I didn't know what I wanted from him, but not that.

He looked at me intently. "Whatever happens, I'll be there with you." I grabbed his hand and held it tightly as we headed to the hospital.

In the emergency room waiting area, I sat with Tyler and Ms. Zohar while Grams filled out what seemed like endless forms. My mother had been whisked away as soon as the ambulance brought her in.

I had already filled Tyler in and after an hour or so, an ER doctor—faceless and nameless to me—came to the waiting room to tell us my mom would be okay physically, but that she'd need a psychiatric evaluation given the circumstances. That would probably take place tomorrow, he told us, because she wasn't lucid yet. I wrapped my arms around Grams as she whispered a prayer under her breath in response to the news that her daughter was alive. Then Tyler helped me update my dad via text, and he responded that his plane had landed. He'd be at the hospital in less than an hour.

"Emma, can I speak with you for a minute?" Ms. Zohar said. "I'll get you something from the vending machines." She grabbed her purse and motioned for me to follow. My reluctance must have shown. "C'mon. Anyone else need anything?"

Grams and Tyler declined. My grandmother remained propped on the edge of her chair, her ankles crossed. She looked dog-tired but refused to leave, even though Ms. Zohar had offered to drive her home. "Not until I see my Rosemary," Grams had said, her manner inviting no argument.

Yes, I had done the right thing, I thought, as I took in Grams' worried eyes. Things would have been so much worse if I hadn't tried. I walked alongside Ms. Zohar with my hands jammed deep inside my pockets. I desperately wanted to chew my cuticles to shreds but knew it wouldn't help anything. This pain couldn't be gnawed away. An awkward silence loomed between us as we navigated a series of halls to the vending machines. I couldn't think of a thing to say. A blankness enveloped me.

When we reached the snack area, several people were already there so Mrs. Zohar led me to a quiet corner.

"We need to talk about Sophie," she said. "I know you've been avoiding me. Not returning my messages." She raised her hands in a pleading gesture. "I know right now is crazy for you, but it's important you understand something, okay?"

My face warmed with embarrassment as I recalled the accusations Sophie had flung. My mother, her father. I tried to slow down my breathing. I wanted to run from Ms. Zohar, but I also understood that wouldn't solve anything.

"Please, Em." Ms. Zohar clasped my shoulders with both hands. "Please, just listen."

I looked away, mortified. Sophie's angry words accusing my mom of destroying her family bounced around my brain. How could Ms.

Zohar stand to have been around me all these years? I would have been a constant reminder of the woman who had betrayed her, of her unfaithful husband.

Ms. Zohar tightened her grip. "The reason I've been trying to get ahold of you is because Fi told me what she said to you." She sounded teary. "I want to apologize. I want you to understand that I don't—that *I've never*—blamed you for anything. Do you understand?"

I slumped against the wall, my eyes downcast. How could she ever forgive me? My mother destroyed her family. Fi had said so. It was all too much. The antiseptic smell of the hospital caused my stomach to lurch. I wanted to disappear.

"I know what Fi told you. She wasn't supposed to—I should have known better." Ms. Zohar let go and sagged next to me against the wall. "But listen, whatever happened between her dad, your mom and me—it had absolutely *nothing* to do with either one of you. I tried to explain that to her." She rubbed at her tired face with both hands. "She's always taken the blame for the divorce. I don't know why. Irrational, right?"

"I think she watched an afterschool special on it once, one of those where the kid blames herself when the parents split," I said through numb lips. "That's what I've always figured."

"Sounds about right." Ms. Zohar lifted her face toward the ceiling and released a low groan. "Fi had a fight with her dad. He told Fi the woman he met recently might be 'the one.' I guess she unloaded on him, blasted him for destroying our family, and he came back at her with the fact that I was the one who filed for divorce, not him. Which is the truth." She paused. "But he left out the part about him sleeping—that he was seeing another woman." She studied the tips of her shoes. "Fi came home angry. Wanted to blame me for everything. That's when I told her why I divorced him." She closed her eyes, her chin on her chest. "I'm so sorry it all came back on you."

I gulped back humiliation. "So," I whispered, "it's true? They did have an affair?" My stomach lurched again.

"Yeah, I'm sorry to say they did. That wasn't something.... Listen, it's in the past. I've long since forgiven them." She puffed her cheeks and blew out. "When it happened, I was angry. But in the long run, I'm blessed to be rid of him, you know? And not once did I ever blame you. *Not once.*" She gripped my forearm. "You must believe me. You were just a child—you had nothing to do with any of it." Tears pooled in her eyes. "You're a second daughter to me, Em. I've watched you grow up—in harsh conditions. Now it's finally getting better for you. I just want you and Fi back together. That's all I want. For you two to try to work this out." She reached for me, and I crumpled against her. I was so tired of running. I knew the truth now.

"But I don't remember anything," I said.

"What do you mean?" Ms. Zohar rested her chin on the top of my head.

"I don't remember anything about an affair." My throat tightened as I forced out the words. "I can't remember ever seeing them together or anything."

"Of course, you don't," Ms. Zohar said, as she smoothed a piece of hair behind my ear. "They were good at hiding." She squeezed me tighter. "I explained this to Fi, but you know how she can be—she wants to lash out. That day was the worst of your life. You lost your sister. You were in complete shock. How could you possibly remember?"

We stood embracing in the hallway for a while. I didn't have my best friend back—but at least I had my second mom. It was something to hold onto.

Chapter 30

Tyler's face loomed on the laptop screen in front of me. I leaned back into the couch in Grams' living room and listened to the conversation blasting in the background. He and his mom and younger brother lived with his uncle's family of five. They planned to stay there while his mom—who was working on an advanced nursing degree—recovered from the divorce.

Based on the ruckus, dinner was almost ready. Living in a loud house filled with bickering and teasing—all the things I could hear going on—seemed like such fun. Compared to what I was used to, it sounded like a party over there.

"You sure you don't want me to come over to Grams' place?" He glanced at his watch, speaking over the noise. "I can be there in five minutes." Someone off screen spoke to him, and he mouthed something back.

"Thanks," I said. "I really appreciate it, but I need to do this on my own. Really." My mom was still in the hospital, and Dad had been spending a lot of time at Grams' house with me. The three of us planned to eat dinner together.

"All right. If you need me, I'm just a text away."

"Got it."

He grinned. That little lopsided grin, the one that made my stomach launch into cartwheels. "Text me later even if you *don't* need me."

"Sure. Promise." Smiling back, I watched his image shrink to black. I placed my phone on the coffee table. My muscles were tight along my spine—from my lower back to the tip of my neck. I stood up, bent over, and slowly straightened into a standing position one vertebra at a time. It was a Pilates stretch Coach used after workouts. I repeated the move, feeling my body relax and give in to the slow, easy movement.

Enough stalling. I eyed the stack of photo albums waiting on the floor next to the couch.

Stop being such a wimp.

As much as it hurt, I had to get started if I ever hoped to pull my crazy life together. Fi had been right when she'd told me I wasn't truly living. I just existed. Which really sucked. It was the difference between observing the ocean versus diving headfirst into its oncoming waves. I had to face Casey's death as well as the moments when our lives had intertwined, even if it reminded me of how short our time together had been. At a recent session, Dr. K suggested I spend time going through family albums as a possible way to jar my memories, to find the thread that would pull those missing moments from the black void together inside my mind.

It was tough. Seeing my family—the one so alien to me now—in moments captured in Pre-CD had the same effect as ramming my big toe into a baseboard. It hurt like hell. I wanted to howl in rage at the injustice of it all. But I knew embracing the pain was a step forward. At least, that's what I hoped.

Settling into the sofa, I took the top album off the pile and placed it on my lap. I opened it as if it were a sacred text not to be damaged. A stale dustiness mingled with the faintest chemical odor of photo developer wafted from its pages. Almost reverently, I ran a palm over the glossy clear plastic that covered the first page of the album. I was a newborn with my parents in the first set of pictures, swaddled in a green blanket as my father held me and stared with wonder at my squished red face. His face exuded adoration—the same expression I'd seen the times he'd taken me outside to gaze at the night sky. In the same photograph, my mom lay in a hospital bed next to him. Her dark hair was cut stylishly, medium-length, loose waves tousled around her oval face, her arm extended so her fingertips lightly touched the crown of my head. She wasn't staring at the camera. Instead, she looked at me.

"At one time, I was her world," I said aloud. I caressed my mom's two-dimensional image. She had been a different person—not just younger, but softer, more approachable. I wished this version were still here. Where had she gone? Was she another casualty of the day Casey died? Or had she already left us by then?

I took my time flipping through that first album, which captured my early years. In one photo, I was a toddler holding my dad's index finger, taking a tentative step down the hallway, one thin arm extended like a ballerina's. Another showed me at maybe four, wearing my mom's chunky black boots and my favorite Kim Possible pajamas as I karate chopped the air in front of me. Still another showed me as a kindergartener, walking into Ms. McCoy's classroom on the first day, glancing back at the camera with a confident look on my face.

I peered into my younger self's eyes. *No fear there*. Instead, a fire blazed within. When had I lost it? That fire? Still another shot showed me with Fi at the kindergarten Winter Party, the same year we became friends, the two of us sharing a plate of grapes, cubed cheese, and brownie bites. We'd been friends all these years, through all the dramas—death and divorce, stupid spats, and even one botched suicide attempt. But could we survive our parents' secrets? I'd like to believe we would, but I wasn't sure anymore.

I grabbed the next album. About five pages in, I gasped. It was a photo of me and my mother—dad had probably taken it—with Mom holding my face to hers while I stared at her pregnant belly with earnest eyes, my small fingers curved over it protectively. The photo was magical. My eyes stung as a memory surfaced of the day after my parents had told me Mom was pregnant. I had bounded through the house, hooting with joy and promising to be the best big sister ever. I wished I had lived up to that promise.

Grams appeared next to me with two mugs of tea in her hands. "How's it going, sweetie?" She put the mugs on the table in front of us and sank down next to me. She pulled me close, and I leaned in.

She studied the photo of pregnant Mom and me and tapped it with a manicured nail, a soft jingle from the bangles on her wrist. "That's always been one of my favorites." Grams smiled and together we made our way through more. There were lots of Casey. I was by her side in most of the shots, where she almost always gazed adoringly at me.

Oh, Case. I'm sorry I let you down.

My shoulders slumped. A part of me wanted to toss these memories aside. I wasn't sure I could keep going. It was almost too much to see how happy our family used to be. To see how much we'd lost.

Grams stopped at a page with an eight-by-ten of me and Casey, our hands in front of us, fingers curved into claws, our eyes squinted with heads thrown back and mouths opened wide, bearing tiny teeth.

"This is another of my favorites! I haven't looked at it in years," Grams said as she grinned and patted the image. "Do you remember this one?"

I stared at it. I had forgotten how intense Casey's face could be when she was in full lion-mode.

"Yeah. Mom and Dad always called her Lion Girl." I shook my head and tucked strands of hair behind my ears. "If they told her to go to bed, brush her teeth, whatever, she'd start roaring."

Look at her. So full of life.

I stared hard at us, two sisters. "I wish I were like her." I choked up but was determined not to cry anymore. I traced Casey's crazy-curly hair in the photograph. "She wouldn't have had these ridiculous panic attacks. Wouldn't be afraid of Mom. She wouldn't have frozen up that day like I did."

Grams searched deep into my eyes. "You don't remember the story behind all that—the Lion Girl stuff?" Her eyebrows lifted in surprise. "You really don't?"

"Remember what?"

She grabbed the next photo album from the stack and rifled through it. Then she stopped on a child's drawing where a stick-figure girl with a thick mane of orange hair stood next to someone, probably Grams, holding a plate of cookies.

"Remember that?" Grams asked.

Still puzzled, I shrugged. Grams flicked a few pages forward, and stopped on a snapshot of me, probably four years old. My bright eyes squinted ferociously into the camera, again my lips were pulled over my teeth, and my arms and hands reached out like a lion's striking paws. "How about this one?" she asked.

I could feel her watching me while she waited for a response. Nothing came to me. I wasn't sure why I'd posed that way. That had been Casey's thing, not mine.

"Casey only did that—turned into a lion—because you showed her how. You taught her to roar, Em. Don't you remember?" Grams twisted toward me. "She wanted to be just like you. When you were three, you learned from somewhere—I don't know, a book or a television show, maybe—that lions were brave."

Something familiar stirred and flickered in the deepest parts of my brain.

"They called you Lion Girl because sometimes you'd wake up in the middle of the night and roar. You'd fight off bad dreams that way. All by yourself." Grams chuckled. "Most kids would cry, but not you. No. You were ready to charge into Hell with a bucket of ice water. Loud and on the attack. I know because you'd about give me a heart attack every time I stayed over to babysit!" She caressed the side of my face. "It was you, Emma. *You* were always the brave one. And, hon, I think it's about time you remembered."

Snippets of memories trickled in—my parents flicking on the light to find me leaning over the bed, bellowing and swatting at imagined-monsters underneath.

"It's coming back to you, isn't it?" Grams asked in a whisper. She stroked my hair and nodded along with me.

Once I had been the fighter, the one punching at the shadow monsters lurking in the dark closet, the faint glow of a nightlight revealing their bulky forms. I had slapped and swiped at the darkness that had threatened me. I remembered.

I was the Lion Girl.

The lion in me had been wounded by Casey's death and had wandered away in search of isolation, a quiet place to lick its wounds. But recently, I'd felt something moving inside me, restlessly circling the recesses of my mind, awaiting the day it was called home, the day it would again face the shadows that threatened the girl. The girl who had always been me.

CHAPTER 31

I t took camping out in the Zohars' family room for three hours to finally get an audience with Fi. For days, I'd texted and left messages on her voicemail, but Fi had ignored them. The ghosting irritated me. So much so, I resorted to enlisting Ms. Zohar's help, of which my second mother was only too eager to do. I wanted to right what was wrong between Sophie and I if I could. She'd realize ignoring me was not an option. I had to make her understand that I had never lied to her about our parents.

She rushed through the front door but stopped dead when she spotted me on the couch, where I sat with her little brother Jacob, feigning an interest in his extensive spiral-bound binder Pokémon card collection.

"What the hell are you doing here?"

Fi's cold words cut through me and a warm flush crept up my neck.

"Language, Fi! *Language*!" Jacob bellowed in a shrill voice. "Mom, Fi's saying bad words again!" He stood up from the couch and covered his ears as he rocked back and forth. Jacob had sensory overload issues, and Fi was being an ass.

"Shut up, dork!" she yelled. Jacob's body stiffened more. "*Leave*—and take those stupid cards with you."

Jacob ran toward the kitchen where I could hear Ms. Zohar trying to calm him.

Sophie dropped her duffle bag in the middle of the hall with a careless thump. "I thought I made it clear. I never want to see you or talk to you again." She placed a hand on her hip and glared at me. I rubbed at the back of my neck and worked out what I should say.

"Careful, Fi. Don't yell at your brother like that." Ms. Zohar appeared in the hallway. "Don't speak to Em that way, either." Her no-nonsense voice was engaged, and she narrowed her eyes. It was obvious where Fi had learned how to make her scary facial expressions. "I invited Emma over here today since you haven't returned her calls." She mirrored her daughter's stance, hands on her hips. "You *will* sit down and listen to what she has to say. You two need to hash this out." I watched mother and daughter continue the staring contest. I smelled meatloaf cooking in the oven and heard Jacob snickering somewhere nearby. Finally, Sophie flicked her eyes away.

"It's, like, whatever, Mom." She looked at the floor and let out a harsh breath. "We can't have Emma getting her feelings hurt, right? She's so *fragile* and has been through so much. Who cares if she's a liar?" She raised her head. "Sometimes I think you care more about her than me."

"I mean it, Fi." It was said as a quiet threat. "I won't have you acting like this. It's an embarrassment. Put on your big girl panties and work this out. You owe it to each other."

"Whatever." Sophie rolled her eyes and turned to me. "Just say whatever you came to say, then leave."

I finally found my voice. "Can you at least sit down? This might take a minute." But Sophie shook her head, her mouth a straight line running parallel with the floor and ceiling. She wasn't going to make it easy. "I just need you to understand something." I paused and tried to gauge the force it would take to knock down Sophie's resistance. "I didn't know about—that there was anything going on between our parents. I'm sorry, but I have no memory of it, Fi. *Nada. Nothing.* And I'm *not* lying. My therapist has tried to help me remember the things that happened that day. But so far, nothing has worked."

"Yeah. You said this already," Sophie shot back. Rage flashed beneath her bored expression.

"But did you listen? You're not *hearing* what I'm saying," I returned the shot. A fire of my own ignited.

Who did she think she was? Did her *brother die because our parents couldn't control their stupid urges? She sure as hell wasn't the only victim from our parents' fling. There were lots of us.*

"If I had known, I would have told you. Not that you would have believed me. I can't even believe it myself. But I would have told you anyway. You know that."

"I would have thought you would, but who knows these days?" She gave a half shrug and hugged herself. "I never thought you'd tried to kill yourself either. Or that you'd make yourself over into some kind of—I don't know—hottie or whatever. I sure as hell never thought you'd be texting my boyfriend all the time." She looked at the floor again. "I thought I could always trust you. But the fact is, you've changed."

"Yes, I have." I jumped to my feet and stood face-to-face with her. My chin jutted forward. "I *want* to change."

"But not in the way you think," I said. "Yes, I tried to kill myself—the stupidest thing I've ever done—because in a weak moment, one of the loneliest moments I've ever experienced, I wanted to finally *stop* the pain I've felt every day since Casey died." My jaws ached from clenching. I breathed deeply and pushed out my breath in measured exhales. "I have blamed myself for Casey's death since it happened. You know that. Can you imagine what it's like to believe you *killed* your sister?"

Sophie looked away, her stance rigid.

"Can you?" I repeated the question. Still no answer. "Well, it sucks. But with help from Doctor K., and some others, I'm trying to change the way I look at my life and everything that happened." I let my words sink in before I went on. "And, yes, Grams encouraged me to change some things about my appearance. I wasn't trying for a hottie look. I just wanted a fresh start this year." I waited for some comment or reaction. Nothing. "I thought you'd support me on that," I said, my voice strengthening with each word, my forefinger now pointed at a startled Sophie. "And for the record? I wasn't texting your boyfriend all the time. He and I were friends. That's it." I was forceful now, frustrated by her lack of response. "From what I understand, he wasn't really your boyfriend anyway. You were *using him* to get Ben. So, who's the real liar here, Fi? Maybe it's *you* who has changed!"

Silence—except for the shallow breathing in my ears—followed my defense. I hadn't planned on shouting that last part.

"Listen, this isn't what I had in mind when I came here. I didn't mean to say you're a liar, Fi…I just…I would never intentionally do anything to hurt you. *Never*. And I thought you knew that."

Sophie lifted her head and sniffed. She shifted from one foot to the other, but she wouldn't speak.

"The main thing is I never deceived you. I don't remember our parents' being involved—not like that. I didn't know for sure about them until your mom told me at the hospital." I extended my arms, palms facing up. "My dad didn't know either. I think he's even more blown away than we are."

Sophie searched my eyes. She seemed to be hunting for the right words.

"It's all screwed up, right? I mean that stuff about our parents," she finally said. She squared her shoulders. "But it doesn't matter. That's not really the problem. I can't tell you how many times I've defended you when our friends made fun of your weirdness. I'm not trying to hurt you—just being honest." Sophie lifted her chin. "Ben even said he couldn't understand why we were ever friends. He says I've carried you all these years, and, honestly, I think he's right."

My entire body stiffened. *Ben* says? *Really?* The words hurt, yes, but the detached way Fi delivered them bothered me even more. What could I say? Had Sophie carried me all these years? Probably. But I had carried Sophie, too, at different times in our lives. That was what friends did, right? Carried each other when they needed it. I had never felt obligated to do it, never resented it, because she was my friend.

"I know you can't stand Ben, but these past few weeks have been some of the happiest of my life," Sophie said with a soft smile. "I've gone to parties, made lots of new friends, laughed my butt off over stupid things like regular teens do. It has been fun, you know? Nothing life or death." She inspected her fingernails. "The best part is I haven't had to worry about you standing alone in some corner or freaking out or whatever." She pushed hair behind her ears. "And you're right about Tyler—I never liked him the way I like Ben. He was more like a brother than a boyfriend. I thought if Ben saw me with another guy, well, he'd get a clue."

"Congratulations," I said, shoving my hands in my pockets. "I guess Ben finally figured it out."

I looked at her with new eyes and my friend, someone I'd considered a sister, seemed more like a stranger. Or maybe not. I realized we'd been drifting apart long before the revelations about her dad and my mom.

Long before this past summer, in fact. This year we each had gravitated toward different groups. Maybe we both had changed. There was no need for anger. We had simply outgrown each other.

"I had no idea you've felt this way for so long. I wish you would have talked to me about it," I said and shrugged. "I deserve friends who don't see me as a burden, and luckily, I think I've found some." Sophie raised both eyebrows. She'd probably expected a different reaction. "I'll see you around, Fi. If you ever need someone to listen, I'll still be there for you. You'll always be family to me, even if we're not friends."

At that moment, Ms. Zohar stepped into the room. Her eyes darted between the two of us. It was obvious she'd been listening to the conversation.

"Emma, would you like to stay for dinner? Maybe you and Fi could talk some more?" she asked, her voice unusually high.

"Thanks, Ms. Zo, but I don't think that would work. I think we've covered everything, right?" I asked Sophie. She gave a curt nod and moved out of the way as I headed to the door.

On impulse, I turned back and gave Ms. Zohar a hug. "I gave it my best try," I whispered into her ear and gave her an extra squeeze. At this moment, I'd miss her more than I'd miss her daughter. "Thanks for everything. You've always been the best."

"You have, too," she whispered back. "I'm so proud of you for finally realizing it."

Yeah, I thought, as I walked away from their house, *I'm proud of me, too.*

CHAPTER 32

I sat on a bench in the locker room with Anne across from me and Aliah and Trini on either side.

"Seriously? You want me to *what*?" I cocked my head as I asked Anne and a bubble of hysterical laughter escaped my mouth. "How exactly does tapping my face help? Did you ever consider it might actually *cause* me anxiety?"

"*Shhhhhhh*. Just do it," Anne said, her face squeezed in concentration. She showed me how to use my fingers to tap on specific meridian points of the body, first on the fleshy part of my outer palm. Then Anne moved her hands to her head and drummed her fingers on top of it—*thrump, thrump, thrump*—and then to the bones on the outside of her eyebrows. She worked her way down her face and body to her collar bone. I tried to keep up but struggled to keep a straight face. "My mother swears by this. She says it releases energy pathways and expands your emotional freedom." Anne tilted her head at me and drawled, "Or maybe it realigns your energy points?" Her brow wrinkled as she continued drumming different points on her body. "God, now I'm confused. But she did say this would stop your panic attacks. It's supposed to help all of us focus, actually."

My body shook with the effort, but I couldn't hold it any longer—another squeal of laughter erupted. Anne looked hurt but Aliah and Trini continued tapping. Aliah just barely held it together.

Anne, whose mom owned a local health food store, had been wonderful since my mother's overdose. She had knocked on Grams' door one evening last week to deliver a gift bag overflowing with blueberry muffins—gluten-free, of course—that her mom had made for us. Also tucked inside the bag was a medium-sized vial filled with essential oil of bergamot labeled just for me. Anne's mom insisted it would subdue my anxiety.

Anne, who smelled like a stick of chewing gum, usually wore peppermint to 'energize' herself. She couldn't wait to give me the vial of bergamot. She made me rub the orangey-lemony oil on my wrists and the pulse points at my neck and behind my knees and ankles. I was covered with it today. I wasn't sure it calmed me like it was supposed to, but I smelled like a cup of brewed Earl Grey, Grams' favorite.

Breathing exercises, biofeedback, fruity oils, meridian-point thumping; I'd do whatever I could if it'd keep my anxiety under control. My mom had been transferred to a psychiatric treatment center the previous day, which had been difficult for Grams and Dad. Both had grim faces when they returned last night. I had spaghetti waiting for them, but they barely touched their plates. Dad stayed over and slept on the couch. I was doing my best to stay positive—even if it meant thumping myself on the head.

Coach walked into the locker room and cautiously approached us. She eyed us with a bewildered expression until Anne finished her final tap.

"How are things going in here?" Coach asked. She tapped her clipboard against her muscled thigh. "Do I even want to know what you're doing?"

"We're clearing Emma's electrical pathways," Anne said brightly. "It'll help her stay calm during the relay."

"Oh?" She nodded, lips pursed. "Huh."

"Yeah. So, uh, my mom says Emma's anxiety may be caused by trapped negative energy, or something like that. Like it needs to be freed?" Anne shrugged. "I can't remember exactly how, but this helps."

"Hmmm. Interesting." Coach said, then abruptly sniffed the air with a puzzled expression. "Wow." More sniffing. "Do you *smell* that?" She pivoted in all directions and eyed each girl in the locker room. "I know someone has tea in here—I can smell it. I don't know who it is but get rid of it now! No beverages allowed in the locker room other than water!" she yelled.

Frozen in mid tap, I made eye contact with Aliah. Unable to contain it, we exploded into laughter, each holding the other's shoulder as our heads almost banged together. Anne and Trini joined in.

Laughter. Maybe that's the therapy I needed, I thought, as I ambled along with my friends to the track. We stretched on the field, reaching our arms toward the sky, the sunshine warming us, the breeze slight but fresh on our skin. We headed to our stations to practice drills and field events. Maybe it was the giggling or the bergamot or the rhythmic tapping or simply mojo. It was hard for me to pinpoint. But this time, when Anne rounded the track to hand off to me, I synced with her pace. No anxiety. The exchange was seamless, even easy, the baton smooth and cool in my hand. I curled my fingers around it, relaxed yet secure, like when I'd grip Casey's small hand with my own.

I hurtled forward toward the finish line and grinned as my team hooted for me as I passed with baton in hand. We had a bond, a connection I hadn't felt in a long time. It pinged inside my brain like the sound of a computer rebooting, coming back to life. Confidence flooded through me. I was part of something. We were ready for next week's track meet, and if we ran like this, and I secured the exchange, we stood a great chance of winning.

Then it hit me. It barely even mattered if we won. I had already gained something far more valuable. I had found a place, a team—a family where I belonged.

Chapter 33

T he sun warmed my cheeks and the tops of my closed lids. I repositioned my head so I'd catch even more of its rays—a sunflower stretching toward its fiery lifeline. I felt the freckles sprouting across my face. My fair skin might burn by the end of the day, but I didn't care. It felt delicious. A light breeze ruffled my hair as I took in the smells of grass, mud and peat along the boggy lakeshore. Somewhere nearby, someone was grilling hot dogs. I sniffed the air again and my stomach growled.

My father shifted next to me. We sat side-by-side on top of a picnic table at Purple Sage Park, a place where I had played as a small child, and, later, with Casey. I used to push her on the swings, making sure she held on tightly to the chains as she sailed higher and higher. This had been Casey's favorite place. She loved feeding the ducks, which nested in the shoreline marsh.

Earlier today, my dad showed up unexpectedly at Grams' house and wouldn't say where he was taking me, that it was a surprise. He had driven to the park and had reached behind my seat to pull out a paper grocery sack with two loaves of bread inside. Excited, I'd jumped out of the car and ran for the picnic bench closest to the lake.

With eyes closed and sunshine on my face, I listened to the sporadic shrieks of children's high-pitched laughter mixing with the modulated quacking of ducks and occasional honking from geese. The sounds and smells of this place brought peace to my soul.

I should have come here sooner. We should have come together as a family.

I squinted my right eye open as I adjusted to the brightness and glanced at Dad next to me. He had his glasses off, and like me, his face turned toward the sun with his eyes closed, his body relaxed. Both of us would probably be lobster-people by the end of the day. But neither of us cared. We sat in comfortable silence until the sound of barking erupted nearby. A dog streaked in front, chased by a young boy and his dad. It headed toward a flock of ducks at the water's edge not far from where we sat.

"We should have done this before," Dad said, echoing my thoughts. He straightened, shielded his eyes, and watched the dog jump into the water. It splashed its people and scattered the ducks in a burst of flapping wings and squawked protests.

"Yep, we should have." I sat up. "Glad you thought of it today, though."

"Me, too." He shifted his gaze away. Something else was on his mind, but like me, he didn't seem to want to ruin the pleasant vibe.

"How's track? The relay team ready for the meet next week?" he asked.

"Yep. We're running great together. They've helped me with ways to control my anxiety. It got worse after Mom's stuff happened." I shooed a flying insect away from my face. "So that seems to be the team's main goal: Keep Emma from panicking during the race." I focused on the flock of ducks that regrouped in the middle of the lake. Even the barking dog wouldn't disturb this calm moment I wanted with my dad.

I observed the ducks as I told him about the deep-breathing yoga techniques and other new-age ideas we were using to keep me relaxed during the relay.

"One of the techniques goes like this." I took my pointer fingers and rapidly drummed against my temples, then the area between my eyebrows. Dad watched me for a moment, stunned, then burst into deep, genuine laughter. I loved the velvety sound of it and giggled in return. "No. Really. You should try it. It's called tapping. It's some kind of meditation technique."

"Maybe I will." He chuckled again. "Sounds like they're a special group of young ladies." He put his glasses back on and watched the ducks, which all moved as one body in a synchronized movement on the lake.

"Yeah. They are." I nodded. "Coach Rodriguez helped a couple of months ago when I was beating myself up over everything." I brushed away another insect that buzzed near me. "She and some of her friends who fought in Fallujah came back messed up with PTSD, but now she's way better than when she first came home." I shaded my eyes from the sunshine, taking a side look at him. "Gives me hope that I'll get through all this someday, too."

My dad nodded. Usually when I reached the subject of panic attacks or any subject connected to Casey's death, he'd abruptly change the conversation or bolt. This time he listened. I studied him, curious to see how long he could pull it off.

"So how are your visits with Doctor K going?" I asked, hoping I hadn't pushed too hard with the blunt question.

He cleared his throat and took a few moments before answering. "They've been helpful, I think." He tracked a family holding hands as they walked along the shoreline in front of us. The mom and dad were swinging a toddler-aged boy between them. The little boy yelped with excitement when his parents lifted him high between them every other step. "He wants me to voice my thoughts more often. Says I need to talk to you about things, about the past and all. Thinks that will help me, but more importantly, he believes it'll help you."

I nodded thoughtfully. I could have told him that—had tried to tell him that—many, many times Post-CD. Guess he wasn't ready to hear it until now. *Besides, Dr. K has a way of making you see things about yourself that you don't necessarily want to see.*

"I do want to help. You're it for me, you know?" He was still looking at the family. "I'm sorry I haven't been there for you since everything happened with Casey. Then last summer happened. I blamed myself for letting you down, and then I suppose I *really* shut down." His voice was hoarse. "You know I love you, right, Em? I'm not sure I've told you that enough."

"Of course, I know that, Dad." I reached for his hand. I'd never felt unloved by my father, just forgotten maybe, or loved from far away. Having him say those words aloud warmed me from the inside out, ten times more than the sun ever could. Hope bloomed within me. "I'm sorry about last summer. It was like an impulse I couldn't control. I was so angry at myself about Casey's death, and I felt hopeless, like my life would never get better. Wish I had a do-over on that." I squeezed his hand. "Things are different now. You don't have to worry about me so much. I'm getting better. I promise."

He pulled me into a clumsy embrace and rested his chin on top of my head. Sitting with him like this—just being together—filled my heart.

"Thank you," he murmured. "We'll make it through this. That's my promise to you."

"Yep. We will." At that moment, I was convinced of it.

He pulled away, taking in the lake again and fidgeting with his wrist-watch. Something else still bothered him. I sensed it. This was the longest "real" conversation I recalled ever having with him, post-CD. I took advantage of it.

"Anything else on your mind, Dad?" I examined his profile, the way his eyes crinkled at the corners.

"Yes, but it's not easy to discuss." It was the type of cryptic statement that usually would fill me with catastrophic dread. But not today. I wouldn't let anything ruin this long-awaited conversation between me and my dad.

"The things that matter usually aren't easy. That's what Doctor K. always says." I looked down at my fingernails, amazed at how healthy my hands looked. I waited as he sorted his thoughts.

Finally, he twisted around to face me, sitting cross-legged on top of the picnic table. He leaned forward on his elbows. "I'm considering legal separation from your mother." His words came out quick and concise. "It's something I've been thinking about for a while, but I never wanted to add more complications to your already overcomplicated life. You've had too much to deal with. But in light of recent events, I can't be around your mom." He steepled his fingers. "Let me rephrase that. I don't believe I can be around her while I heal. I don't think you can either." He sighed. "I wish things were different, but, looking back, I don't think I've ever been able to forgive her. I want to. I understand she has an illness, and I know she never meant to hurt anyone. It's just— I need distance. But I'm not leaving unless you're with me. I can get us a condo nearby so that you can stay at your school, still be near friends, near Grams."

"Wow." I stared hard at him. Again, I was amazed my parents had stayed together as long as they had, especially with mom's issues and dad's habit of disconnecting. For whatever reason, he took care of her even though she unintentionally sucked the light out of everyone near her. My mom was an emotional black hole. It was no wonder my dad always seemed empty. Even knowing that, the finality of him leaving her caused a strange twinge in my gut.

"I get it," I told him. "But what will Mom do without us? She might unravel. She needs serious help, but I'm still not sure she understands that." I lightly rubbed the cuticles on my fingers. "I wish she'd get on meds, or whatever therapy she needs. And she needs to stop drinking—it makes it worse. Grams says she self-medicates, and that Gramps did it, too."

"Yes, I'm afraid that's correct." He sat perfectly still. "I'll still help if I can, try to get her to understand the disorder and, hopefully, come to terms with it. I should have done that all along, but I was blind." He looked down. "I won't abandon her. I promise. I'll help, but it'll have to be while we live apart. It's best for all of us."

Dad was right. We both had been living under the shadows my mother cast for far too long. Mom would have to head toward the light on her own. Some steps had to be taken alone, and if Mom made it out of the darkness, we'd be there, waiting for her. After watching Grams all these years, I had hope. After all, I came from a family of tenacious women. The same blood running through Grams also coursed through me, Casey and, yes, my mother. Even if the battle appeared unwinnable, I had to hope my mom would triumph someday.

I didn't want the day to end on a sad note, so I jumped off the picnic table. I stretched my arms to the sky, then reached back. "Can you pass me the bag?" I asked, and he handed me a loaf of bread. "C'mon. Let's feed the duckies."

The flock swam toward us with purpose. I couldn't help but grin. I recalled a moment long ago when Casey and I were here, surrounded by geese. An aggressive gray gander had pushed its way to the front of the crowd to chase after Casey, who held the bread bag in her small hand. She had flapped her arms like wings, the plastic bag swinging to-and-fro as she honked back at it, trying to scare it away. But the pushy gander loomed closer, blaring full volume as it snapped its yellow-orange bill an inch from her nose. Casey, maybe two at the time, opened her eyes wide, pivoted and ran full speed into the safety of my arms. As the tubby, deranged bird followed, I had done the only thing I could think to do. I had placed Casey safely behind me, let out my most menacing lion roar, and charged the bird. Its tail feathers puffed as it half-waddled, half-flew away from me. We had whooped and hollered, Casey and me, as it landed ten feet away and smoothed its ruffled feathers as if nothing had happened.

With my dad nearby, I tore off pieces of crust, getting ready as the first group of ducks stepped from the lake, shook water from their gleaming feathers and shuffled single-mindedly toward me. They gulped down the bits of bread tossed their way and I smiled. Casey would have loved it.

CHAPTER 34

I hadn't seen my mom in over a week. As soon as I entered her room on the fourth floor of the treatment center, I knew she was in one of her dark moods. Something about the way she angled her chin and tracked me across the room, the fake smile more worrisome than an intense glower. Throughout my life, I'd learned to read these signals, which were as clear to me as bright yellow road signs that read "Danger Ahead." As always, when the signs appeared, they'd crash into my senses with unrestrained force; probably the same type of alert a gazelle felt when catching the first whiff of a predator's scent. I almost tasted the bitterness—or was that acid on my tongue?—that emanated from my mother's pores. My heart revved on an adrenaline spike, a *whooshing* of blood thrumming in my ears.

Maybe I shouldn't have come today.

"Hey, Mom." I forced myself to sound casual, another defensive measure, and sat on the edge of the faux-leather chair near the bed. I tested a false smile of my own. My stiff lips barely cooperated. "Feeling okay today?"

Mom, who sat in bed, didn't answer. She wore a quilted blue robe, one that we had bought her for Mother's Day a few years back, now rumpled. Her dark, disheveled hair framed a tired, lined face. Her lips transformed into a stoic line. I bent the inside of my wrist toward my nose, trying to be nonchalant, and took a deep hit of bergamot oil. I needed to stay calm. Just as I read her signs, my mother could also read mine.

Her hands shook slightly on her lap, and a fine sheen of sweat glossed her cheeks and upper lip. "I've seen better days, but I guess you already know that." She glared at me. "Especially since you and your father put me directly in Hell." Mom looked around the small room for dramatic effect before quoting the Monopoly "Go to Jail" card. "You know—Do not pass 'go,' do not collect two-hundred dollars."

My flight instinct was screaming for me to leave the room. *Say you need to use the restroom but keep walking. Nothing good can happen with her like this.*

I ignored it and stayed planted in the chair. The running from her had to stop. I forced myself to remember when I battled the scary shadows as a girl. But this wasn't a coat hanging inside the closet, creating a shadow monster. This was my mother. She embodied "frightening" when she was in one of these moods.

"What? Nothing to say?" Mom asked. False innocence clouded her eyes, her voice abrasive.

As a child, I'd learned people should never stare a strange dog directly in its eyes. It might consider that a challenge. I used this same tactic with my mom, shifting my eyes downward, locking in on the jagged nail on my mom's left index finger. It needed filing. I saw that she no longer wore her wedding band. When did that happen? Had Dad told her we were moving? I'd have to ask him.

"Can I bring you anything?" Changing the course of this visit was my primary goal. "Do you want anything from the house?"

"Yeah...a big, blue bottle of Skyy, for starters. That would do it," she snapped.

"That's not funny, Mom. You almost died," I said, my voice grim. It was the first time I had ever heard her acknowledge her alcohol use. She usually pretended her cocktails were as harmless as iced tea. No one ever talked about it, or the unpredictable mood swings of her illness—her ability to burn violently hot and, within seconds, transform to ice. Mom hurt anyone near her when she was like this, but I wanted to at least try to help. Maybe her acknowledgement of the vodka was a first step toward getting better.

"Yes, I almost died. But you botched that up, too, didn't you?" My mother verbally swung at me. "You should have left me alone. It's what I wanted. But you always screw things up. Always have."

I flinched, then shoved my hands under my thighs to keep fingers away from my teeth. I hadn't chewed on my cuticles in months, and I didn't want to start now. My mom sat for several minutes in silence.

Tired of waiting in the quiet, I snuck a quick glance at her face. She'd been waiting for the contact.

She launched the next verbal attack in a brittle voice. "Did you know you almost weren't born? When I found out I was pregnant with you, I didn't want you." She smoothed the sheets around her. "I mean, why would I? I was doing what I loved. Taking photographs, covering meaningful assignments. Traveling all over the world, meeting interesting people. My life was fun, exciting. Your father somehow convinced me to keep you, to get married." Her voice trailed off, the last word sounding distasteful. "Having you...that was the biggest mistake of my life," she proclaimed coldly, as if the thought had just occurred to her.

The blow almost knocked me out of the chair. For years in Post-CD, I'd suspected she didn't want me around, but now she had confirmed it. My mother had never wanted me. The cruel words and their reality pierced deeply into me. I felt my soul being slashed, something ripping, something coming undone inside me. This was how my mother hurt others the best. Deconstructing us all, piece by piece, until we believed we were nothing, we were no one.

"Okay." I rose on shaky legs. "I thought I could help but...." My heartbeat drummed erratic in my chest. A panic attack was imminent. It reached around me like an old friend closing in for a smothering embrace. I had to get out of there. "This isn't working."

"Go ahead, Emma. Run. That's what you always do. Except when it counts. Like when you just stood there...you stood there and just watched as Casey...." She stopped, released a mournful sob and used the edge of her sleeve to dab at her eyes before quickly regaining control. My mother appeared unhinged, a wide-eyed intensity pinning me down. Her intention was to flay me, figuratively, but with the same physical pain attached to the act. Then her eyes narrowed down to slits. "You didn't run then, did you? You just ... let her go... let her die," she finished with a rough, broken whisper.

I sucked in air in ragged measures. I couldn't maintain normal breathing. It felt as if I'd been repeatedly speared in the gut, my stomach clenched in pain from invisible puncture wounds. My teeth chattered as adrenaline again flooded my body. I had to get away. Before I knew it, I moved halfway to the door. The world was a blurry swirl of water-colored images splashed against a tilted canvass. But Mom wasn't finished with me. Not yet.

"All you had to do was keep an eye on her. That's it. Let her have a fucking tea party, watch the damn TV. But, no, you couldn't be bothered to take care of her. It's your fault she's dead," she shouted, her cheeks flushed a deep red. "If you had only told me. Why didn't you tell me she was back there...behind me? *Why?*" She ran hands through unruly hair. "I would have hit the brakes. I would have!"

As she screamed the last sentence, it felt like I slammed into some invisible wall, jarring my entire body. A flurry of images from another time and place unleashed inside me. A rushing current of white static filled my brain. It drowned out whatever else she was screaming.

Instead, I focused on sights, sounds, and sensations, all which flickered inside my brain: Casey spilling water out of a white, plastic teapot with a pink rose decal peeling off the side, jabbering sweetly to stuffed animals set in a circle in front of the TV. Mom sweeping past me, car keys jingling in hand, the smell of her Red Door perfume trailing behind as she dashed out the front door. The sound of a ringing telephone, its plastic receiver smooth and hard against my ear, against my cheek. A man on the other end—a familiar voice, but not Dad's—whispering something I didn't quite comprehend but knew it was wrong. *So wrong.* The creak of a storm door hinge. My heart drumming inside my chest once I registered that Casey had left the tea party.

Where did you go? Case, where are you?

The thudding of bass coming from the SUV in the driveway, windows rolled up, Mom's ponytail bobbing up and down in rhythm to loud pop music blaring from the stereo. Casey clutching Bear as she circled behind the SUV, a high-pitched, determined voice calling out, "Casey go, too, Mama! Casey go, too!" Then a series of tiny, determined *roarrrrs*. The high-pitched whine of the SUV's engine thrown into reverse, drowning out those tiny roars. An animal-like wail released from my lips.

Please, God. No!

A feeling of hopelessness, of crumpling, buckling under blackness, of being trapped in a tunnel of muffled sound, suffocating, encased in darkness, then, finally light and images seeping through again. A fuchsia-colored cowgirl boot glinting in the sunlight, near the left back tire. A small, plump hand with fingernail-polish the shade of bubble gum, peeking out from under the SUV, Bear lying just out of its grasp. Blackness.

I pressed my palms to my temples and squeezed.

No more. No. More.

The whirring of the white static ended like someone flicked off the power. My mother yammered on, but she could not hurt me any longer. I moved my hands away from my face, my jaw set. I now knew who I was, what I was capable of. My body tingled all over again, my fight response kicking in. I shook with inner rage. My mother continued screaming that she would have hit the brakes. She was unwavering, incessant.

"Enough!" I screamed back. Some people were born with a lion's taste for blood, unafraid to lunge, fixated on the pulsing jugular; while others, like gazelles, bolted from danger. I shared traits of both. I had been a gazelle for far too long, had tried to outrun the past, had lost myself to avoid its threats. I had forgotten that along with the legs of a gazelle, a lion's heart pounded beneath my skin, with its power rumbling even now. I'd never forget again.

I faced my mother, a fury overtaking me. I could smell my mom's musky sweat, her illness a fog cast into the air around her, almost visible. Her breaths quickened.

"Enough," I whispered through gritted teeth to my mother, to myself. I stared directly into her eyes. I thought about the conversations I'd had with my father, with Tyler, with Fi, with Grams, with Coach Rodriguez, with Dr. K. Deep in my soul, I knew I wasn't to blame for Casey's death. My mother knew it, too.

I moved toward her, my steps slow. "I can't stand your lies anymore." I stopped at the foot of the bed. "You know the truth, Mom. I do, too. I was too young to realize what was going on at the time, but now I get it. I know."

I could see her trying to get a reading on what had changed. My mother froze, only the quick rise and fall of the lapels on the robe indicated unease.

"Are you hearing me, Mom? I *know*," I said, pinning her with the ferocity of my gaze

I want to hurt her; to make her feel the pain I've felt all these years.

I balled my hands into fists, keeping them tightly against my body so I wouldn't be tempted to strike her.

"You know what? That I was making a quick run to the store and—" she started to say.

"Enough." My voice was a deadly soft. "You're not listening. I told you. I *know*." I circled to the side of the bed, moving in closer. I kept my voice low, my words controlled. "I know you weren't going to the store that day. That was a lie. I know *why* you were in such a hurry, *why* you changed clothes, *why* you put perfume on that day. You were sleeping with Fi's dad, and you couldn't wait to get to him, could you?" I worked my jaw a few times, biting back the fury that clamored for escape. "He called back. Did you know that?" Mom ducked her head. "On the telephone. I answered, and he thought I was *you*." I let the words sink in. "Your lover spoke to *me*, thinking it was *you*."

I waited. "I was a kid, Mom, *a child*. It shook me, the dirty things he whispered. I took my eyes off her for a second—that's it, *a second*—then she was gone. So, don't tell me I couldn't be bothered to watch Casey. I *loved* her. It was you. You couldn't be *bothered* to take care of us, could you? You couldn't be *bothered* to stay loyal to Dad. You couldn't be *bothered* with the notion that maybe having sex with my best friend's dad would destroy their family." My mother darted her eyes around, desperate, cornered. "Just like you destroyed ours. All your choices. Not mine."

With each sentence I uttered, my mother flinched. The shaking of her hands increased. She tried to bury her face, tears sliding down her right cheek onto a portion of exposed neck where her carotid artery visibly pulsed. Silent sobs wracked her body. But she said nothing.

I thought I'd feel better lashing out, watching her cry. God knows she deserved it. But all I felt was emptiness. I didn't have the stomach to destroy another person. I watched her weeping, not wanting to comfort her, but finished with the chase.

"I know other things, too, Mom." I was still forceful, but the bite had disappeared from my voice. "I know you've battled demons—as Grams puts it—for a long time. Just like your dad did. I'm sorry for that—but you need professional help. You don't need alcohol." Still nothing but sobs from her. "And you do need to get treatment for your bipolar disorder."

"I know Casey's death was an accident, and you never thought that it would happen. But it did." I stood over her. "So, no more secrets, or blaming me, or telling yourself lies about why Casey died that day. No more projecting your guilt onto me. She wouldn't want that and neither do I. She'd want us to help each other heal, to get on with living." I regarded her with pity. "Mom, if you don't get help, you'll lose another daughter. It's your choice."

Just then, Casey came into view in the corner of the room, hunched low, her eyes wide and alert. I nodded at her before I left, ignoring our mother's hysterical crying, knowing she would have to overcome the past and get proper help before she could ever get better. I wasn't the only one who needed to learn that lesson.

I retraced my path down the hallways and felt lighter with each step. I opened the door to the lobby. The bright sunlight caused me to squint for a moment before I saw my dad. His head popped up, and he immediately put down his magazine, rising to his feet. He must have seen it on my face—maybe the flushed cheeks gave it away—because he walked over and, without a word, took me into his arms. He gently rocked me back and forth, whispering, "It's okay, baby. It's okay."

It was then I finally cried. Not because of what had just happened with my mom, but because it seemed a lifetime ago since my dad had held me close and called me baby.

CHAPTER 35

R aindrops pelted the window with gentle spatters outside my bedroom as a late spring storm rolled through North Texas. I stood near the glass, temporarily lost in its lulling rhythmic sound. The gray weather matched my melancholy mood.

So much had changed in the past few months. Not long after the confrontation with my mom, Dad had filed for legal separation. Even though I knew it was coming, the news still rattled me. A sense of unfinished business nagged at me, like working a jigsaw puzzle, nearly finished, only to discover pieces were missing, the creation incomplete.

I hadn't been there when my dad had told my mom, but from the expression on his face when he'd arrived at Grams' house that night, I guessed it had been hellish. He had walked through Grams' front door looking pale and shaken. Grams had wordlessly wrapped him in her arms, tears on her face as he folded his tall frame and sobbed into her frail shoulder. I had encircled them both in my arms and lay my forehead against Dad's damp stubbly cheek.

"Em?" My dad called out. The sound of his footsteps clomping down the hallway brought me to the present. "We need more packing tape and extra boxes. I'm running to the store. Need anything?"

"Nope. I'm good."

"I'll swing by the deli and pick up dinner." He stood at the bedroom door. "Want your usual?"

"Yeah. Definitely." His face was so relaxed. Making the decision to leave my mom—and the house with its painful memories—had lifted much of the worry from his face. He looked like a young forty-five, handsome and eager to start something new.

"Got it. Be back in a few," he said as he headed out.

I was almost finished packing my room. I continued wrapping knick-knacks in newspaper and placing them in boxes. It was difficult to believe it was happening. The movers would be there in a couple days, and I'd no longer live in my childhood home. My dad had signed a lease on a three-bedroom townhouse near my school. I knew it was best for everyone, including my mother, who'd been released from the treatment center last week. She had taken a taxi home, filled a suitcase, and left for the airport, Grams said. The story was she planned to visit a photographer friend in the northwest. She had phoned Grams but hadn't come to her house to say goodbye to any of us. When we had come home yesterday to start boxing up stuff, we found the unopened bottles of her prescribed medication from the treatment center. Mom had left them standing upside-down on the kitchen counter. *Message received.* It seemed my mother needed time and space to figure things out, too.

I regarded the wrapped picture frame in my hand. My treasured family portrait. I encircled it with more layers of newspaper to keep it extra protected and placed it in a box filled with puffy Styrofoam peanuts. I had marked it on all sides with the word "fragile" in bold letters, aware of the symbolism. I looked up, and there Casey stood in the doorway, hesitant. Today, she looked older, about my age, and she resembled our mother even more than usual.

"Hey, Case," I said, lightly. An ache for my sister, and maybe for the mother I'd probably never know, filled my chest. Nothing would ever satisfy that void, but I knew I had to move forward, not stay trapped in the past. Like always, Casey seemed to sense my mood. She stepped back into the hall and gestured for me to join her as she moved toward her room.

"It's almost time, isn't it?" I asked, as I peered into Casey's bedroom.

Our house would be on the market soon. My mom might return from wherever she had disappeared to. Or maybe not. No one could predict what was ahead. Most of Casey's clothes, toys, and furniture—except for things with sentimental value—would be dropped off at the Salvation Army. Some other child would sleep in Casey's 'big girl' bed, the one she was so proud of. Another girl would grow up in front of her dresser mirror, maybe someday standing before it, her hair in an up-do, decked in a prom dress. All things my sister would never experience. I bit at the side of my mouth to keep from tearing up, resigned to what would never be.

The room wasn't as immaculate as it usually was since my mom had been in the treatment center. A thin layer of dust covered the dresser top. I wiped it off with the hem of my T-shirt, then saw Casey in the mirror right behind me. We stared at each other's reflection. "So," I whispered, "Mom couldn't even say goodbye. She just left." I swallowed the lump in my throat. My sister's eyes—luminous and deep and tender—held mine for several more beats. "You heard her, right? She never wanted me. Just you. She made that crystal clear." I rubbed at the top of the dresser, a distraction for me as I spoke. "She never got over losing you. None of us did. I guess you already knew that, too."

Casey reached out, but stopped, her arm falling limp to her side. She shook her head with an emphatic no, then jerked it toward the bed, motioning for me to look under it. I didn't understand why she wanted me to do that, but I kneeled and reached underneath, not sure what I might find. I didn't feel anything there. Not at first, but I extended my arm farther and combed back and forth with outstretched fingers. I touched the corner of something hard and smooth pushed up against the baseboard. *A book?* I glanced back at Casey, whose face remained impassive, then tugged it out bit by bit. It was another album—the black, oversized kind our mother used for her most prized photos and as a professional portfolio.

I stood up with it in my arms and took it back to the dresser, where I laid it out in front of me. The smell of it—that tang of chemically processed photo paper—brought back images of my mom coming out of the darkroom as she wiped her hands on torn jeans and hummed a tune. She was happy when she worked. The darkroom had been her refuge.

I looked back to make sure Casey was still there. Then, with caution, I opened the album. I flipped through the first three or four pages, my mouth gaping as I saw photos of myself. Lots of them. Candid photographs taken Post-CD, my mother's signature style in each shot.

"What is this, Case?" I scanned more pages. "I don't—Wait. How did she take these? She was never there with me. I never saw her." They were photographs taken with one of my mother's huge telephoto lenses. One image was snapped at Sophie's eleventh birthday party at the skating rink, a zoomed-in shot of me helping Fi blow out candles, my face freckled and fine-boned like my father's. Another was me as a sixth-grader walking by myself on a school field trip at the Perot Science Museum in Dallas. I stood a lonely figure surrounded by hordes of others, my look despondent despite the gleeful faces around me. There were many more of me in various places.

The last photograph was taken just last week at a track meet, the day my mother was released from the treatment center. So she hadn't left town right away. Somehow she'd managed to go to the track meet first. The photo showed my limbs blurred in motion, the baton clutched in my hand. Most striking was the crispness of my face, perfectly in focus, a steel intensity in the set of my jaw, a ferocious blissfulness springing from my eyes. It portrayed my love of the chase—filled with hope and promise and joy. I couldn't believe it. My mom had captured exactly what I felt when I ran.

In fact, Mom had caught many of my moods through the years—all of them post-CD. All the years after Casey had died, I'd believed she'd abandoned me, which she had by traditional parenting standards. Maybe these photos were how she had expressed herself. Maybe it was the only way she knew how. It was evident the artist loved her subject, even if from a distance.

"I had no idea," I finally said into the mirror. "I don't know what to say."

She nodded again, her face radiating love and empathy. She reached for me but stopped short of touching my hair. Casey's elegant, long-fingered hand, which also looked so much like our mother's, hovered about an inch away from my head—not making contact, but just close enough that something like static electricity gently pulled strands of my hair outward, toward her outstretched fingers. I gasped as I felt the tickling sensation of hair rising and falling.

She had never reached out to me like this before. Casey's reflection flickered in and out, and then she was gone. It lasted less than a minute—the simple gesture of one sister caressing the hair of the other, offering comfort—but its significance meant so much more to me. I sensed a love begin to fill the void that I'd felt only moments ago.

Chapter 36

The restaurant was in the historic district of town. It had an Austin vibe to it. Colored lights were strung from the ceiling and Texas-themed music of various genres played over the speakers. A few couples and groups, many wearing hipster glasses or dressed in fashionable clothes, ate nearby.

"I'm glad you're here today." With the flick of a finger, Tyler spun a packet of sugar on the table. "I thought maybe the egg comments had come off—I don't know—like really lame." He watched the spinning white rectangle, with dark lashes that cast faint shadows on his cheeks. It made him look more vulnerable than usual. "Or maybe you thought this retro diner place idea was, I don't know, kind of weird?" He squirmed in the booth. "For a first date, I mean."

I sat on my hands to keep from fidgeting. So, it was a date—I hadn't been sure. I was tongue-tied and jittery. Bad combo.

"I'm glad I came, too," I managed. "I just had to work out a few things. You know, a lot of stuff going on right now."

"Yeah. I get it. One hundred percent." Tyler peeked up at me, grinned calmly and returned to the sugar packet. I watched, too, hypnotized as it cartwheeled in circles atop the shiny Formica. "So, this *is* a first date," he said, his voice much more confident. "That's a relief. I thought I'd blown it with the egg puns."

As the packet came to a stop, I ducked my head and feigned interest in the napkin dispenser.

Our waiter appeared. He was stocky with gray hair pulled into a man-bun, his suntanned face leathery and comfortable like a pair of well-worn boots. He wore a short-sleeve T-shirt, and on his left bicep sported a scarlet and gold lion. It was the Gryffindor crest from the *Harry Potter* series, which I had obsessed over as a kid, reading each of the seven books at least five times. Harry Potter was technically my first crush.

"Hey." His twinkling eyes followed mine. "You like my tat? I'm a huge Potterhead. My grandkids think it's the coolest." He handed us menus, pulled a pad from the back pocket of his jeans and a pen from behind his ear. "We do breakfast 'round the clock here, but we do dinner items, too. I vouch for the chicken-fry. Everything's homemade." He held his pen, readied to jot something down. "What can I get you to drink?"

I ordered a sweet tea, and Tyler said that was his favorite too. The waiter strolled away and quickly reappeared with two glasses.

"That's one interesting dude," Tyler said as he watched the waiter return to the kitchen.

"I know, right? And how awesome was that Gryffindor crest?" I whispered. "I want one, and I don't even like tattoos."

"Yeah. That reminds me of something I wanted to tell you."

"What's that? Something to do with Harry Potter or a tattoo?" I laughed, more relaxed after talking to the waiter. I slid a sugar packet back and forth between my two hands.

"Last night I was watching the National Geographic channel." He held his hand up as I raised my eyebrows. "Hey, no judgment. Nerds are their own kind of cool, okay? I love me some documentaries." He reached out and swiped the sugar packet from me.

"Hey, give it back!" I chuckled and tried to pry it away. He let go of the packet and grabbed my hand. His fingers wrapped lightly around mine while my stomach performed a few tumbles. The feeling wasn't fight-or-flight this time. It was something much different. Tyler had that lopsided little grin on his face. I couldn't stop staring at the small freckle just under his left eye.

"Okay," he said, "so back to my story. I'm getting distracted." He squeezed my hand, then placed it back on the table. He took a swig of tea. "Now what was I saying?" His face appeared as flushed as mine felt. "Oh, yeah. There was this documentary on African lions—about their social behavior. Apparently, they're more social than any other cat—did you know that? More like dogs. It made me think about what we talked about on the phone last week."

"Be more specific. We've talked about a lot of things."

"What Grams told you about that nickname from when you were a little kid?"

"Oh. Yeah."

"Well, the interesting thing about lions is they don't do well on their own. They're communal creatures, like humans. If lions are alone—like if they've been injured or forced out of the pride—they usually don't make it. They're extremely vulnerable. Ultimately, lions need other lions to survive."

"Is that so?" I wondered where he was going with this.

"That got me thinking." He reached for both of my hands. "You've been like a lion without a pride. Because your parents were kind of screwed up and all, right?" He laced his fingers with mine. "But not anymore, you know? You don't ever have to go it alone. Not as long as

I'm around." I let my hands relax in his and gave into the waves of goose bumps that rippled across my skin.

The waiter was there again, clearing his throat. "You kids know what you want?"

"I do," Tyler said as he wiggled an eyebrow at me. "How 'bout you?"

That odd heat again.

"I'll have the house breakfast. Eggs scrambled, please. Turkey bacon, if you have it," he told the waiter.

"And I'll have the same." I still felt the warmth of his gaze.

After we finished eating, Tyler suggested we walk to a bookstore nearby. That sounded perfect to me. We had another hour before his mom picked us up.

As we left, the waiter called to us, "Y'all come back and see us again!"

"Yessir! We'll be back!" Tyler said, holding the door open for me.

"Thanks." A giddiness enveloped me. The muscles in my face hurt from smiling so much. I was aware of the goofy look on my face but didn't care. This is what "happy" felt like.

"Anytime," he said softly. He reached for my hand, and I swayed toward him, my forehead coming to rest against his collarbone.

"Em," he said, his voice soft and serious. "I have a question. It's important."

"What is it?"

He lifted my chin and held it gently. I drank in his eyes, which sparkled with good-hearted mischief, and something else, too. "So—" He cleared his throat. "If you're a lion girl, does that make me a lion boy?"

I blinked at him, then snorted. "Now *that* was goofier than any egg pun!"

His smile faded into longing as he moved toward my mouth. His warm breath skimmed my cheek just before he kissed me, the firmness of his lips sparking another wave of warmth inside me, my heart galloping at full speed. He pulled away and caressed the side of my face. "You know, I've always had this weird thing for big cats."

"Really?" I raised an eyebrow. "The more you speak, the stranger it gets." His fingers continued to stroke my face. "Maybe you shouldn't talk so much."

"Maybe you're right," he said.

This time, I reached up, entwining my fingers in his hair, and pulled his face toward mine. I moved in even closer for another kiss, as a warmth spread throughout my body. I'd be the first to admit I was no expert on the subject of romance. This was my first serious kiss, after all. But even though I didn't have a brother, in my opinion, Fi had been *wrong, wrong, wrong*: as far as I was concerned, Tyler's kisses seemed as far away from brotherly as I could imagine.

Chapter 37

A late afternoon sun shone on the crowded bleachers. The sixteen-hundred-meter relay was the final event of the regional meet. The spectators' anticipation pitched through the air like a kite tossed around in a springtime gust. Coach Rodriguez huddled us together and gave each one of us specific instructions. If we won this race, our team would qualify for the state meet, a first in school history for the four-by-four-hundred.

Coach lightly grabbed my shoulders and applied a reassuring pressure. "All right, Watters, besides running like the wind, what's the most important thing you need to do?"

"Manage my nerves. Don't take off unless I have the baton." I lifted my chin higher. "Don't worry, Coach. I've got this."

She searched my face, then nodded in agreement. "I believe you do."

Again, she pulled our relay team together until our heads touched one another's. "No long speeches, girls. Just this. Remember how hard each of you has worked to get here. This is your time to shine. Make it count."

Relay runners on the first leg began moving to the track. Aliah headed to the starter block and began stretching her quads. She'd alternate standing on one leg, folding the other back, and holding the top of her foot against her backside. All the while, she watched her opponents.

I had to keep my muscles warm, too. I shook my arms and called to Aliah, who was setting up on an outside lane. "You've got this!"

She planted her feet on the block, crouched down at an angle, extended her arms for support, and placed her fingertips lightly on the track in front of her. She glanced over at me, baring her teeth in a fierce smile before returning her concentration to the lane ahead. Her expression hardened as she zeroed in on the space ahead. She clutched the red aluminum baton in one hand; her body poised for launch. The firing pistol cracked, and the runners sprung from their blocks. Aliah flawlessly rocketed off, a blur of long thin braids flying past the crowd, her powerful sprinter's legs and arms pumping furiously.

"Go, Aliah! Go!" was screamed from the sidelines and bleachers. She was the epitome of strength and beauty. She rounded the first curve and took the lead.

Trini was waiting in her lane, ready for the second leg of the race. As Aliah entered the exchange zone, Trini shuffled, motioning for the hand off. Still in the lead, Aliah sprinted with everything she had, her contorted face flushed as she pushed to pass the baton. Just as she extended it for the exchange, her spike caught the track, causing her to lurch forward, the baton bobbling at the end of her fingertips. I watched in horror with the rest of our team, as an equally horrified Aliah stumbled a few steps before skidding down on one knee. Thankfully, she remained in the lane and somehow still clutched the baton, avoiding team disqualification. A shaken Trini doubled-back toward her. She wrestled the baton from Aliah's frozen grip and charged after the runners who had flown past them.

"Run, Trini! Dig in!" We pulled a limping Aliah into our circle.

I patted her back. "Shake it off. No worries. We can catch them."

Coach walked up, still confident. "Knight, get that knee checked out when this is over."

"Coach, I don't know—what happened." Red-faced, Aliah struggled to speak between gasps. Her knee was scraped and bloody. "I just—"

"It happens, Knight. We'll just have to make it up." Her focus returned to the race. Trini couldn't make up all the ground they'd lost. When the pack of runners formed on the inside lane, she was next to last.

Anne bounded onto the track and awaited her position. Winded, Trini negotiated the last curve and dashed toward her. She placed the baton into her outstretched hand.

Everyone knew Anne was the slowest on our team. She ran hard, working to maneuver her way between two runners just ahead of her, but they squeezed her to the outside. She took the second curve, her face scarlet from exertion, her arms and legs driving rhythmically. She managed to pass another runner and inched the team into fifth place.

I took my position on the track and stood calmly, waiting for my position. With a quick scan of the bleachers, I spotted my dad, Grams, Tyler, and Ms. Zohar sitting together in the second row. Led by Tyler, they hooted and hollered, "Go, Redhawks!" Tyler had been waiting to catch my eye. He waved and gave me a double thumbs-up. I gave him a nod, and watched Anne taking the third turn, holding her own. I was ready. I had never been more ready in my life. I knew what was at stake and what I had to do.

Anne, running as hard as I had ever seen her, passed another opponent who had stumbled in front of her on the last bend. We had moved into fourth place. I kept my eyes on the red aluminum baton clutched in her hand. I inhaled the familiar smell of rubberized track and bobbed on the balls of my feet. As Anne neared, I began loping sideways, my open left hand reaching back. The familiar, cold metal landed solid in my palm, and I shifted it to my right while simultaneously rocketing toward the runners ahead of me.

I entered my zone. My lungs took in air, pushed it out; my spikes lightly dug into the track, propelling me. A breeze caressed my face. I moved steadily, determinedly onward, my gaze focused beyond the lead runner, ablaze with one purpose. Stuck on the outside on the second curve, I overtook a runner. As soon as I spied an opening, I'd make my move for the inside. My muscles screamed but sang simultaneously; this was what they were meant to do. My long stride, coupled with speed, allowed me to move past the next runner. I now had a solid hold on second place.

Rounding the last curve to the straightaway, I stayed laser-focused on the finish line. I tasted the salty sweat that glided down my face, some of it catching at the corners of my mouth. My nostrils flared, desperate for oxygen, as I blasted at full speed and tried to catch the elusive opponent in front. It wasn't easy. The runner—a blur of dark hair and purple singlet—remained a few steps ahead, refusing to relinquish the lead, showing no signs of weakening.

Then I spotted her. Casey stood just beyond the finish line and waved. *Move, Em, move*, I heard her yelling inside my brain, encouraging me, cheering me on, always rooting for me. I kicked into true pursuit mode, a bucket of adrenaline through my veins. My body no longer consumed oxygen; it fed on something else, something nameless. I wanted this for myself. For Casey. For Coach and my team, and my school. For my dad and Grams. For Ms. Zohar and Tyler. For Dr. K and Ms. Poskey. And even for my mother, who remained paralyzed by the past, buried under a rubble of mistakes, indiscretions, and the difficult illnesses she struggled to face. I fought for her, too. I *needed* this win, *tasted* it. This was the kill I craved, hard-fought, but bloodless. My lungs and legs burned with fire, but I transformed the pain into fuel and pushed even harder. Pain only had the power I gave it, and from here on, I'd no longer let it hold me back. Instead, I'd use it to power forward toward a better life.

I was almost to Casey, who stood with both arms extended wide. Like she was the big sister now, waiting to scoop me up—just as I had done to her countless times. Just a little farther, a little faster, and I'd be inside her embrace. I widened my stride and drove my arms, giving everything, my heart banging and clanging deep inside my chest, egging me on for one last push, energizing me as I took those final...*one...two...three*...steps past my opponent, lunging over the finish line. Bounding right into, and then through, Casey's outstretched arms. I beamed as I passed through my sister's spirit, an invigorating blast of cool air, tickling like a thousand butterfly kisses, light and feathery against my skin, followed by the sensation of sunshine warming my body, and enveloping me, encircling me, forever encircling me. I didn't need to see Casey anymore to know she was there. She had always been. Would always be.

I slowly coasted down the track, panting, a happiness I couldn't begin to describe exploding within. My teammates stormed me from behind, hands reaching out, lifting me, carrying me on their shoulders in front of the bleachers. Cheers from the crowd rained down.

Tears welled in my eyes, but they were the best kind, the kind I'd never experienced before in Post-CD—they were tears of pure joy. I tasted them, sweet like drops of honeysuckle nectar on the tongue, grateful for what they signaled. I found my dad and Grams, and the others whom I loved, some of them hugging each other, others calling from the bleachers. I raised an arm in acknowledgment, grinning at them, the ones who had believed in me, stood by me, waited for me.

Inside my head, I heard a series of growls—like the ones I recalled Casey making so long ago—noises that progressively grew into a loud victorious roar, no longer in the voice of a child, but one filled with the fierceness forged only by enduring trials. Forged only by living, and loving, and sometimes losing. For I knew the lion, scarred but restored, had returned to the girl, had returned to me, even stronger than before. It had survived. It had found its way home.

Acknowledgements

The characters and the specific scenarios described in *Lion Girl* are fictional, and any errors in this book are entirely my own.

This novel is dear to my heart. When I was a small child, I channeled my inner lion whenever I needed courage. I'd roar as loud as I could and throw myself at whatever threatened me—whether a shadow monster in the closet, an older sibling who picked on me, or that unfortunate nurse who once tried to give me a shot when I was five. Some of the threats were real, some perceived, but in those moments, I *was* a lion. (I'm pretty sure I came up with the whole lion thing after seeing the film "Born Free" on television.)

I grew out of it by first or second grade. But I kept that ferocious spirit nearby, releasing it when I needed a boost of courage. It has helped me get through many dark times. It's my hope that we all can find our inner courage when faced with challenging circumstances or when we see injustice. Like lions, we need to have each other's backs if we want to survive. So, *roar* when it's needed. No backing down. Your voices matter.

I'd like to express my gratitude to all who have helped me with this novel. There are many, so bear with me! And please forgive me if I've left anyone out.

I'm grateful to my late parents Joe and Jane for allowing me to be the Lion Girl as a child. Thanks for humoring me and encouraging my wild imagination. (I apologize about that nurse who tried to stick me with a needle. I know you had lots of explaining to do!) Love you both forever.

Thanks to my late mother-in-law Joyce Moses, aka Granny to those who loved her. Parts of Grams are loosely based on her, especially her vibrant personality and colorful manicured nails. You are missed, Granny, and the world is less vivid without your sparkle.

To my late uncle, Frank Augustini, I miss solving the world's problems with you over pasta and Lambrusco. You rarely gave compliments; your belief in my writing meant more than you'll ever know.

To Michele Jeter, thank you for reading this manuscript multiple times through its evolution. I'm grateful for our rambling conversations, our paint nights, our laugh sessions. You're a true friend and a blessing in my life. And to Emma Adams, thank you for loaning your first name to my main character. Like you, she's gifted with grit.

To my writer gal-pal, Maureen O'Mahoney, thank you for hours spent hashing out characters and plots at the local coffee shop. You made the creative process a blast, and I know *Lion Girl* is stronger for it. Also, I'm thankful to Heather Ellett, who provided constant encouragement as this novel made its lengthy trek toward publication. I appreciate your friendship and support through the years. (Ever consider specializing in "writer therapy" sessions? There are many of us in need!)

Thank you to Sally Kemp, who edited the earliest version almost eight years ago. And special thanks to my dear friend Julie Nichols, who edited it after I pulled it out of a drawer and tweaked it. The thing about tweaking a manuscript is you often add more mistakes. (At least, I do.) So, I appreciate you using your skills to give *Lion Girl* another glow-up, Jules. I'm also grateful for your enthusiasm to get this novel into the world after the pandemic. I was listening. And many thanks to Sean Hooks for the final polish.

Props to beta readers Amy Wilson, Julie Hollywood-Burkett, and Robin Best for making time in your extremely busy schedules. Your comments and suggestions have made it a stronger novel. You're rockstars!

As always, endless gratitude for SMU's The Writer's Path, where this novel began, and a special shoutout to instructors/authors Suzanne Frank, Amanda Arista, and Keith Goodnight. The program, although no more, was essential to the creation of *Lion Girl*. To the writer peeps I met on the path, thanks for your constructive criticism. Peeps include Maureen, Heather, Rick Hynes, Dawn Tufenkjian Capitel, Kristin Cicciarelli, Stephanie Chambers, and Justin Moore.

I'd like to thank the following educators from Vandeventer Middle School in Frisco ISD: Counselor Dennis Thorpe; now-retired Coach Jamie Siess; and Paige Hoe, former principal. I appreciate you talking with me multiple times for this project. Can't say thank you enough. Educators are real superheroes.

I've been lucky to have lots of amazing cheerleaders along the way. A shoutout to Tammy Bird, Deborah Alvarenga, Jean Yaeger, Anna Cox, Donna Ericson, Candice Clark, Chloe Zonis, all the Ridgeview game night ladies, and my Augustini-Best-Moses-Herrera-Howard-Flores extended family members. I'm grateful for your constant encouragement.

Brooke Carlock, thanks for your hard work on the cover. I love it. It perfectly captures Emma's story.

Kent, I appreciate your endless support in helping me cross the finish line with this novel. I wouldn't have managed it without you. Thanks for listening, for the countless reads and edits, and mostly, for believing in me. I'm blessed to be married to an exceptional writer who can edit! And special thanks to Annelise, our talented and creative daughter, whose love of reading young-adult fiction inspired me to write *Lion Girl*. I love you both to the moon and back, times infinity.

About the author

Gina Augustini Best is an independent writer and former newspaper journalist. She holds a bachelor's degree in Humanities from the University of Houston-Clear Lake and a master's in media and communications from Texas Tech University. She completed The Writer's Path, a two-year, novel-writing program at Southern Methodist University.

A Texas native, she lives in the Dallas area with her family. Her writing often explores themes of unconditional love and complex family bonds. Despite stories that tackle realistic, and sometimes gritty issues, her works focus on hopeful and empowering messages. *Lion Girl* is her second novel. Her first published novel was *More Than Ivory*, an upper YA mystery/thriller.

Visit the author at **ginaaugustinibest.com** and/or follow her on social media.